VEGA

ROBERT BARNARD

VEGA

ROBERT BARNARD

Summary: When a series of bizarre and prophetic dreams begin to haunt first year law student Nathaniel Shaw, he discovers he may be the missing piece in solving a decades-old mystery in Burlington, Vermont.

Genre: Mystery, Horror, Romance

ISBN: 9781072934530
Publisher: Cherry Valley Publishing

"Where the devil can't succeed,
he'll send a woman."

- Old Polish Proverb

I had a normal life once.

Though it seems impossible to imagine now, there was a time when my family could look at me as if I weren't crazy. A time when I was a promising student—gifted, some professors told me—a time when I could dress myself in the morning without being watched by an orderly, when I could drive my car and buy groceries and go to the movies all on my own. A time when I could brush my teeth without supervision and wear shoes with laces, when I could walk through empty city streets without the ceaseless, unnerving certainty that someone was *watching* me.

But that was once upon a time and long ago. And although I'm constantly inundated with phrases by doctors and therapists alike—you know the ones—"you're showing promising signs of recovery, Nathan," and "you're making improvements every day, Nathan," and "baby steps, Nathan, baby steps," it feels as if my life will never be the same again.

I'm writing this, after all, from the hospital bed that I'm ordered to remain in between the hours of three and six, every afternoon. Nurse Schroeder even allowed me a pad of paper to call my own and a pack of crayons to write with.

Someday soon, hopefully, they'll allow me a pencil.

But for now: baby steps.

And I hope this doesn't come off as sounding overly desperate. I don't want pity. I don't want sympathy for the fact that my dinner tonight will consist of a lump of cold, bland instant potatoes beside a ketchup-coated brick of mystery meat that the hospital staff insists is meatloaf. I simply want to tell my story. That's all I've wanted to do since the start of all of this—tell my story.

1

And if you're reading this, it means you're interested in listening, and that's more than I can ask for. Maybe you want to know my side of things—why, in the fall of 2012, so many important people close to me died—or maybe you're interested in *her,* maybe you're one of the few that believes she exists at all, or maybe you're certain you've met *her* or someone like *her* in the past. Maybe you've been told that you're crazy, too. And maybe you need some validation that you're not.

Forgive me. Even after all this time, I find it hard to say her name. But this will be a very dull read for you, my friend, if not once do I mention her by name, like she's some nefarious villain. And although she was a lot of things, the jury is still out on whether or not she was a villain at all, so that might be an unfair accusation to make. Perhaps she was, but part of me insists that somewhere in her were good intentions all along.

But, I'm getting ahead of myself.

So, let's go back. Back to the summer of 2012, back to the last time I remember my life being sane, simple, average, and ordinary.

Back before all of that would change forever.

Back before the day that I met Vega.

ψ

My father passed away when I was just nine years old. Lung cancer. He came from an era where cowboys in television commercials lassoed bulls as they drew puff after puff from a filtered cigarette. He smoked a pack a day, quitting briefly around the summer of 1990, when I was born. By Christmas of that year he had picked the habit back up again, and nine years later he was dead.

My memories of my father are loose, fleeting, and fuzzy at best. The human mind's ability to recollect doesn't really activate until the age of five, and he was gone when I had barely turned nine. That left me with a precious four-year's worth of memories and experiences with the man half responsible for bringing me into creation.

Most of my knowledge of my father came from my mother. According to her, he was a tough as nails son of a gun. And, when it came to the cancer, he truly gave it hell. Fought the good fight. Didn't go quietly into that dark night and yadda, yadda, yadda.

In the spring of 2003, my mother remarried. If I said that was an easy thing for a brooding thirteen-year-old who sorely missed his father to accept, I would be lying. My mother could have married Superman, and I'd still have spent every afternoon locked up in my bedroom, listening to loud and angry music and scoffing at his inability to handle exposure to Kryptonite.

"Kryptonite," I'd have said to myself, a snarky smile etched across my face. "What a loser, what a doof. Who has trouble being around Kryptonite? *My* father could have stood around Kryptonite all damn day and not been bothered by it."

So no, my mother didn't remarry to Superman. In all honesty, she married someone much braver, though I wouldn't fully understand that for some years to come. His name was James Patel. Lieutenant James Patel, of the 29th infantry division for the United States Army.

In early 2002, Lt. Patel, against the wishes of his family, completed enlistment in the United States Army. By March he had been shipped off to a part of the world that I could not point out on a globe if it would win me a million dollars.

In mid 2002, Lt. Patel had his right leg, from the knee down, blown to kingdom come after stepping on an improvised explosive device buried in a patch of sand by a group of people who meant him dead.

In late 2002, he met my mother, a nurse who cared for him during his recovery at St. Thomas' West Hospital in Albany, New York. By the following spring, Lt. Patel had not only made a full recovery, but had a prosthetic leg fashioned beneath where his God given leg had once been. He used that leg to do something all of us take for granted, something he couldn't have done on his own for many months: kneel. And the first time he knelt was the precise moment he asked my mother to marry him, in the Veteran's recovery ward of the St. Thomas' West Hospital.

Two people, brought together by what would otherwise have been heartache, violence, and tragedy.

Hell of a love story, yeah?

Some of us get better than others.

James and my mother got a great one.

ψ

Although James was a terrific man—no denying that—it was hard not to wish I had my own father in his place when it came time for me to move in the summer of 2012.

It was the first day of August, and I was preparing for the biggest move of my life. Nathaniel Shaw was finally flying the coop. I'd been accepted into the Marshall College of Law, and my first term was set to start in less than a month. Marshall wasn't in Albany; hell, it wasn't even in New York. It was over a three-hour car ride away, across the state border in Northern Vermont. A little city called Burlington, and I couldn't wait to get there.

Not that I'd had a problem living at home; my mother and stepfather halved my tuition costs by letting me stay with them while I earned my bachelor's degree. The SUNY Albany campus, the fine institution where I completed a bachelor of science in pre-law, was a mere thirteen-minute car ride from my front door.

Most students my age would scoff at the thought of spending their prime party years under their parent's roof, but for me, it wasn't a big deal. It just worked out that way. I had friends who were struggling to pay rent and keep clean clothes on their backs, who ate ramen noodles cooked in coffee pots for dinner.

My mother insisted on washing, drying, and folding my laundry. James cooked barbecue on the grill out back on Sundays. Pulled pork and brisket. And if you don't think free laundry service and meals aren't alluring enough temptations to ditch dorm life, then you've never tried James' honey-barbeque-glazed brisket.

Both of them were helping me prepare for the big move in their own ways that balmy August afternoon. They helped me pack old cardboard boxes to the brim with lamps and loose clothes, then wrap them tightly with shipping tape. Each tried their damnedest to dispense sage advice to me, a young man about to be let loose in the world for the first time in his life.

My mother was a blubbering wreck, but James tried his best to be stoic and thoughtful. He wasn't a college-educated man himself, but I could tell he was eager to wear the hat of old, fatherly mentor.

During a pause in the hustle and bustle of packing, James stopped to put a hand on my shoulder, look me square in the eye, and try to spill some of that paternal wisdom he wanted so dearly to dole out.

"You know, Nathan," he said, in that voice that sounded like old car tires rolling over loose gravel, "this isn't easy on your mother, you leaving here and all."

I nodded. Mom was downstairs brewing a pitcher of iced tea. But there was no shortage of cold beverages on that warm summer day, so I suspect she was simply tired of crying in front of James and I, and needed a break from watching her one and only child pack up his childhood bedroom.

"It's not easy on me, either," I replied. "I just do a better job of hiding it."

James laughed. "Can't bottle that sort of stuff up. It'll kill ya."

I smiled and stuffed a pile of old sweaters into a box. Vermont got cold, I was told, much colder than what I was used to in New York. Burlington was situated beside Lake Champlain, and the lake effect snow in the winter was enough to freeze your nose off. At least, that's what some travel blogs and online forums had told me.

"You're a damn smart kid," James continued, "and you've turned into an exceptional young man. You've always made us proud. Life dealt our family a miserable hand—each of us—and you never used that as a crutch or an excuse."

I didn't know what to say to that, so I smirked dumbly, metered off a foot of packing tape, and sealed shut my box of winter clothes.

"But, you're gonna have a place of your own now. Far from the eyes of your mother and I." He hesitated as he chose his words. "There's gonna be an awful lot of temptation—"

"Oh, Jesus," I huffed, and I waved my hands. I had a funny feeling, judging by James's tone and delivery, of where the conversation was headed. "I'm twenty-two years old," I said, and I chuckled. "With all due respect, I know all about the birds and the bees—"

"Hey, now, let me finish," James interjected. "We're not worried about you showing up over spring break with a Nathan Jr. attached to your hip."

Who says I'll be back here during spring break at all? I thought.

"But there's more to it than all that. I know how…how *liberal* these college campuses are these days," James said. "You're going to be around a lot of pot and God knows what else."

He thinks I've never smoked. He thinks I finished four years of undergraduate coursework without being in the presence of marijuana.

"And the ganja that goes around now, Nathan, it's not like when me and your mom were kids," James said. "It's ten times stronger, ten times more potent."

It was nigh impossible to picture Lieutenant James Patel of the United States Army kicking back with a tightly rolled joint at any point in his life, leg or no leg, as a kid or as an adult.

"We won't be close by," James went on, "is all I'm trying to say. If you ever needed bailing out, that is."

"Understood, sir," I said. He hated when I called him that, but it was so hard not to, with his buzz cut and square shaped face. He was more G.I. Joe doll than human being, the very caricature of an army man.

"But that said, if you ever are in trouble, if you ever need help or just someone to talk to, we're here for you, Nate. Always." James released his grip from my shoulder and gave me a mighty pat on the back.

"Anyone want tea?" my mother asked, as she carefully carried a tray of drinks up the staircase outside my door. When she reached the second floor landing, her eyes studied my room, the closets emptied and square shaped stains on the walls where posters once hung. For a moment I thought she might topple over. James must have thought so, too, because he darted toward her, grabbed the tray of drinks, and set them on a stack of boxes in the corner of my room.

"I feel like I'm losing my little boy," my mom blurted, and a fountain of tears erupted from her face.

"You'll never lose me," I said, and I wrapped my arms around her. James joined in, too, and the three of us shared a long and somewhat awkward hug.

That night, after the last of the packing was finished, we gathered around the kitchen table one last time over grease soaked wedges of pizza and cold beers. We laughed, told stories, and hoot and hollered, each of us in our own way refusing to accept that come morning I'd be gone.

ψ

The day I moved out of my childhood home in a quiet suburb of Albany, New York, was one of the warmest summer days we'd had on record. Looking back now, I wonder, was it her? Was she with me even then? As we grew to know each other, it became abundantly clear that Vega possessed a certain amount of magic equal to her charm, a warmth that followed her the way the smells of summer followed the rare and infrequent breezes that morning.

"Are you sure you have everything?" my mother asked, and she tapped the top of my beat-up SUV.

I affectionately called it The Beast, but it was in fact a Jeep Cherokee, and it was almost as old as I was. My mother and James bought it for me as a high school graduation gift four years earlier. It was a manual with a funny transmission that sometimes slipped between first and second gear. The red body had been faded by years of sun exposure, its hull peppered with rust and wear from harsh

New York winters. It wasn't glamorous, but it was (for the most part) reliable, and that was good enough for me.

I ran my hand along the hood of The Beast. "I've got everything. I'm sure of it."

"And you'll call as soon as you get to Burlington?" my mother said.

I nodded, then patted the pocket where my cell phone was. "As soon as I step out of the car."

My mother crossed her arms. Again, she was fighting the tears.

"I did a quick inspection this morning, Nate," James said. "Checked your oil. Brakes. Tire pressure. She's all set."

"I appreciate it," I said.

"You're gonna have to do that on your own now, you know. It's important. The roads over in Vermont are a nightmare in the winter, and you can't be running out your front door in the morning on bald or deflated tires—"

"I'll check once a week," I said, and I slapped James on the shoulder. "I was taught by the best."

"So this is really it, then," my mother said, and her voice cracked.

I nodded, opened the driver's side door of The Beast, and climbed in. I rolled down the driver's side window—The Beast had neither power windows nor a functional air conditioner—and jutted my arm out.

"I'll be fine," I said, and I gave a little wave and started the car. The Beast made a clunky, tired groan and the engine turned over. Behind me, a puff of smoke shot out of the exhaust.

James sidestepped close to my mother and wrapped his arm around her waist. They stood beside each other at the end of my driveway as I backed out onto the main street. When I shifted into drive, it was hard not to watch them in my rearview mirror, both of them waving together in unison until the road bended and they faded from view entirely.

ψ

The ride from Albany to Burlington took a little over three hours, the longest one I'd ever driven on my own. I kept the radio tuned to a classic rock station the whole way, bobbing my head to screaming guitars in an effort to keep my mind focused on the endless miles of road ahead.

The GPS function on my cell phone guided me through every sleepy little town and country back road between Albany and Burlington. When I'd first earned a driver's permit six years earlier, the Smartphone was still a full year away from invading every cell phone consumer's pocket, and the idea of your phone guiding you with turn by turn directions was still the stuff of science fiction. It was the end of the dark ages, and if me and some buddies from school wanted to take a weekend joyride into New York City, or a camping trip up into the Adirondacks, we'd have to print out the directions from a computer beforehand, lest we chance getting lost. Can you imagine?

After three hours of piloting The Beast through narrow, hilly passages and rural farmscapes, I was pulling up in front of the worn down bungalow at 126 North Ave in Burlington, Vermont. I'd found the home on an Internet classified two months prior, and couldn't resist. The ad read:

"I have one room to rent in my home in Burlington, VT. The ideal roommate will be 420 friendly, tidy, and easy to get along with.

10

Home is a ten-minute drive from downtown Burlington and twenty minutes from the University of Vermont. Rent is $400 a month and includes WiFi, cable, access to common areas, and use of washer and dryer."

The author of the advertisement listed himself as David Barger, and at the end of the listing he provided his phone number. I couldn't dial it fast enough. I'd spent weeks poring over online classifieds and forums in search of a reasonably priced room to rent, and all my efforts had got me nowhere.

When I called, a friendly, thin voice picked up. He didn't say hi, hello, or any formal variation of the greeting. In what I'd soon learn was typical Dave fashion, he answered simply by saying: "Yo."

"Hi," I said. "I'm calling about the room for rent."

"Oh, yeah, that?" Dave said, sounding a bit surprised. "You're interested?"

"Sure am."

"And you saw the photos I posted of the place?"

"I did," I said.

"And you're *still* interested?" Dave said, and he chuckled so hard he snorted.

Most folks probably would have hung up by that point, but I could just tell the two of us would get along if given the chance. More importantly, Dave had the cheapest rent for a bedroom in Burlington by about two hundred bucks.

Dave and I exchanged pleasantries, and I told him when I'd be moving in (August) and why I was moving to the area (to be a student). He sounded thrilled to have a renter—the place *was* a bit of a dive, and in hindsight, I was probably the first person to call and show genuine interest in it—and he said he was excited to meet me in person.

"One last thing," Dave said, before hanging up.

"What's that?"

"You're not a cop, are you, Nate? A narc?"

I laughed. "Farthest thing from it."

"Eh," Dave said, "I'm just fuckin' with you. See you in August."

When I parked The Beast, the first thing I noticed was that the photos of the house Dave used in the ad were incredibly outdated. I felt duped. The pictures must have been taken, at the very least, a decade prior. I knew I wasn't renting out the guest quarters of a mansion, but the house looked worse for wear, even more troubled than it did in the advertisement. A blanket of leaves, twigs, and branches clung tight to the home's roof and rain gutters. The green paint on the clapboard siding was cracked and peeling from years of neglect. The two windows on the front of the home, on either side of the front door, looked like tired eyes staring back at me. There were wide water stains on either side of them, and the window closest to the driveway had what looked like blooms of mold growing beside it.

Before I'd stepped completely out of my car, Dave was already bustling out the front door and hurrying toward me.

"Howdy," he said with a wave. He wore only a bathrobe and slippers, despite the fact that it was early in the afternoon.

"Hey," I said, and I hopped out of The Beast and extended a hand to shake his.

"Oh, no, we don't do that formal stuff here," he said, and he reached out his arms and gave me a great, big bear hug followed by a slap on the shoulder. That took me aback, but it seemed sincere.

"What we got here?" he said, and he eyed the boxes crammed into the rear seats and trunk of The Beast.

"Clothes, a computer, some books. One of those boxes is full of old Nintendo games."

"Nintendo!" Dave said, and his eyes lit up. "Oh, yeah. We'll get along just fine. Here, let me give you a hand."

I popped open The Beast's trunk and grabbed my first box. "Oh, no, I couldn't let you—"

"Please," Dave said. "You don't have much. With the two of us, we'll be done in five or six trips."

Dave insisted, and he helped me carry the dozen or so boxes into the guest room on the side of the house. Truth be told, the interior was nicer than the outside let on. The carpet was old and stained and everything needed a fresh coat of paint, but there was a charm to it all. *This is my first place,* I distinctly remember thinking, and there was a mild sense of pride that came with that.

The guest room was partially furnished. There was a desk that I could use for my computer, a full-sized bed pressed against the corner of the room, and an office chair. The rollers on the bottom of the chair were cracked and worn, rooted deep into the high-pile rug.

Tacked upon the wall beside the bed was a tattered poster of Kate Upton, sprawled out across some exotic beach, tucked into a bikini that seemed deliberately a size or two too small for her.

"Oh, that," Dave said, and he looked embarrassed. "Belonged to the prior tenant. He must have forgot to take it down."

"Leave it," I said. "The way my love life's been, I would appreciate the companionship."

"Ah," Dave said. "Not my place to pry."

"It's all right," I said. "Bad breakup, earlier this spring."

For the first time all weekend, I thought of Christine Harper. I had buried the thoughts of my last serious relationship beneath the chaos of the move to Vermont and the unique heartache of leaving home.

Christine and I had met that January, and what should have been puppy love turned into a fairly intense fling. By March, the two of us had entered some kind of pact to not see other people—something I thought we were both taking seriously. By June, it'd come to my attention that she was having an equally hot and heavy relationship with a guy in the microeconomics class we both shared, and that was that. What we had was fast and fleeting, and I wasn't at all prepared for it to be over when it was. I'd had little interest in the fairer sex ever since, and I figured that was for the best. The first year of law school is the hardest, and as far as I was concerned, I'd be better off without the distraction.

"Well," Dave said, and he clapped his hands. "Let me give you the grand tour."

Dave led me down the narrow hallway beyond my bedroom door and past the guest bathroom. Thankfully, him and I wouldn't have to share it—he had his own, in the master bedroom across the house—so I was free to leave my toothbrush, soaps, and towels in there and use it whenever I pleased.

My bedroom hallway opened up into the kitchen. Like the rest of the house, it was dingy. The cabinets were of a style and pale color that was all the rage in the 1970's. The appliances looked equally as old; the refrigerator made a loud hum as it strained to keep whatever few groceries were inside it cool. The stove hadn't been cleaned in ages. There was no dishwasher, just a single basin sink, beside which was a microwave caked with grease.

"Everything here runs on gas," Dave said. "Nothing's electric. It'll take some patience and getting used to. The pilot light on the stove goes out from time to time. Kind of a pain in the ass, but, I make do."

From the kitchen, we stepped out toward the living room. In the corner was a small table to eat at with two chairs on either side of it. In the center of the room was a big, flat screen television with a dozen or so video game consoles and DVD players plugged into it. Wires and cables snaked out of the television and onto the cabinet it rested on. Opposite the television was a recliner and a couch, both of which looked like something Dave must have found at the local Goodwill.

"This is the entertainment hub," Dave said. "Feel free to use whatever. My girlfriend, Hannah, comes over from time to time. We order in, smoke out, watch bad movies and play video games. You're always welcome to join, if that's your sort of thing. Beyond that, it doesn't get too rowdy. I don't ever seem to have too many people over."

I felt like Dave was trying to get a read off of me, so I offered: "I don't think I'll be throwing too many parties here either, bud." And that was true—I was new to the area and didn't know anyone. Any of my friends and classmates back at SUNY Albany had zero interest in driving all the way to Upstate Vermont for law school, no matter how prestigious Marshall was. I'd like to say that Marshall, being one of the top law schools in the nation, was my only reason for applying there, but I'd be lying. I was long overdue to get out of the house and be on my own. And, it didn't hurt that I'd be three hours away from Christine Harper and the bittersweet memories I had of her.

But that's the damnedest thing about memories: no matter how hard you try, there's just no running from them.

ψ

15

It was about an hour after Dave had given me the grand tour of our humble little abode that my cell phone rang. I groaned, immediately realized that I failed to call home upon my safe arrival in Burlington. I was setting up my computer when it rang, and of course when I fished it out of my pocket, it was my mom on the other end.

"Hey," I said, and before she had time to say anything, I apologized. "I'm so sorry for not calling. I was unpacking and it slipped my mind."

"You had me worried half to death, Nate," my mom said, and I knew that was only partially true; if she'd truly been worried, she'd have called much earlier. This was guilt, not worry, pure and simple. "Not even a full day out of the house and you've already forgotten us back home."

"Not true!" I said. "Really, I just got carried away."

"That's what James insisted happened. He begged me not to even call."

"Well, I'm glad you did."

"How is it?" she asked. "The house?"

"Oh, it's great," I said.

"And the drive wasn't too bad?"

"Not at all. You'll see for yourself when you come up during the holidays."

There was a pause on the line. Maybe she'd just assumed that I'd be coming down to visit over breaks, not the other way around. But in the weeks before, James had mentioned how it'd be nice to take a road trip, the two of them, and that maybe they'd come up around Thanksgiving.

"That's...that's good, Nate, really," she said. "So we're all good then?"

"We're all good then."

"Okay. Have a good night, hon. And stay out of trouble."

I did stay out of trouble, but my first night in my first apartment was anything but good.

It started off good, at least. Dave and I took a stroll down North Ave, toward a short row of shops and eateries.

There was a convenient store with a couple of bums hanging around the bus stop out front. When we passed by it, a pair of rats came scurrying out of a rain gutter attached to the store. I yelled, Dave laughed. I made a tasteless comment about how I'd never shop there.

Beside the rat infested convenient store was a bar, and beside the bar was a SubTub. Dave insisted that SubTub had the best sandwhiches in all of Burlington, so we ordered a couple to go and took them home. Afterward, Dave retired to the living room couch to have a smoke and play some video games. He invited me to do both but I declined, and decided to turn in early. I still had some unpacking left to do, and I was exhausted from the morning's drive.

I wish there was something I could have blamed that night's terrors on. Something in my sandwich from SubTub? But it tasted fine, and besides, Dave didn't get sick. Second hand exposure to the marijuana smoke that wafted toward my bedroom from the living room? Unlikely. The stress of moving out from home? Maybe.

When I'd made my bed and started to drift to sleep, Kate Upton watching me from her exotic beach above me, I fell into a terrible nightmare.

It started warmly enough—at least, where I remember it starting, dreams rarely have beginnings and ends that are easily defined—but it quickly turned revolting.

17

I found myself at the edge of a deep, dark wood. Ahead of me were endless miles of trees, their gnarled branches twisted and entwined with one another. In the middle of the wall they formed was a single, narrow trail. Clung to the trail was a milky blanket of fog.

Of course, had I encountered such a wood and such a trail during waking hours, I'd turn around and run in the other direction. But one's own motivations and logic rarely make sense in dreams, so I pressed onward, squeezing between the braided branches and roots of the sprawling wood.

Soon, I reached a clearing. A flat patch of forest where the sinister trees gave way to a perfectly stamped circle in the middle of the woods.

Standing in the center of the circle were two deer, and it was in the middle of that awful dream that one of my few, precious memories with my father returned.

We'd been on a fishing trip—him, my mother, and I—the fall before he passed away. Mom had packed a little picnic for us, and we all piled into the family minivan one early Saturday morning to drive upstate, admire the colors of the changing autumn leaves, and wrangle a Catfish or two.

By afternoon we were hungry and hadn't caught a single damn thing, so we cracked open the picnic basket mom brought. We sat on the shoreline of the Mohawk River, eating tuna sandwiches and drinking lukewarm cans of Coke, when they appeared: a pair of deer, beautiful and dignified, emerging from the woods behind us with barely a peep. It was as if they'd materialized from thin air. We sat together, silently admiring them from afar, shooting them not with rifles—hunting season was still open that weekend—but with the faulty cameras in our minds, those lenses of memories that always

18

remember the bad times as having been not so bad, and those rare, truly golden moments as ten times more beautiful than they really were.

It was a story we told again and again, a truly once in a lifetime moment that I'm thankful the three of us shared before my father's sudden departure from this mortal coil one year later.

It occurred to me, standing in the dark field of my bizarre dream, that the pair of deer staring back at me were not entirely imagined, but identical to the two from our fishing trip along the Mohawk. They were exactly as I remembered them. The buck stood two feet taller than the doe at his side, his antlers reached high up into the air. The doe, with her soft hazel eyes and white mottled coat, stood calmly beside the buck.

"What are you doing here?" I cried out; which, in the context of the dream, I guess made sense.

Startled by my shout, they dashed into the woods behind them and vanished.

That's when it first caught my eye, the bright crimson orb shooting across the night sky above me.

Across a blanket of twinkling stars it soared, burning hot and red, a tail of rust colored glitter trailing behind it.

Was it headed for earth?

Was it headed directly at me?

It was beautiful, hauntingly so, and I could have kept my neck craned toward the heavens for hours just watching it, were it not for the startling, panicked grunts of injured animals.

I looked back down at the clearing. Where the deer once stood were two birch colored pikes, planted like trees in the soft soil, their sharply pointed ends aimed at the falling star above.

19

On one pike was the severed, impaled head of a doe; on the other, the buck. Lengths of sinewy, blood-soaked flesh dangled from beneath their necks. High-pitched shrieks and screams left their mouths, their extended tongues undulating as they screamed.

Standing between the two was a figure, cloaked head to toe in black, still as a statue. It raised a hand in my direction, pointed at me, and called out three words:

"Come to me."

I woke up, wrapped in a pile of blankets, my t-shirt drenched in sweat and my chest heaving. I yanked my cell phone from where it charged on the nightstand beside me to check the time. 3:30 AM.

I stood and paced back and forth for a moment, trying to shake the brutal and violent imagery of the nightmare from my mind.

When I finally caught my breath, I walked toward my bedroom window, wedged my finger between the slats of the blinds and peered out.

The night sky was dark and cloudy, not at all like the clear blanket of stars in my dream. Still, I stood and waited, bathed in moonlight, half expecting to see a shooting star fall down toward earth.

ψ

My first morning in my new apartment fared much better than my first night there.

I'd awoken around a quarter 'til eight, just a few hours after falling back to sleep after my nightmare. Soft morning light flooded my bedroom—it would be a good thing to invest in some curtains, preferably dark ones, I thought—and I could hear the sound of bacon sizzling in a fry pan. I hopped out of bed and followed the aroma of morning breakfast, like a cartoon character might follow the scent of fresh-baked apple pie back to the windowsill it cooled on.

When I'd made my way to the kitchen, Dave was standing in front of the thirty year old stove, busily cooking a giant breakfast. I didn't have to ask if any of it was for me—I didn't want to be rude—but unless he was planning on eating a half dozen eggs and a pound of bacon by himself, I assumed he was cooking for the two of us.

"Hey, bucko," Dave said. "How was your first night on your own?"

"Pretty good," I lied, and as I rubbed my eyes I remembered Dave telling me he had a girlfriend, Hannah. Maybe this was a Saturday tradition of there's, and she was on the way over?

"Do me a favor and pour us some O.J. from the fridge. I'm almost finished here, and I'd hate for it to burn."

"Can do," I said, and I fished the carton of orange juice from the refrigerator, then grabbed a couple of glass tumblers from the cupboard beside where Dave stood cooking.

"Now, don't go on expecting this kind of treatment every weekend," Dave said, as I filled our glasses to the brim. "But it's the least I could do, it being your first weekend here and all."

Dave was one of the good ones, I was learning that fast. The guy didn't send off a single negative vibe. His house was old, but he kept it tidy. His hair was always a moppy mess, but he kept groomed, kept impeccably white teeth and never stunk. He was around the same age as me, and my best guess was that he came from a life where he never had much, but that didn't stop him from being proud of what he *did* have.

21

"I appreciate it, Dave, really," I said, and I carried our glasses of juice to the small, oak dining table between the living room and the kitchen.

Dave followed close behind, plates of scrambled eggs and perfectly cooked bacon balanced in his hands. We sat across from each other and, in the absence of any female companions or family members, ate like the undomesticated men we were. We talked with mouthfuls of food, pounded at the table when we laughed, and devoured our plates of breakfast with the same manners as our cavemen ancestors.

When we finished our food, Dave said, "I hate to run out so fast, but I should get to work soon. Would you mind cleaning these dishes?"

"Course not," I said. "It's the least I can do. Where's work?"

"Remember where we got our subs last night?"

"SubTub, really? That's where you work?"

"No," Dave said. "The convenience store next door, where the bums hang out and wait for the bus."

"Oh," I said, remembering the comments I'd made on our walk home the night before. "The one I called—"

"Dilapidated and rat infested?"

I could feel my face flush red.

"Don't worry about it," Dave said. "It *is* dilapidated and rat infested. But I've worked there for years. I carve out a decent enough living ringing up beer and lotto tickets for the town drunks. Hey, what is it you do?"

I didn't know how to answer that. A lot of people aren't aware that most every law school prohibits their students from working during their first year. The course load is simply too heavy to balance school and a work schedule.

22

"I don't have a job lined up. I probably won't start a paid internship until next summer."

Dave looked understandably surprised. "Hey, Nate," he said. "The check you gave me for first month's rent...that's going to clear when I deposit it, right?"

I smiled and nodded. The whole thing was very hard to explain. The summer of 2005, James' father passed away, and when he did, a significant portion of his estate passed down to James. My mother and him didn't fall into that trap that you always see people of modest means falling into when they inherit a windfall. Instead of moving the three of us to a palatial estate in some snobby town like East Violet, or buying a vacation home, or a yacht, they banked the cash. All $1.2 million of it, after taxes. James' father had patented some kind of indulgent hand sanitizer in the early nineties, and his family had been set for life. James—not content with a life of luxury—left home to serve his civic duty and chase very bad men through unforgiving desert hellscapes. From what I understand, it created quite the rift between James and my surrogate grandfather, but not enough of a divide to cut James out of his father's will entirely.

On my eighteenth birthday, after being handed the keys to The Beast, James sat down with my mother and me, and presented me a check for $80,000.

"It wont' be enough," James had instructed me, "for a fancy car, or to pay for all of your tuition. You'll earn those things. The tuition will be covered by scholarships and grants, of that I'm certain. Your grades will take you far. But it will cover your day-to-day expenses, if you're smart. It will keep food in your stomach and gas in your car, and you won't have to work a single day until you're holding your

Juris Doctorate in your hands. Your mom and I have discussed it at length."

I was flabbergasted, didn't know what to say. Sometimes at night, I'd overhear the two of them talking about the inheritance. But, I always thought it was a small figure. It wasn't my business and it wasn't my place to pry. When that Christmas James bought my mother a diamond tennis bracelet and myself the latest Xbox, I guessed that his inheritance was for forty grand. I don't know why I chose forty, but my curiosity and imagination demanded a number.

And the man had just wrote me a check for double that.

I didn't explain all of those details to David, but I did give him a roundabout answer.

"You'll never have to worry about me defaulting on my rent," I told Dave, kindly. "I have a small trust"—a lie, even after four years of undergrad work it had over fifty-thousand dollars remaining—"and I keep careful accounting."

It didn't occur to me that telling Dave, a stranger to me less than twenty-four hours prior, that I had a trust setup in my name might be a risky maneuver.

"It's all gravy, baby," Dave said. "I'm sorry for prying. It's just, when a new tenant tells me that he doesn't have a job in sight for over a year, it's a cause for concern." He stood and brought his dishes to the sink. "Nate, you never struck me as the spoiled college type. I should have asked more for rent."

"I grew up very modestly," I said. "My college trust was a recent phenomenon. From my stepfather."

"Say no more," Dave said. "I've already peeked into your business enough. I get off around three this afternoon, so I'll see you sometime after that, yeah?"

24

I nodded, wished Dave a good day, and he was out the door in a flash, hurrying down North Ave toward the convenience store with the bums outside.

Dave had only been gone for a matter of moments before a particularly bothersome sense of loneliness rose up beside me. The house at 126 North Ave was quiet. Too quiet. I did the morning's dishes to take my mind off things, but that bought only a five-minute reprieve from the sudden dread of lonesomeness.

I remembered the blinds in my bedroom window. They were white, vinyl, and some of the slats were cracked or crooked. The window could stand to benefit from a set of heavy, dark colored curtains, so I strolled back into my bedroom and plucked my phone from the nightstand.

I opened the Internet browser and typed in the words: "window treatments for sale near me." A list of a dozen or so retailers within a ten-mile radius filled the screen.

Now, up until that day, had you asked me if I believed in fate, my answer might have been unclear. Somewhere between a yes and no. Was it fate that two beautiful deer crossed the path of myself, my mother, and my dearly departed father on that one perfect autumn afternoon many years back? Was it fate that my stepfather, James Patel, ran off into war, only to have his leg blown off? That was awful, of course, but had it not been for his injury he'd have never met my mother, the woman he fell so hopelessly in love with.

I can say now, unequivocally and with total certainty, that I believe in fate. Because out of the dozens of fine retail establishments that I could have bought curtains from, I chose the Dianne's Fabrics at the Burlington Town Mall. I could have just as easily chosen to shop at the Target across town or the Wal-Mart one city over.

As soon as I decided to drive to the Burlington Town Mall, I surrendered myself to fate.

And, although I didn't know it then, fate was barreling down on me at a hundred miles an hour.

ψ

It took three tries to get The Beast started before my trek to the Burlington Town Mall that Saturday morning. At the time, I was livid; the Jeep sputtered and made a high-pitched whine in its desperate attempts to start.

On the third attempt, the engine roared to life. I suspected that the battery might need replacing soon.

Burlington was entirely new to me, so I plugged the coordinates of the shopping center into my phone's GPS and let it guide me there. It was both strange and exciting, coasting over unfamiliar landscapes in The Beast. Burlington was at some points quaint and scenic, and at others sprawling and bustling. I cruised along Battery Street, and Lake Champlain opened up wide to the right of me. Sailboats dotted the water; picnickers sprawled out across the shoreline on checked blankets. It was truly beautiful, so much so that not once did I think of how horribly lost I'd be without the help of my phone shouting turn-by-turn directions to me in its robotic voice.

In no time flat I was at the Burlington Town Mall, a modestly sized shopping center near the edge of the city. The rust brick façade on the front of the mall hinted that the structure had been built in the 1980's, or possibly even earlier. Some updates had been added, that was obvious, and the parking lot had recently been repaved. But the structure itself screamed of a bygone era, when brick and mortar shopping establishments ruled the country, before anything you'd possibly wish for could be delivered to your doorstep upon a few clicks of a computer mouse.

I parked The Beast in a parking spot close to the front entrance of Macy's and hurried my way inside. The interior of the mall was much larger than the outside suggested it might be, and in total there were four different wings of shops that all intersected at a food court in the center of the building. As lost in the mall as I was on the streets of Burlington, I found a directory, scanned it over until I found the location of Dianne's Fabrics, and marched on over to the store, which, as luck would have it, was close to the entrance I came in at.

Luck smiled on me again when I entered Dianne's and found that they were having a massive sale on Cavern brand blackout curtains. They were normally twenty bucks a panel, but today they were ten, so I bought two and made my way to a register at the front of the store.

A gentleman in his early forties rang up my purchase. He smirked at the curtains as he bagged them.

"College kid, huh?" he asked.

I shrugged. "Sure am."

"Oh yeah," he said, handing me a shopping bag. "These are all the rage with you college kids. None of you want to see the sun before noon."

"Sure don't," I said, and the cashier handed me my receipt and I was on my way.

I could have left the mall that day and drove back home, watched bad television, and played one of the dozen video games Dave left out on the living room coffee table. But I was so enamored by wanderlust from the drive over, and the weather was so nice—if not a bit too warm—that I didn't want to retreat back to the four walls of my bedroom in Dave's bungalow.

When I searched the mall directory for Dianne's, I had spotted an Orange Julius in the food court. I thought of how nice it might be to grab a frozen drink, drive over to the shoreline of Lake Champlain, and just spend an hour or two watching the boats come and go, watching kids toss Frisbees back and forth, and greeting dogs and their owners as they passed my bench.

So, I headed to the Orange Julius, ordered a strawberry smoothie, and turned to head back towards the Macy's that I parked near. With my shopping bag in one hand and my smoothie in the other, I must have looked like a bit of a putz, walking gleefully through the mall's corridors. But, what can I say—simple things always made me the happiest, and I was overcome with a tremendous amount of relief and joy that day. Relief that my roommate was a normal, happy guy who sometimes made breakfast and not some troubled looking serial killer type, and joy to be fortunate enough to live in such a beautiful little town and attend such a great law school. My life was starting to feel like a box of puzzle pieces that were all clicking together.

On the walk back towards Macy's, I passed a Happy Body gym. It might seem funny for a gym to be in a mall, but remember, this was the summer of 2012, and malls across the country were closing left and right. Had the space not been rented out to a gym, it'd probably sit there vacant.

Happy Body had long floor to ceiling windows along the front of it, which was a pretty clever marketing trick. Dopes like me could pass by, sipping on a smoothie that had the caloric equivalent of a double cheeseburger, and peer inside at all the hardworking folks, and maybe feel shamed into walking inside and asking about a gym membership before leaving the mall for the day.

The gym had been empty the first time I passed by, but now it looked like a spinning class was about to begin. An instructor took his seat in the center of a row of incumbent bikes. Behind him were a dozen or so gym members, mounting their bikes, preparing for the arduous workout ahead.

And I'd almost passed the last window, almost overlooked this otherwise innocuous spinning class, before *she* caught my attention.

She was sitting all the way to the right in a pair of tight black leggings and a red tank top that looked like it could have been painted on. Her hair was pulled back in a high ponytail, but a few strands of bangs hung curled in front of her face.

She was fire. She was sex. She was rock and roll.

My smoothie, slicked with condensation, almost slipped out of my hand. I caught it before it had the chance to splat against the floor, and it was only then that I'd been awoken from some kind of hypnotic trance, and the utter embarrassment that I had been *staring.*

In everyone's life, there will be a few genuine moments of surprise, good or bad. When, on my eighteenth birthday, my parents sat me down and handed me a check for eighty thousand dollars— that was a moment of genuine surprise. Up until then, it might have won the gold medal for the most surprising thing to ever happen to me. But what happened next, that balmy afternoon at the Burlington Town Mall, was a very close silver.

The girl in the red tank top had indeed caught me staring, but rather than glare or roll her eyes, she stared back. And after what felt like ten thousand years of locking eyes with one another, she leaned forward on her bike, and winked.

I smiled and offered a stupid little wave in return. She smiled too, and I hurried away from the tall windows of the Happy Body Gym and toward the exit of the mall.

In that moment, I figured I'd never cross paths with her ever again. Which was kind of dumb—Burlington was beautiful, but it wasn't very big.

In fact, I would meet the mystery woman from the Happy Body gym two weeks later, on my very first day of attendance at the Marshall School of Law.

She would introduce herself to me as Vega.

ψ

The rest of my Saturday afternoon went exactly as I'd planned it. I drove to Lake Champlain, parked The Beast, and found a bench along the edge of a park that overlooked the lake. I sat there with my smoothie, which by then had mostly melted into a watery slosh, and watched the sailboats come and go. There were kids tossing Frisbees. There were people walking dogs. One couple passed by with a great big Labrador named Charlie, who was as excited to greet me as I was to greet him. I gave Charlie a pat on the head and a scratch to his back, then thanked his owners—a well dressed couple in their fifties—for letting him visit me.

With my smoothie long gone and the early afternoon sun starting to dip, I walked back to The Beast and drove myself home. My watch said it was a little after three, so I figured Dave would be home, and it'd be nice to have the company. The drive was careless and simple, just a few turns that I remembered from earlier in the day. I didn't have to rely on my phone for directions once.

I parked The Beast in Dave's driveway and walked inside. It was weird, having my own key to my own place. Twisting the handle of a lock and not seeing James and my mother on the other side of the door was a strange feeling that would stick with me for weeks.

When I was just about to push the door open, I heard a rustling in the shrubs beside the front of the house. I put my keys back in my pocket, closed the door, and walked over to investigate.

The shrubs were gnarled and overgrown, so it was hard to tell what exactly was lurking inside of them. I inched closer, my curiosity getting the best of me, and the thought crossed my mind that I had no clue whether or not snakes and other vile creatures were native to this part of Vermont.

I crouched and pressed my hands into the shrubs, prying apart some branches to get a better look at the soil below. As I did, I heard the most innocent sound cry out at me: the meow of a small kitten.

"Hey, buddy, where are you?" I asked, pushing apart more branches.

A pair of glowing, emerald orbs looked up at me and widened. The kitten meowed again.

I reached into the shrub and pried the creature out. It was small enough to fit in the palm of my hand. And, no wonder it'd been hard to spot in the shrub; it was black, head to toe.

I brought the critter up against my chest. It purred and butted its head against my chin. Growing up, I didn't have a lot of high maintenance pets. Goldfish. A hamster. At one point, an iguana. When I was very young, we had a family dog, but he passed away before I could make any reliable memories of him. In my teenage years, I'd pushed heavily for a cat, but James was allergic.

"What are you doing out here?" I asked, in that cooing baby-talk voice folk tend to use while speaking to very small animals.

The kitten meowed again, then curled up in my hand and squinted its eyes shut.

I opened the front door and made my way inside, carefully carrying the creature. Dave was sitting on the living room couch—a place I'd almost always find him in the weeks to come—playing a video game. He paused his game and turned to me.

"Hey, man. Were you just talking to someone?"

"Just this little guy. Or girl. I'm not sure yet." I held out my palm and showed Dave the kitten, not once considering whether or not he might have an allergy or some other aversion to felines.

"Where'd you find that?"

"In the shrubs out front," I said.

Dave shook his head. "Litter box is staying in your room."

"What?" I said.

"If you could see the goofy look on your face right now, you'd know that there's no chance in hell that cat is going back outside or to a shelter. Litter box stays in your room. And please, get it checked out for worms or mange or whatever it is those things can carry."

I felt embarrassed. "Dave, really, the thought to keep it hadn't even crossed my mind."

"Cool," Dave said. "Then I'll keep it. But the litter box is still staying in your room."

I smiled. "You're really okay with this?"

Dave stood up and walked over to the kitchen, poured himself a glass of water. "Are you sure *you're* okay with taking care of a newborn animal before you've even had twenty-four hours of freedom to yourself?"

I nodded. "Cats are easy. They do most of the work for you."

Later that week, I'd bring our newfound roommate to the Burlington Veterinary Clinic. It'd be checked carefully for a microchip, in case it belonged to someone else. It didn't. It'd also be checked for fleas, worms, feline leukemia and a laundry list of other conditions. For a tiny kitten found wandering around outside, it sure had a clean bill of health.

The little fluff ball turned out to be a girl; not that it really mattered. Dave and I had affectionately referred to her as Shadow in the days to come, so either way that coin landed, the name would fit. Shadow seemed appropriate, not just because the girl didn't have a speck of white or any other color on her, but because of the way she followed Dave and I, night and day. We were inseparable.

"Listen," Dave said, and he returned to the couch with his glass of water. "Sit down. I wanna have a talk, man to man."

I sat on the recliner across from him. Shadow had fallen asleep against my chest.

"I still feel bad about this morning. About prying."

"You had every right to," I assured him. "You're my landlord. You should know that you'll get paid each month."

"Yeah," Dave said. "But I don't like the way I went about it. I figured, it's only fair that you know a little more about me. About where I'm from."

I nodded. "Sure, Dave. But that isn't necessary."

"You think it's strange that a twenty-four year old guy who works at a convenience store has a house all to his own?"

I shrugged. "I never really thought about it."

"I never knew my mom," Dave said, bluntly. "She left when I was little. Really little. It was just my dad and me, here, since I was a baby."

Dave took a sip of his water. I had no idea what to say, so I said, "I'm sorry to hear that."

"Ancient history," Dave said. "It's all gravy, baby."

"So then...my bedroom," I said. "The Kate Upton poster...the former tenant was—"

"Me," Dave said. "And I really meant to take that poster down. I'm embarrassed."

My mind raced at all the possible reasons Dave's father was no longer in the house. The most obvious seemed clear. Dave and I were part of the same terrible club, the membership of which cost years of heartache and sorrow.

"My father passed away last year," Dave said, confirming my suspicion. "The house was paid off. It went to me. So, like you, I know how it feels to just be...handed something. There's an odd sense of guilt that comes with it, you know?"

I nodded.

"My job at the Quick Mart down the street...it's enough to pay the taxes, keep the lights on. Keep beer in the fridge. But I needed a roommate to skate by. In a couple of years, I want to sell the place. The land is worth more than the house that sits on top of it, but it'd be enough to get out of here. Get a fresh start."

"It's so beautiful here. Where would you go?"

"Hannah and I were thinking Florida. Orlando, maybe. It's beautiful here, Nate. But the winters are hell. Hannah and I have been together a few months now, and it's getting serious. She has the same opinion about winters and snowstorms as I do. They're better off viewed from your cell phone screen, while sitting on a beach and sipping an ice-cold beer."

"They never bothered me much," I said.

Dave nodded. "Oh, you'll be sick of it someday, buddy." He let out a long, tired sigh. "That's about the long and the short of it. What's law school? Three years?"

"Three years," I said.

34

"I doubt we'll be out of here before then, so you won't have to worry about finding a new place, assuming you like it here."

"I do like it here."

Dave raised his water glass toward me, a mock cheer. "Here's to our time together then, my pal. May it be long and prosperous."

It wouldn't be. What was it John Lennon said? "Life's what happens when you're making plans." Yeah, that tired old adage.

I wanted all of Dave's plans to work out, I really did. He was one of the good ones, and he deserved the best. But Dave would never get the chance to sell his home. A few weeks later, the little two-bedroom bungalow at 126 North Ave would burn to the ground in one of the worst home fires in Burlington's history.

ψ

The two weeks between the Saturday I moved into Dave's house and my first day of law school came and went in a flash. I spent much of that time doting after Shadow. I bought her a perch that I kept in the corner of my bedroom, a scratching post, and a litter box. We were a couple of peas in a pod. It helped that Dave had grown a fondness for her, too. Though the litter box remained in my bedroom, Shadow had free roam of the house and could come and go as she pleased. She often sat between Dave and I during late night video game romps, snoozing and grooming herself to her heart's content.

On more than one occasion I met Hannah, the apple of Dave's eye. She was a lovely girl in her late twenties. I found out that she was studying nursing at the University of Vermont, after a long and stalled career in retail. The big box electronics retailer that she worked for since high school was shuttering their doors, and Hannah had taken that as a sign to change careers. There had been talks about the two of them moving into Dave's master bedroom together someday, but Hannah was trapped in a lease until the summer of 2013 at the earliest. The two had asked me "if I'd be cool with that next summer," to which I replied I would be very cool with it; they were the nicest couple my age that I'd ever met. Though their relationship was young, anyone who spent five minutes with them knew that they genuinely cared for each other, that they were one of the rare duos meant to last.

The Sunday night before my first day of classes, my mother gave me a call. I was sitting at my desk, Shadow napping beside me, studying my schedule for the next day alongside a map of the Marshall campus. The college was huge but the layout was simple, and I was fairly certain I wouldn't have a hard time finding where my classes were.

"Hey," I said, answering my phone while still studying the map.

"Hey, sweetie," my mom said, in her usual sing-song voice. "I just wanted to see how you were doing before your big day. You sound busy."

"Never too busy to talk to you," I said, and I closed my laptop screen. "How are you, mom?"

"Well," she said, "good. It's just so quiet around here without you."

I expected her voice to crack, but it stayed strong.

"I'll have to surprise you some day," I said. "I'll come over late at night and start banging some pots and pans."

My mom snickered. "I wouldn't put that past you, Nate."

"How's James?" I asked.

"He's good, he's good. He finished installing some new cabinets in the kitchen this weekend. You know, those cabinets have needed

36

replacing for years. I think he's just trying to distract himself now that you're out of the house."

"I never expected him to be so sentimental."

"You know, Nate, he thinks of you as his son."

That line in particular always made me feel bad. James had always been terrific to me, and I always thought of him as a fatherly figure, but never as my *dad*. And I never called him dad. Always James. Even after the guy wrote me a check big enough to carry me through college. I could just never bring myself to do it.

"I got a cat," I blurted, desperate to change the subject.

"Is that so?" my mom asked, after a short pause. "What brought that about?"

"I found her roaming around the front of the house a couple weeks ago. Had her checked out at the vet and everything. She's fit as a fiddle, so we decided to keep her."

"Huh," my mom said. "Nate—what color is it?"

"Black, why?"

"Now *that's* funny," my mom said, and again the phone went silent.

"Why is that?" I asked.

"Oh, it's nothing, it's just—well, it's silly." Another pause. Finally, my mom said: "I had the most peculiar dream a couple of weeks ago. You, your father, and I...we were all sitting along the Mohawk River, eating tuna sandwiches, when those two deer approached us, you remember that?"

I felt the skin on my forearms turn to gooseflesh. "Of course I remember."

"And I swear, that dream was so lifelike, it was like we were all back in time in that very moment, the three of us, together again. Only one thing was different."

37

"What was that, mom?"

My mom laughed, then said: "Cupped against your chest…you were holding a black, baby kitten."

ψ

I didn't have any nightmares that night. No twisted, sick retellings of long lost childhood memories. No shooting stars scraping a sinister path through the sky. In fact, I didn't have any dreams at all. I hardly slept a wink the night before my first morning at Marshall. Which is odd, I guess. I'd never had any nerves about a big, first day at school before. Four years of undergrad work came and went without nerves. What was it about law school? There was a pressure to it that I'd never felt before and have yet to feel since.

That Monday morning I woke up, fed Shadow, then tiptoed to the kitchen to quietly feed myself. One room down, I could hear Dave's snoring. His shift at the Quick Mart didn't start until later that afternoon, so there was no surprise breakfast feast waiting for me at the stove. Instead, I settled for a cold bowl of cereal.

Shadow walked a figure eight between my feet as I stood in the kitchen, contemplating the phone call with my mother from the night before. It was strange, right? What are the odds that she'd dream I found a black kitten before I ever had the chance to tell her so?

Well, that was the rub, wasn't it? She hadn't dreamt I found one, only that I was holding one. The fact that both shadow and the cat in her dream were black could be thought of as coincidence. I'd wanted a pet feline of my own for ages; it wouldn't be unreasonable for her to think I'd get one as soon as I was on my own, far away from James' allergic reactions to pet dander.

As for the rest of her dream? Again, not uncommon that we'd both experience a subconscious retelling of the fishing trip that her, my father, and I went on so many years before. It was a treasured memory between the three of us, one that we'd each dreamt of many times before. It wasn't unusual that we'd have similar dreams in the same two-week span of time. And they *were* similar, not identical. Hers ended much happier, after all, with the deer merely visiting us, as they had that autumn afternoon long ago. Mine ended with their severed heads planted upon pikes, still bleating and shrieking as that dark figure beckoned me forward.

The whole thing left an unsavory taste in my mouth, no matter how hard I tried to chalk the whole thing up to coincidence. I'd say that it felt paranormal, or supernatural, or some other modifier like that, but the truth is I'd never been much of a believer in those sorts of things. To believe in ghosts, or an afterlife, or other mystical phenomenon would require believing in a God. And what kind of God would tear a boy away from his father—his hero—at the age of nine?

There was a time, I suppose, that I believed in ghosts and ghouls as a child. But that was long ago, and it was a thought I didn't like to revisit.

Shadow purred, bumped her head against my ankle. How long had I stood in the kitchen, reflecting on such morose and awful thoughts? Long enough for the cereal in my bowl to turn soggy and the milk it floated in warm; long enough for the clock on the kitchen microwave to indicate that if I didn't get moving soon, I'd be late.

My seven o'clock drive through town was quiet and peaceful. Burlington hadn't woken up for the day, and there were few other cars on the road. Streetlights had darkened, yet the early morning light glowed soft. It was that razor's edge between night and dawn that's infinitely more beautiful when experienced in a small city.

I turned off of North and onto Hampshire. The city receded behind me, and the two-lane highway snaked through a dense patch of pines and elms, a winding route with many bends.

Twelve minutes later, The Beast and I were pulling into a parking lot in front of a grand, old building. Its brick face was weathered from a century and a half of Vermont winters, but it was still strong and dignified. Rows of fir trees stood before it, and behind it were a half dozen or so other buildings, all equally as old and as elegant.

I took a long, deep breath and savored the moment.

I'd finally made it to the Marshall College of Law.

My first class was in Bircham Hall, near the rear of the campus. Although I arrived to the auditorium fifteen minutes early, it was already half-filled. Each aisle of seats was peppered with sleep-starved students, some of who were dressed very professionally, and some of who—myself included—were dressed like they cared too much about looking like they didn't care too much. One girl in the back of the auditorium was wearing pajamas.

I scanned the seats and took my place somewhere in the middle of the auditorium. It was a safe place, I figured; close enough to hear the morning's lecture and participate if I wanted to, but far enough back from the lectern that I wouldn't be singled out specifically.

There were still ten minutes left before class started when I heard the big, metal doors on the side of the room clank open. I don't know why I turned so quickly to see who was walking in, but it was like all the air had left the room at once.

All this time later, I can remember exactly what she was wearing. A shiny pair of black heels; they looked expensive, and they had little straps that wrapped around her pale ankles. A slim, red dress that clung to her hourglass frame. A rose-gold colored watch was fastened to her left wrist. A necklace in the same shade as her watch draped loose around her neck. And, atop her head, was a black, floppy, wide-brimmed hat. It's a bit dumb to admit, but I wondered where that hat was going to go when the lecture started. Would she wear it throughout the whole class? It looked too expensive to drop on the floor.

We made eye contact with one another, and she smiled, then made her way toward the row of seats I sat in. My pulse quickened.

"Hey there," she said, and she gave a little wisp of a wave with her fingers. She eyed the seat next to mine and asked: "Are you saving this for anyone?"

"I'm not," I said. I was so proud of myself for not stuttering.

"Fantastic," she said, and she set her bag down on the floor in front of her and took a seat. "It's good to see a familiar face on the first day of class."

"Is it familiar?" I said.

"I never forget a face. Especially one that gawked at me while I worked out."

I extended a hand. "Nathaniel Shaw. Sorry for gawking."

She returned the handshake. Her hand was firm and warm. "Vega Rowland." She cleared her throat. "So you admit you were gawking then?"

"I wouldn't call it gawking—"

"Then what would you call it?" she said. "Staring awkwardly?"

I could feel my face blush. I hated how I turned red in moments of embarrassment.

41

"Tell me, Nathaniel Shaw," Vega said. "Do you often stare awkwardly at women while they exercise?"

If a frog had climbed out of my throat at that very moment, it could have delivered a better reply than whatever I was trying to come up with.

"Oh, for crying out loud," Vega said. "You should see the look on your face. Chill. I'm just toying with you." She bit her lip, and her smile flattened. "Besides, if you'll recall, I stared back. Now, tell me, why are you sitting here at 7:45 AM?"

"Same as you," I said. "To study torts."

"Mmm, yes, that is the class," Vega said. "I mean, why didn't you register for Chelsea Harmon's torts class? She teaches late in the afternoon, she's a total babe, and most importantly, she's not McManus the Anus."

I laughed and pulled the class schedule I'd printed from the notebook on my desk. I studied it, found the professor's name for my morning torts class.

"Mick-man-us," I said. "I think that's how it's pronounced."

"You're new around here, aren't you?"

"I am," I admitted.

Vega smiled. "Everyone around here pronounces his name Mick-*mane*-us, partially because it annoys the hell out of him, and partially because it rhymes so perfectly with anus."

"What's so terrible about the guy?" I asked.

Vega popped a piece of bubblegum into her mouth, then looked at the clock above the whiteboard at the front of the auditorium. "We got some time," she said. "You really want to know?"

Her voice was like velvet; smooth, but it had a cool rumble underneath. Truth be told, I could have listened to Vega Rowland recite the ingredients off the back of the granola bar tucked inside my backpack for the ten minutes before class began, and I'd have been happy with it.

"Yeah," I said. "Hit me with it."

"He's a mean old bastard," Vega said. "He doesn't give anyone in his classes an A, ever. It's part of some fucked up philosophy of his. He thinks an A is symbolic of perfection, and that the modern school system has coddled students into expecting them, instead of earning them. He thinks they're handed out too easily, and so he challenges his students to accept the fact that they won't always get one, even if they turn in excellent work. No one has left his class with higher than a B+."

"How do you know all this?" I asked.

"I studied at the University of Vermont," Vega said. "He taught pre-law classes there part time. I took a class of his that he taught on contracts. I witnessed this all first hand."

"So he's a tough grader," I said, and I shrugged. "I can deal with that."

"It's more than just his grading policies," Vega said. "There were a lot of unsavory rumors that swirled around him back at U of V. Dude's a bit of a pervert."

"Now you have my attention."

"Do I?" Vega asked. "Back in the eighties, he dated one of his students. Joyce Nicholson. Got her pregnant, apparently. She died in a car wreck a few weeks before she was supposed to deliver. Did you take Hampshire on the way over here today?"

I nodded.

"Then you drove past the spot where she wrecked," Vega said. "She drove straight into a ditch on one of the bends in the road, about a mile from the front of campus."

"That's awful," I said.

43

Vega snapped the piece of gum in her mouth. "What's worse is that, according to legend, she drove into the ditch herself. Despite carrying McManus's baby, the dude was still going to flunk her for failing his torts class. She was already struggling in a couple of other classes, so she was going to lose her scholarships, her grants, and be put on academic probation for it."

"Bullshit," I said.

Vega raised her hands. "Listen, I'm just telling you the same legend all us U of V students have to hear. Fact is, the guy never married, never had any other kids. And to this day, he's a colossal prick. Joyce Nicholson got her revenge on him, sure. Now we all have to suffer his wrath twenty-some-odd years later."

"It's a better story for a campfire than for a college auditorium," I said. "Had I known ahead of time, I would have brought marshmallows and graham crackers. I bet he's not so bad."

Vega laughed. "My guy, you're in for a surprise if you really believe that."

"I've had terrible professors before," I said. "I still passed my classes just fine."

Vega tapped my desk. "You got a phone?"

"Who doesn't?"

"Hand it over, smart ass."

I pulled my cell phone from my jeans pocket and handed it to her. She slid her thumb across the screen, tapped the icon for my phone book, and started to type.

"This is my number," she said. "If this class finishes, and you walk out of here without desperately wanting to drop it, you owe me a coffee. And don't be cheap—I'll be able to tell if you're lying."

I smiled, and probably blushed again. "Deal."

44

She was friendly, she was flirty, and she was so far out of my league you'd get a nosebleed looking for her. At the time, I wished I had some answer or explanation for why Vega Rowland would want anything to do with a schmuck like me. In hindsight, that first day of law school was page one of a very short and extremely complicated love story.

But, of course, I didn't know that then, so I leaned deep into my seat, slipped my phone back into my pocket, and waited to see if Professor McManus would prove his reputation true.

ψ

All in all, I had three classes on my first day at Marshall: Torts, Real Estate Law and Contract Negotiations. On alternating days I had classes that dealt with family law and criminal procedure. None of the classes were easy, by any stretch of the definition, but none of them were exceptionally difficult, either. I was confident that, with a little extra discipline than I'd exercised in my undergrad studies, I'd keep my head afloat for the semester.

Torts was by far the most intimidating. Not because the subject matter was impossible to learn, but because McManus was every bit the anus that Vega claimed he would be.

McManus was well into his sixties by the time I had him as a professor. He showed up to class that Monday morning, two minutes late, looking like he dressed on the drive over. His button down was half untucked from his slacks, he wore a navy blue blazer with a funny white stain on the lapel, and he hadn't bothered to shave. It was hard to picture a young Joyce Nicholson—or anyone, for that matter—falling in love with the guy.

And, without fail, McManus was every bit as mean as he was unkempt. He spoke with a tone that was always rife with indignation, as if he was annoyed to be there, or that he was doing us all a favor by gracing us with his presence. He called on students at random to answer questions they had no chance of answering—it was the *first day,* remember—and belittled them when they answered incorrectly. Luckily, I was spared any embarrassment; but, I feared that would change by the end of the next class.

I didn't see Vega again that day. After class ended, we parted ways, but not before she studied my face and insisted that I owed her a coffee.

The prospect of forming some giddy, schoolboy crush on Vega worried me. I'd done a pretty good job of avoiding the fairer sex since Christine and I broke up earlier that year, and without all those little distractions that relationships bring, I had done all right for myself.

I had an hour-long break between my class on real estate law and my class on contracts, so I took the time to visit Marshall's lunch hall and grab a bite to eat. I placed an order at the campus SubTub— "Subs as big as a tub!"—and found a table in a somewhat quiet corner of the hall to sit and eat at.

I opened my laptop, careful not to spill slices of tomato or lettuce onto the keyboard (the subs really were as big as a tub, and as messy as they were delicious), and opened up my Internet browser. The details of Vega's story lingered with me; McManus was, by all measures so far, a giant anus, but I questioned the validity of the finer points of Vega's campfire tale.

Consumed by curiosity, I first did a search for Joyce Nicholson. I was doubtful that the infamous student even existed at all, and that if she did, the details of her life (and supposed demise) had been greatly exaggerated.

As it always is with the Internet, the first search result yielded pornography. Apparently, Jenny Nicholson is the name of a very popular adult film actress, and my Internet browser—which assumed I typed Joyce when I meant to type Jenny—directed me to Miss Nicholson's personal webpage. Jenny was cute, no denying that, but she was also about a decade and a half too young to be the infamous Joyce Nicholson, so I exited off the page quickly before a passing student could notice the risqué photos that flooded my laptop screen. I didn't need to be known as the guy who looked at naked women on his lunch break while eating his sub sandwich.

I leaned back and crossed my arms. Vega had said that Joyce killed herself in the 1980's, hadn't she?

I pulled up my Internet browser again and typed "Joyce Nicholson, 1980's" into the search engine.

The results this time weren't pornographic, but they were also completely unrelated.

The first hit was an archived news article from the L.A. Times concerning spiking gas prices in the summer of '88. The authors of the article were listed as Ben Nicholson and Joyce Burke, thus their inclusion in my search results.

The second hit was a consumer report for the 1988 Pontiac Firebird, authored by Joy Nicholson. A fine looking car, sure, but far from what I was looking for.

I let out a defeated little sigh and refreshed the search engine. This time, I entered the words: Joyce Nicholson, 1980's, Burlington, Marshall.

Bingo. The first result was a direct hit.

Joyce Nicholson had indeed been a student at the Marshall School of Law, and she had indeed passed away in the fall of 1988, although not by her own hand. In September of that year, during a particularly brutal and unseasonably early snowstorm, Joyce lost control of her 1981 Plymouth on the drive into Marshall, when a moose leapt out in front of her car. The Plymouth couldn't brake on the ice-slicked roads, and the two collided. The half-ton moose burst through Joyce's windshield, and its antlers separated her head from her body. The news article spared not a single, gruesome detail, yet still found it necessary to point out that she was dead on the scene, so as not to be confused with other incidents of moose-antler decapitation where the victim survived.

The article indicated that Joyce was with child at the time of the senseless accident, and that, like its mother, it did not survive. I wondered if it was true that Joyce and McManus the Anus had been romantically involved? The possibility seemed to exist.

I finished my lunch and went about with the rest of my day. By the time I'd completed my contracts class and was headed back out to the parking lot to go home, I'd nearly forgotten Vega's urban legend from that morning. I'd been too busy, too swamped by the onslaught of my new classes, to focus on much more than the inner workings of the American legal system.

I was halfway back to The Beast when my cell phone buzzed. I plucked it from my pocket and found a message from Vega. It read: "Don't think I've forgotten about that coffee."

I texted her back, told her that she was right, McManus was truly an Anus, and that even though I didn't have much say in that little bet of hers, I was willing to hold up my end of the bargain.

A short while later she messaged me again, asking if I had any plans that night. When I told her I didn't, she said we should meet up. I replied, asked where she had in mind. In no time flat, I received a simple three-word response:

"Where we met."

ψ

Before I stepped foot in my front door that afternoon, I could smell the overwhelming odor of marijuana smoke. It crept through the gaps of the doorjamb and wafted outside. It was pungent and thick.

I unlocked the door and shouted: "Police!"

Dave and Hannah sat on the living room couch, eyes glued to the television set, unamused.

"Hah hah," Dave said. "Very funny."

I hopped into my bedroom and set my bag down on my desk. Shadow was napping at the foot of my bed, uninterested in the company in the common area of the home.

"Hey," Hannah called from the living room. "Come play Crash'n'Bash with us."

I stepped back out of my room and into the main hall. The living room was flooded with electronic beeps and blips. Occasionally, I could hear Dave curse under his breath. Apparently, Hannah was winning that round of Crash'n'Bash.

"I can't," I said. "But you two have fun."

"Oh, come on," Hannah said. "Dave is such a sore loser. Come, give me a real challenge."

I grinned. "I wish I could, but...I have to be somewhere."

"Ah," Dave said. "What's her name?"

"It's not like that," I said.

Hannah shook her head. "Then what's *his* name?"

49

"Oh, Hannah," I said. "You know Dave's the only man in my life. But, if you two must pry, I'm heading down to Burlington Town Mall. Meeting a classmate. Her name is Vega."

"Did you hear that, Dave?" Hannah said, and she set her video game controller down on the coffee table. "Our little Nate is running off to meet a girl." She rubbed her eyes and pretended to cry. "He's growing up so fast."

"It's not like that," I said again.

"Then what *is* it like?" Dave asked.

"I'm not sure yet," I said, "but I'm really interested in finding out. She's way, way out of my league. It's like when a stranger makes small talk with you at a bus stop, and you just want them to cut to the chase. Are they going to ask for a buck, or try to bum a cigarette off of you?"

Hannah smiled. "You know, Nate, there's always the slim possibility that this girl has an actual interest in you. As a person."

I shook my head. "Highly unlikely. We don't even know each other."

"You don't give yourself enough credit," Hannah said.

Dave stood up from the couch, pointed to Hannah, and then to me. "Is there something I should know about here?"

Hannah giggled. "You've got nothing to worry about, Davey. Nate's sweet but I'm forever yours." She wrapped her arms around his waist and gave him a kiss on the stomach.

What Hannah and Dave had was real, it was clear every time I was graced with their company. I'd seen it before in my parents, and I saw it again between my mother and my stepfather, and I was seeing it between the two of them.

I took a quick shower and changed into a fresh set of clothes. By the time I headed toward our front door to leave, Dave and Hannah were napping on the couch together. Dave was leaned back, his feet on the coffee table, and Hannah had passed out with her head in his lap.

I tiptoed to the front door, but quietly as I tried, Dave's eyes blinked open.

"I'm sorry," I whispered.

Dave shook his head; no apology necessary. "It's all gravy, baby."

The front door opened with a squeak, but before I could leave, Dave called out for me in a hushed voice.

"Hey," he said. "Have fun."

ψ

It was late evening by the time I hit the road for Burlington Town Mall. Vega had asked if we could meet at 7:30, and I didn't want to be a minute late. Or did I? If I showed up too early, that might look desperate. If I showed up late, I might look like an ass.

The Beast was operating at full power that night. No engine stutters or stalls, it made the fifteen-minute trek to the mall without so much as a squeak of the breaks. I passed by Lake Champlain, caught glimpses of the sailboats coasting toward shore, eager to make landfall before the sun set that night for good.

I drove carefully up Hampshire, the memories of Joyce Nicholson's demise still fresh in my mind. I caught myself eyeing the sides of the road for signs of moose and imagined how I'd react if one sprung into the middle of the road.

It was 7:26, according to the digital clock on the dashboard of The Beast, when I parked in the Macy's parking lot at Burlington Town Mall. It was 7:31, according to the clock on my cell phone

51

screen, when I was walking toward the Orange Julius and passing by the front windows of the Happy Body Gym. On a bench in front of one of the windows sat a neatly dressed girl fiddling with a cell phone screen.

Vega.

"Hey," I said, the word leaving my mouth unevenly.

Vega looked up. "Nate," she said. "You made it."

"If you'd ever seen the car I drive, you'd know that's a cause for celebration."

She smiled. "Come on," she said, and she stood from the bench. "I want to pick your brain."

Together, we walked across the food court. We waited in line at the Beans-and-Things and ordered a couple of coffees to go. I gladly paid for them, but before I had a chance to tip, Vega stuffed a crumpled handful of dollar bills into a glass jar beside the register.

Vega pointed out a little table for two on the side of the Beans-and-Things, facing the food court, and suggested that we sit there.

"You're new here, Nate. I figured you could use a friendly face to show you around the place. Where are you from?"

"New York," I said. Whenever I told folks I was from New York, they immediately assumed the city, so I quickly added: "Albany."

"You're not too far from home then," Vega said. "Just across the lake."

"Nope. I suppose I'm not. What about you? Where are you from?"

Vega let out a little burst of air; half giggle, half sigh, all exclamation. "At this point, it might be easier to list the places I haven't lived."

"Go on," I said.

"Well, I was born in Oregon. Grew up near a little town out there called Grand Ridge. Middle of fucking nowhere. Around five, my father and I moved down to California. San Diego. I spent my middle school years in Arizona and my high school years in southern Florida. I finished the first half of my undergrad degree back in California at UCLA—go Bruins!—then transferred out here to finish at U of V. Now, here I am at Marshall. Living the dream."

"Oh my God," I said. "I lived in Albany all my life. And then…I moved here. Not nearly as exciting."

"I'd trade with you in a heartbeat, Nate," Vega said. "There must have been some stability to that."

It's true, there was. Growing up around the same kids, in the same town, in the same school brought a certain constancy and comfort. It also brought monotony, dullness, gossip, and small town politics. Plenty of big fish all sharing the same little pond. I missed some of my childhood friends, sure, and I constantly missed my mother and stepfather back home. But Burlington was the fresh new start I'd been yearning for.

Vega said, "So what brings you out to our fine city?"

She brushed away a strand of hair that had fallen in front of her face. I caught myself staring at that simple gesture for a bit too long. It was hard to not be hypnotized by her, even the little things she did.

"I—well. So I can attend Marshall," I said, after much too long of a pause.

"Yeah," Vega scoffed. "That much is obvious. We have the same class together. But why Marshall? Why law school at all?"

"I want to help people."

Vega crossed her arms. "Please, Nathaniel. I'm sure you can do better than that."

"I want to speak up for people who can't speak for themselves—"

"Stop," Vega said. "These are canned and amateur answers that I'd be disappointed to find on a law school application essay. Be real with me. Why do you *want* to go to law school? Like, Batman fights crime because his parents were murdered, right? What is it that makes you tick?"

I didn't know how to answer that right away. It was the first time Vega ever challenged me, and it wouldn't be the last. God, it was her trademark. Everyone else—friends, family—coddled me. Everyone else would have been happy with my answer that I wanted to help people, and they would have given me a hard pat on the back for being so goddamned noble.

Not Vega.

And it occurred to me, shortly after her line of questioning, that I *did* know how to answer her, but I was uncomfortable in doing so. Admitting my reasoning to her, and admitting my reasoning to myself, would not be easy.

"I—my father died when I was a kid," I said, and even thirteen years later those words couldn't escape my lips without a quaver to them. "He smoked. Like a chimney. And as a kid, I guess I needed a villain to blame. As I got older, that villain looked more and more like the big tobacco companies. I watched class action lawsuit after class action lawsuit get thrown at the industry. None of them stuck. I got interested in consumer advocacy law so that maybe, just maybe, I could help the little guy. However that might be. So, maybe, there'd be some nine year old kid out there who wouldn't have to grow up without his dad."

Vega smiled. "Now *that's* an answer."

I shrugged. "What about you?" I asked, but as I did, I swung my hand out across our little table and knocked her coffee over. The styrene lid popped off the paper cup, and a river of steaming, brown liquid gushed forward, a small stream of which reached the end of the table and dripped onto Vega's lap.

"Shit!" Vega sad, and she swatted at her dress.

"Are you okay?" I asked, panicked.

Vega bit her lip. "Yes. Yeah, I'm fine—"

"Stay here," I said, "I'll go get you some napkins. And a new coffee."

"That's okay," Vega said. "Really, I was finished anyways."

I was already standing up from our table. "Then at least let me grab some napkins."

I hurried between tables full of shoppers who gave me funny looks as I ran by. When I'd made it back to Beans-and-Things, I grabbed a handful of white paper napkins from a dispenser, smiled at the barista who'd helped us just a short while earlier, and hurried back to our table.

When I arrived, I was surprised to see the mess was gone. Vega's coffee cup sat on the table, lid attached, and the brown pool of water that formed had vanished.

"What happened here?" I asked.

"A mall custodian passed by," Vega said. "Right after you got up. He saw your smooth move and helped clean up the table right away."

"I was only gone for a minute or so," I said.

"He was good at what he does. I hope the mall pays him well."

"Huh," I said, and I set the napkins down on the table and took my seat. The top of the table was bone dry.

55

Later that night, after I finished my coffee and we stood from our little table in the food court, I offered to throw away our cups. Mine was light and empty, but when I picked up Vega's, it was filled to the brim. And though that makes sense to me now, it really bothered me at the time—I had watched every last drop of coffee pour out; the cup was knocked flat on its side, the lid popped off completely, and its contents emptied. It had happened fast, but it most certainly happened.

When I tossed our cups in the nearby garbage can, and I heard hers hit the bottom of the bag with a *thunk,* I wanted to ask then and there what was going on. But we were walking close, side-by-side, our arms almost touching. She was watching me with those wide, dreamy eyes of hers, and I quickly pushed the thought out of my mind.

ψ

After we had our coffee, Vega and I spent an hour or so strolling the mall together, making jokes about McManus and the awful way he parted his hair, and when that got stale, the conversation turned towards our favorite movies, our favorite books, our favorite musicians. Was it a date? Hell if I knew. If the two of us had only remained friends from that moment forward, I'd have been happy with that.

About a half hour before the mall's close, I walked Vega out to her car. She drove a little, two door Mercedes. The car was jet-black and looked fast enough to fly. Vega was wealthy, that much was clear. Not "stumbled into an eighty-thousand dollar inheritance" kind of wealthy, either. Her clothes, her jewelry, her vehicle—they all screamed of extravagance, even if Vega herself didn't carry the kind of snobby attitude stereotypically associated with such luxuries. I

56

pictured her father, whoever he was, standing at his desk while reviewing his credit card statements each month, then having to catch a nearby chair to keep from doubling over.

Vega thanked me for the coffee and for the laughs, climbed into the driver's seat of her little coup, and sped off. I walked two lots over to where The Beast was parked and drove myself home, wearing a stupid grin the entire ride.

I came through my front door just as Hannah was getting ready to leave. She was giving Dave a peck on the cheek and throwing on a light jacket.

"Gone so soon?" I said.

"Nine o'clock on a Monday night is pushing it," Hannah said. "Besides, we've had enough fun for one day."

"You owe me that game of Crash'n'Bash," I said, and I pointed at the Nintendo in the living room, still bleeping and blooping.

"And you owe me all the gossip on your mystery lady," Hannah said. "Maybe sometime you can convince this one to leave the house. We could have a double date!"

"Oh, yeah, that would be *so* fun," Dave said sarcastically, and he held the door open for Hannah. She gave him one last kiss on the cheek, and she was gone.

Shadow came prancing from my bedroom and purred at my feet. I picked her up and held her tight against my chest. She let out soft, gentle little purrs. She'd gotten so much bigger in just the last two weeks.

"We ordered Chinese," Dave said. "There's some leftovers in the fridge if you want any. Help yourself."

"Thanks, but I had a big lunch. SubTub."

"Subs as big as a tub!" Dave exclaimed.

57

"Yep, you really got me hooked. Listen, I think I'm gonna turn in early."

Dave nodded at his bedroom door. "Same here, buddy. But before I hit the hay, how was your little get together?"

"A lot of fun," I said, "aside from the part where I spilled scalding hot coffee on her."

Dave shook his head and smiled.

"I don't know what it will lead to," I said, "if it even leads to anything at all. But, it's nice to have a friend on campus."

"Well, good luck with that," Dave said with a wink. He turned down his bedroom hallway, but before he could get far, I shouted after him.

"What's your secret?" I asked. "You and Hannah."

Dave stopped, but didn't bother to turn around. "Ain't no secret, man. People who say love has to be this dark, treacherous, complex thing are full of shit—that's just a plot device in pop songs and movies. When you click with someone, you just feel it. Feels right. That's all there is to it, just clicking."

I headed back towards my room, but before I got to my door, I heard Dave say: "Well there is one secret, I guess. I keep a very open mind when Hannah wants to try out new things...you know...sexually."

"More than I needed to know," I shouted back.

On the other side of the house, I could hear Dave chuckling. "Good night," he said. "And, oh, you might want to clean the kitchen counter real good before you use it next."

"You didn't," I said, loud enough for him to hear.

"If I said we didn't, would you believe me?"

I'm not sure if I would have or not, but just to be certain, I didn't touch the kitchen counter for the next three days.

That night, sleep came easy.

Shadow curled up at the foot of my bed, and the two of us fell into a deep and well earned slumber. I was absolutely exhausted. I had tossed and turned the night before, and if I was lucky, slept for a total of three or four hours at best.

By ten o'clock, I had completely knocked out, lulled to sleep by Shadow's rhythmic purring and the gentle wind outside my window.

I found myself seated at my desk in the torts auditorium at Bircham Hall. Everything was so perfectly in place, so lifelike, that it took me a moment to realize I was dreaming.

The auditorium was dimly lit, not at all how it looked in the morning, flooded by buzzing fluorescent lights. At the front of the room McManus paced pack and forth, muttering under his breath and scribbling a jumble of words onto the blackboard. Only he wasn't using chalk, was he? He was using the pointed end of a pocketknife, one that he gripped so tightly his palm was starting to bleed. Back and forth he went, carving letters into the chalkboard with scrapes so shrill they made my skin crawl.

I felt someone beside me, so I turned in my desk. It wasn't Vega sat next to me, as it had been in the morning, but someone else. Someone I'd only seen once before, in a photo in a newspaper obituary. Though the photo was black and white, she appeared to me in glorious color. Her red hair feathered at her shoulders, her face was full of freckles.

"You know who I am?" she asked.

"Joyce," I answered. "You're Joyce Nicholson."

"I used to sit right here," she said. "And listen to his lectures. My, the years have been unkind to him."

The silence between her words was punctuated only by McManus's knife tap-dancing across the chalkboard.

"What's he writing?" I asked.

"I guess we'll find out soon," Joyce said, and she sighed.

I squinted, focused on McManus as he finished. Carved deep into the chalkboard was the declaration:

THOUGH WE ARE BLIND, YOU CAN SEE JUST FINE!

"What does that mean?" I begged, and when I turned to Joyce, her face was missing from her top lip up. Her head had been dashed to bits, leaving nothing but a bloodied, mangled stump.

"You can see," Joyce said, her bottom lip undulating, "for those who cannot." Her tongue fell from the orifice that was once her mouth and hit the desk in front of her with a slap. She slumped out of her chair and collapsed onto the floor of the auditorium.

I stood up, horrified. McManus turned from the black board to face me. His shirt was half untucked, his hair was combed in that stupid part he wore, but his eyes were missing. Where they should have been were deep, black pits.

"Going somewhere, Mr. Shaw?" McManus asked.

"What's going on?" I shouted.

"The dead can't tell the living their secrets," McManus said. "You'd have more luck catching a shooting star."

The floor of the auditorium shook, and the ceiling above us peeled back like the skin of an orange. The star littered sky was empty, save for a single ball of flames streaking through the atmosphere. It felt like it was aimed directly at me, and I raised my hands out in front of me as it rocketed closer.

"What is it?" I screamed.

McManus cackled. "It's a Tuesday pop throwback to Christina Aguilera."

"What?"

"Everyone remembers this classic gem," McManus said. "Genie in a Bottle debuted fourteen years ago today."

I opened my eyes. Above me, on the nightstand, a DJ spoke through the single speaker on my alarm clock radio. I was twisted in my sheets, face down on the bedroom floor. Sunlight burned through the narrow slat between my blackout curtains. Shadow sat nervously in the corner of my bedroom, watching with curiosity as I woke up.

"Shit," I muttered. "I overslept."

ψ

My morning had been ruined by my nightmare. I'd overslept by twenty minutes before the dulcet vocals of Christina Aguilera's old chart topper rattled me awake. I'd awoken on the floor, my neck stiff and my body sore.

The shower I took was so fast the water barely had a chance to warm. By the time it was finally hot, I was stepping out and toweling off. I skipped breakfast completely.

The Beast was kind enough to start on the first try, and my ride to Marshall was rushed. I stomped the accelerator when traffic lights turned yellow, I took turns too fast, I passed slow drivers and muttered obscenities under my breath.

I didn't stop speeding until I rounded the wide bend on Hampshire, the one a mile or so before campus, the one I was certain Joyce Nicholson lost control of her car on so many years before, even though there was no memorial or marker for the accident.

I thought of her, young and optimistic, her whole future a blank canvas, before a cruel twist of fate in the shape of a northeastern moose took that all away. It didn't seem fair.

Visions of my nightmare crept back, though I'd tried my best to deny them all morning. I didn't much care for the paranormal, never paid much mind to ghost stories or tales of apparitions, but it was feeling more and more likely that whatever visions visited me while I slept were more than just a jumble of the day's frustrations.

It felt like someone was calling out to me from somewhere far away.

It felt like they needed help.

When I arrived at Marshall I parked The Beast in the lot near the rear of campus, behind the Bircham building. Before I stepped out, I pulled a slip from my bag that had my day's schedule printed on it. I took a moment to study it, get acclimated with what classes were at what time and in which buildings, and headed out to start my day.

Criminal procedure was first; a fine class with a lovely professor, not at all like old man McManus. His name was Mark Cooper, and within the first two minutes of his lecture, it was clear that he was a man who loved what he did for a living. He spoke with passion and enthusiasm. He treated his students with respect.

After criminal procedure I had a two-hour break, and again I used that time to order SubTub for lunch. Their subs were delicious and really did feel as big as a tub. I worried that if I ate there too often, I'd be as big as a tub, too.

After my two-hour break was Ashley Guerrero's family law class. While not the most interesting subject—to me, anyhow—Professor Guerrero was on equal footing with Professor Cooper when it came to treating her students with respect and compassion. I wish I could say that I enjoyed the subject matter more, but I didn't. It was hard enough when my father left my mother and I, pulled from us by forces beyond our control. Were it not for his death, they'd have had a long and happy life together, of that much I'm certain. The thought of two people wedding—and then divorcing—one another was preposterous to me at the time. What can I say? I was young.

After family law, my day was done. Finished. Five classes, Monday through Thursday, which met on alternating days. That meant my Tuesdays and Thursdays would be short, while my Monday's and Wednesday's would be crowded. It was a juggling act, but it all went by at a clip that I was sure I could keep pace with.

Barring any exigent circumstances, that is, such as car trouble. Which is precisely what happened that afternoon.

I had made my way back to the parking lot after Guerrero's family law class and climbed into The Beast. Before I even plugged the key into the ignition, I knew something was wrong. My nostrils tickled at the sickly-sweet scent of gasoline wafting through the air vents. I tried to start the car, and it made a pathetic little whimper. I cranked the ignition again, and again the old Jeep groaned and sputtered. On the third attempt, the engine didn't try to turn at all. Instead, a loud electronic beep came out of the dashboard, and the engine light clicked on.

I smacked the steering wheel of the Jeep and watched as the parking lot emptied. Lucky bastards, free to go home or out with friends, or wherever they pleased now that their day was done.

I pulled out my cell phone and started to search for phone numbers of local tow truck companies. I'd found one that looked reputable enough, and was just about to dial it, when a familiar looking black Mercedes drove by.

The Mercedes stopped just before it would have turned onto the two-lane section of parking lot that connected Marshall to the main road out front. It turned abruptly to the left, and circled back towards me.

I was embarrassed, okay? Vega had it all. It hadn't occurred to me before that moment that she'd never seen The Beast, and I was suddenly, for the first time ever, ashamed of it.

The Mercedes pulled up next to me, our driver's side doors facing one another. A dark, tinted window slid down smoothly. Behind the steering wheel, of course, was Vega.

"Hey, loser," she said with a grin.

I rolled down my window with the hand-crank beside the door handle. "Hey."

"You know," she said, "most of us drive out of here when we're done with class. You got some sentimental attachment to that parking spot or something?"

"Har, har," I said. "She won't start. I'm about to call a tow."

Vega bit her lip, shifted her Mercedes into park. "Don't do that."

I narrowed my eyes. "You want me to pop the hood? We'll take a look at it together, you can help figure out what's wrong."

"I feel like, judging by your tone, you're implying that I wouldn't be much help to you because I'm a woman. It's 2012; misogyny jokes are out of fashion. They don't suit you, bud."

"I didn't mean it that way—"

"Of course you didn't," Vega said. "Give me a second. Don't call anyone."

She pressed her cell phone to her ear and her window slid back up. Thirty seconds later she opened her door and stepped out of the car.

"What's going on?" I asked.

"I know a guy. He'll come give it a tow and bring it back to his shop."

64

"*You* know a guy?" I nodded towards her car. "Something tells me the brand new Benz doesn't have to be brought to the shop very often."

"Well, I don't know a guy. My father knows a guy. And this guy may or may not owe my dad a favor or two. As for my car—you're right. It doesn't need to go in for service often. But the envy suits you about as well as the misogyny." She patted me on the shoulder. "Be good."

"A lot of guys owe your dad favors?"

"A few."

"Is he—like, The Godfather?"

Vega crossed her arms, unamused. "You know, you're a regular fuckin' Conan O'Brien today."

There's always a bit of fun to that, isn't there? Meeting someone new, when there's still a mystery to them. Figuring out what buttons can be pushed and which ones can't, what they find funny and what they find annoying.

It didn't take a rocket scientist to figure out Vega was teetering more towards annoyed than amused, so I eased off the throttle just a bit.

"This is going to be really awkward if you just sit there in your car like a goober while we wait," she said.

I stepped out of The Beast and leaned against the rear panel of it, facing Vega. "You don't have to wait with me."

Vega pulled a pair of Wayfarers from her purse and perched them on her nose. "You don't want the company?"

"I'd love—I'd really like the company," I said. "But, you must be busy."

"Eh," Vega said, and she shrugged. "I've got nothing going on the rest of the afternoon. My Tuesday and Thursday schedules are light."

"Mine too."

"But my Monday's and Wednesdays are a real bitch."

"Mine too!"

"Wow, we're like, twins!" Vega said, in a mock, sing-song voice.

"On second thought, maybe I'd be better off without the company," I said.

Vega curled her lips. "Yeah, Nate. You wish."

ψ

Vega stood with me for a little less than half an hour while we waited for the tow truck to arrive that afternoon. We passed the time together, talking about our Tuesday classes and about the work that was already starting to pile up despite us being only two days deep into the semester.

A little before 2:30 PM, a tow truck almost as old as The Beast came rumbling into the front parking lot at Marshall. Vega waved her arms back and forth, an air traffic controller guiding takeoff, and the truck nosed towards us and sputtered across the parking lot. The driver backed the rear bumper of the tow truck until it was almost touching the front bumper of my Jeep, then stepped out. A squat, older gentleman with a bushy mustache and silly comb-over hopped out of the driver's seat and toddled towards Vega.

"Vega," the driver said, in the kind of croaky voice that only comes after years of smoking. "How good to see you."

"Good to see you too, Greg."

"How's your father?"

"He's just fine."

"And what have we got here?" Greg said, and he nodded at The Beast.

"The engine won't turn over," I said.

"Could be a bad battery. You want a jump?"

I shook my head. "My stepfather checked the battery just a few weeks ago, before I moved up here. You're welcome to check, but I'm afraid it's more serious than that."

"Do me a favor," Vega interrupted. "Take it into your shop and give it a once over. We've got a bitch of a semester coming up, and my friend here can't be missing class over car problems."

"Your wish is my command, Miss Vega," Greg said, clapping his palms together. He squished a meaty, grease-covered hand into a pocket on his overalls and handed me a business card. At the top, in blocky lettering, were the words GREG'S TOWING & AUTO REPAIR: BURLINGTON'S FINEST. Beneath was an address and phone number.

"I can't promise we'll get to look at it today," Greg said, and he glanced at the watch fastened to his wrist. "But as soon as we do, I'll give you a call." He stuck his hand in a different pocket and pulled out a short yellow slip and a ballpoint pen. "Fill this out with your particulars, and I'll get back to you as soon as possible."

I pressed the yellow slip against the hood of The Beast and filled it out. As I did, Vega crossed her arms.

"Is something the matter, Miss Vega?" Greg asked. A nervous smirk crept over his face. His bottom lip was trembling.

"I understand how busy your shop gets, Greg," Vega said, and she made a small, little pout. "But do please take a look at Nate's Jeep for me today, won't you? It would mean so much."

Greg nodded enthusiastically at Vega, and then at me. "Of course," he said. "I'll make it our top priority."

I unhooked the key for The Beast from my key ring and handed it to Greg. He pocketed it, along with the yellow slip I had filled out, and carefully connected The Beast to the rear of his tow truck. In no time at all, my old Jeep was high up on the bed of his tow truck, and the two were pulling out onto the main road.

"Well," Vega said. "Let me give you a ride home."

Vega brought me back to the old house I shared with Dave, and had just as much to say about its worn and tired look as she did about the Jeep, which was nothing. I felt bad, waving to her as she pulled out onto North, that I'd made such assumptions about her. It was becoming more and more clear that although she had nice things, she cared very little about them, and even less about the things of others.

When I came in the front door, I found Dave curled up on the couch, his hands wrapped tight around a tall, glass bong.

"Yo," Dave said with a cough. "I didn't hear you drive in."

The Beast's old engine was loud. You could hear it coming from a mile away. "Well," I said. "That's because I didn't."

"Everything okay?" Dave asked.

"Hell of a day, that's all," I said. "The Beast died in the Marshall parking lot this afternoon. I had to get a ride home."

"You should have called," Dave said.

"You don't have a car."

"Nah, man. But Hannah does. She doesn't have class until six on Tuesdays. We could have swung by."

"That's nice of you," I said. "Really. But it was no problem, Vega happened to drive by."

"Ah," Dave said. "Your lady."

68

I thought of how plainly Vega introduced me to Greg the tow truck guy as her friend. But hey, that's all we were then, right?

"I wouldn't quite call her 'my lady.'" I said.

"Then your knight in shining armor," Dave said, and he laughed. "Wait—what do you call it when a lady is a knight?"

"I think just 'a knight.'"

"Right on," Dave said. "Right on."

A meowing fluff of fur appeared next to my feet. "She give you any trouble?" I asked.

"Nah," Dave said. "Shadow and I have been hanging out all day."

I picked her up and carried her toward my room. She nuzzled my shoulder.

"Hey, wait," Dave called. "You wanna hang?"

"I wish I could," I answered. "But my class work is already starting to stack up. I better get at it."

Dave threw a little salute with his hand. "It's all gravy, baby."

I had sat down at my desk and plowed through about an hour's worth of reading for my family law class when my cell phone rang. Shadow, who had fallen asleep on the foot of my bed, shook her head in disgust when the sound of the phone startled her out of sleep.

"Hello?" I answered. The number was unfamiliar, but it had a Burlington area code.

"Nate," a scratchy voice said. "It's Greg."

I glanced at the alarm clock that sat on my nightstand, shocked at how little time had passed. Greg really did make checking out The Beast his top priority.

"Hey," I said. "How are you doing?"

"Better than you are, kid. Your Jeep has got some problems."

"Oh," I said. "Hit me with it."

"You sittin' down?"

I slammed my family law textbook shut. "Yeah, Greg, just spit it out already."

"You were right, it wasn't the battery. Battery's fine. Your fuel pump and starter are shot to shit though. A real one-two punch. Both are gonna need total replacement. Honestly pal, it's amazing it's been running this long."

"Okay," I said, hesitantly. "What's the damage looking like?"

"Well," Greg said, "that ain't the long and the short of it. We can put in a new pump and starter by the end of the week, no problem, but there's more. The wiring in the rear of your engine is torn to shreds. I've seen squirrels build little nests in engine blocks before, but they usually get crushed or flee before they can do any real damage. This is something else, kid. It's real far out. Like nothing I've ever seen. It looks like some animal got into the rear of the engine block and chewed out the primary cables that run from your battery to the dashboard."

"Okay, Greg. Just hit me with it. What are we looking at?"

"The fuel pump and starter are gonna clock in at about seven hundred bucks after parts and labor. But the wiring, whew…" Greg paused to whistle. "I couldn't even quote you on it until my electrical guy comes in tomorrow morning. It's gonna be a big job. You're lookin' at a grand, easy. Probably more. Say, have you given any thought to buying a new car?"

I let out a long, exasperated sigh. Could I buy a new car? I could buy a decent enough used one. I tried to dip into the money that my mother and stepfather gave me as little as possible. Taking even five or seven thousand out for a reliable enough used car would put a

70

bigger dent into my savings than I was willing to make. Two thousand dollars in repairs was enough to make me sweat.

"Just do the work," I said.

"Are you sure?" Greg asked. "I mean—I'm not one to turn down business, bud. But it feels...uh. Unethical. That's more work than the car is worth."

"Please," I said. "Just do it." And I hung up the phone.

ψ

The next morning, Vega offered to pick me up for class. I hated having to accept, but I had few other options. She asked if I'd heard anything from the repair shop about The Beast, and when I told her they quoted me upwards of two thousand dollars to get it back on the road, she burst out laughing.

"And you're going through with it?" she asked.

"I don't really have any other choice," I said.

She simply nodded.

When we got to McManus the Anus's torts class, it was clear the old buzzard was in a particularly cranky mood. He was sitting at a desk at the front of the auditorium, reading the morning's paper, his furrowed eyebrows peeking out over the sports section.

Vega and I walked into the auditorium side by side and took seats at the same desks we'd sat at on Monday.

"He never gets to class early," Vega said. "What do you think that's about?"

"Oh, I'm sure we'll find out," I said.

The auditorium filled with students, and at precisely 7:45 AM, McManus set down his newspaper and approached the lectern at the front of the auditorium.

71

It was the first time I'd seen McManus since the nightmare I had of him two days earlier. My mind filled with flashes of his eyeless face staring at me, a crooked, knobbed finger pointed in my direction. *I am blind, but you can see just fine.*

"You want to be lawyers, the lot of you," McManus said. "You'll spend day and night reading and writing. So, we better be sure you know how to read and write then, shouldn't we? I'm not convinced half of this room knows how to." He scoffed, then scanned the auditorium. "Marshall used to abide by a strict code of admission guidelines, and now, well, just look at yourselves. It's amazing some of you know how to tie your shoes in the morning." He stopped scanning the room and pointed to a girl in the rear of the auditorium. "You there?"

A slim girl in a pink sweatshirt and grey bottoms stiffened in her seat. "Me?"

"Yes," McManus said. "You. Introduce yourself to us."

The girl leaned forward. "Alison." She cleared her throat. "Alison Graham."

"Alison," McManus said, and he clapped his hands. "Would you mind explaining your attire to me, Alison?"

Alison shook her head. "I don't think that's necessary, do you?"

"I do or else I wouldn't have asked."

"It's hardly appropriate to spend class time talking about what I'm wearing—"

"Pajamas, Miss Graham. You are sitting here, amongst your peers, preparing for a lifetime of service to the legal profession, and you have the audacity to arrive in pajamas."

"They're not pajamas," Alison said defensively.

"You are to exit my room immediately," McManus said, coldly. "You will never set foot in it again unless you are wearing what you

72

would wear to court. Or, at the very least, what you might wear to a ball game or a movie. Is that too much to ask, Miss Graham? Tell me, am I asking too much?"

Alison was stuffing a notebook and a folder full of papers into her bag and standing from her seat when she said: "I'll have you reported to the dean for this."

"It would be my pleasure if you did," McManus said, amused. "I have worked here for over three decades. I am tenured and I am a necessary cog in the machinery that is Marshall. Tell the dean I scolded you for dressing inappropriately. Tell him I disrobed and tap-danced across the front of the auditorium afterward. Whatever you tell him, I assure you, it will not matter much to me. Now, please leave."

Alison charged down the stairs of the auditorium in a huff, then slammed open a door and vanished.

"Now," McManus said, "if we are through with the theatrics, we may carry on, yes? As I was saying, you will spend countless hours reading and writing in your next three years at Marshall and in the professions you go on to afterward. That is why I begin each semester with a mandatory research assignment so as to assess each of you individually based on your ability to read, write, and think for yourselves. You will be given the name of a prominent attorney who is either well known in the public eye, served in a position of high, political power, or who argued on a landmark case. In two weeks time you will hand me an essay on the attorney you have been assigned that shall not be less than thirty-pages, typed. You will explain their importance in regards to the field of torts, and you will explain the impact they've had on the legal community."

The class let out a single, collective groan. A thirty-page paper in two weeks time would be no easy feat.

McManus held up a stapled set of papers. "I have assigned an attorney to each of you before hand, so have your pens and papers ready, as I do not like to repeat myself. Listen for your name, and for the attorney you've been assigned. Ready?"

McManus proceeded to rattle off student names followed by attorney names one after another, with no enthusiasm and hardly any chance to catch his breath between them. When he'd rattled through the alphabet long enough to reach last names that began with the letter S, he finally took a pause.

"Nathanial…Shaw," McManus said, and he looked up from his lectern, focused a pair of tired, grey eyes on me. Quickly, he glanced at Vega, and smirked. Then, he returned his attention to me. "Your paper will be on Mr. Dominic Bloom. Have fun with that."

In that moment, I didn't understand what he was alluding to—how could I have? But, in time it would all make sense.

I was a fly caught in a very wide web, and McManus the Anus was keen enough to notice, even if I wasn't.

ψ

Later that night, I met Vega at the front of campus, beside Bircham hall. I had sent her a text asking if she'd mind dropping me off at home. She told me it wouldn't be a problem, and at the end of our day, we drove away from Marshall together.

"A thirty-page paper due in two weeks," Vega said, and she scoffed. "What an asshole."

"It's starting to make more and more sense why his nickname has stuck with him for so long."

Vega steered her Mercedes out onto Hampshire. To the left of us was Lake Champlain. The sun was hanging low in the sky, nestled

74

behind layers of cotton candy colored clouds. Millions of little diamonds glittered on the surface of the lake.

"And what was that authority complex all about, with that Alison girl?" Vega asked. "The man is a pig. There were at least half a dozen guys in class today wearing basketball shorts and tank tops. He could have just as easily given them a hard time."

"You spend a lot of time in class today noticing what other guys were wearing?" I said.

"Oh, shut up," Vega said. She flicked on the headlights of the Mercedes; outside, the night sky was getting darker with each passing second.

"The man clearly has issues."

"More issues than Playboy," Vega said. "If you ask me, he should consider retirement."

"Have you looked into the attorney you were assigned yet?"

Vega shook her head. "Haven't even had a chance to Google his name. Some guy, Carl Albert. What about you?"

"The same," I said. "But the name sounds familiar. Bloom—I think he's local. I hear radio ads for his law firm all the time."

"Dominic Bloom," Vega said, and she drummed her fingers on the steering wheel. "He has an office in Burlington. Maybe you can really blow old Anus's socks off and get an interview with him."

"Yeah," I said. "That'd be something. But, uh, I'm probably going to shoot more for a bare-minimum sort of thing with this one."

"Don't set your bar too low," Vega said, and she pulled up in front of my house to drop me off. "If you start the semester with a low grade, you'll never pull it back up. That's McManus's trademark, supposedly."

"I'll be fine," I said, and I hopped out of the car. Before I shut the door behind me, I told her thanks, and she told me not to worry about it. I stood at the end of the driveway and watched the tail lights of her Mercedes disappear down North.

Dave wasn't home that night. He was working a late shift at the Quick Mark down the street.

I bunkered down at my desk and opened up my laptop. A quick internet search for Dominic Bloom returned a billion different news paper articles, websites, videos, and advertisements for his firm. It was overwhelming. I wasn't sure where to start.

Dominic Bloom, as it turned out, was more than just a local attorney. Much more.

Mr. Bloom graduated from Harvard Law School in the spring of 1984. Before beginning his career as an attorney, he worked as a hedge fund manager for no fewer than three investment firms in New York City. In 1986, he opened up his first law firm in New York, Davenport & Bloom. In 1988, he inexplicably uprooted from New York to move out west, to Seattle. Davenport & Bloom remained intact and operational in New York, but in Seattle, Dominic Bloom also launched Bloom and Associates. It's no easy (or inexpensive) feat to launch multiple law firms in the same state, let alone across the country.

In 1995, Dominic Bloom planted roots in Burlington, Vermont, where he founded The Bloom Law Firm. All three firms run concurrently to this day, but it was Burlington where Dominic stayed put, and it was Burlington where he oversaw the day-to-day operations of his firm.

Mr. Bloom's first big case—and where he made a name for himself—took place during his time in Seattle, back in the early

76

1990's. Bloom & Associates represented a fledgling tech company known as Vidtronix Games. Vidtronix had manufactured a virtual reality themed arcade machine called "Phantasos" and was testing the cabinet in several different arcades when trouble started to brew. The Phantasos machine was top heavy and had fallen forward on over half a dozen children at different arcades. One machine in particular even overheated, catching fire and burning down a small arcade in Oregon.

Bloom & Associates successfully represented Vidtronix, helping to mitigate the damages and court costs that the video game company would ultimately have to pay. Vidtronix walked away from financial ruin—for the time being, at least; the company would ultimately be liquidated several years later—and Bloom made quite the name for himself. It's no light task to defend a client accused of hurting children, but Bloom did it without breaking a sweat. What should have been millions of dollars in payouts turned into small, out of court settlements in the tens of thousands. Suddenly, every manufacturer accused of negligence wanted some of that Dominic Bloom magic.

Dominic Bloom had quite the reputation as a successful attorney, as his Wikipedia page had gone to great lengths to explain. But what was more interesting were the seedier websites that turned up after pages and pages of digging. A reputation as big as his doesn't form without pissing a few people off, and Dominic Bloom had plenty of detractors—clients who felt scammed, opposing counsels who felt bullied, there was no shortage of folks who hated the man.

Most amusingly was an Internet forum I stumbled over, wherein one of the members wrote a longwinded post accusing Bloom of being Satan incarnate. At first, I thought the forum post was a crude joke, a jab in the vein of that old gag about hell overflowing with lawyers. But, the forum poster was persistent—he thought Bloom was *literally* the devil.

I took all that I had studied on Dominic Bloom, all that I had learned—good and bad—and rolled it out into a paper that night that was approximately three and half pages long, a mere twenty-seven shy of the mark. I hadn't the slightest clue how I could crank out a thirty-page paper on the man in two weeks; but, as it would turn out, it wouldn't matter. My assigned paper would never get turned in.

None of ours would.

ψ

She was topless, her upper body framed by whatever little streetlight made its way through the blinds of my bedroom window.

"You might want to pick your jaw up off the ground, buddy," Vega said.

I sat cross-legged on my bed in wonder. It's not that I'd never seen a member of the fairer sex nude before, no; there were plenty of instances of that skipping as far back as sophomore year of high school. It's just, well, I'd played that colloquial game of baseball more times than I cared to count, but I was a lousy batter. I was great at getting to first. Had a slightly less remarkable track record of getting to second. And, on just a few occasions, made it to third.

But, the way she slinked through the darkened bedroom, the way the words left her velvety lips, the way she looked at me—they all felt like the foreshadowing of a home run, knocked clear out of the park.

She climbed atop me, straddled me, inched her hips closer and closer to mine. With her arms wrapped around my neck, she drew her lips beside my ear and whispered: "Are you ready?"

I nodded, pressed my palms into her lower back.

78

"Good," she said, and Vega nuzzled her lips against my collarbone and started to kiss, slowly making her way up my neck.

I pulled her closer, tried not to shudder as she brushed against me. With my arms wrapped tightly around her, I felt a pinch against my neck. It was small and hardly noticeable at first—like a needle at a doctor's office—but soon it doubled in pain.

"What are you doing?" I asked.

Vega didn't answer. The pinch worsened, and I heard what sounded like...

Chewing.

"It's hurting," I said, and I tried to push her away.

Her teeth sunk deeper into my neck, and the more I struggled, the harder she bit.

"Please," I said, and I grabbed at her bare waist and shoved.

Vega released her grasp and leaned back, cackling. Between her lips was a chunk of human flesh—*my* flesh—and from the corners of her lips dripped thin trickles of blood.

I grabbed at my neck and shoulder, and my hands slicked wet with blood. It poured down my chest, formed little pools between my legs.

Vega wiped her mouth with her forearm and swallowed. Her eyes glowed bright green.

I raised my arms out in front of me, but to no avail. She lunged forward, this time planting her teeth into the opposite side of my neck, and a short moment later I woke up screaming.

"It's seven thirty in the AM on this fine summer morning," a radio announcer said. "We've got a little traffic build up on state road seven, but other than that, you should all be in for a nice commute. Coming up next, we've got some classic AC/DC—"

I slapped at the alarm clock on my nightstand, and the radio shut off. On the desk chair across from me, Shadow was curled up in a little ball, sound asleep.

"Must be nice," I said, and I sat up in bed. Instinctively, I scratched at my neck.

Still intact.

I walked out into the kitchen to grab some breakfast before my morning shower. On the couch, Dave sat in his pajamas, playing Nintendo.

"Nate-dog," Dave said. "Just in time for a quick game of Crash'n'Bash."

"I wish," I said, and I emptied out some cereal into a bowl.

"Hey, don't use the stove," Dave said, not bothering to look over from the TV screen. "It's been acting funny. I can't keep the pilot light lit."

"Luckily, boxed cereal and milk doesn't require much heat," I said. "Hey, can I ask you something? I need an honest answer."

"Sure," Dave said. "What's up?"

"Have you been out here at night, smoking, like…a lot?"

Dave giggled. "Man, I'm out here almost every night smoking. Is it a problem?"

"It's just that, these past few weeks, I've been having some really wild dreams. I thought they were from the excitement of leaving home, but they're reoccurring and getting increasingly…fucked up."

"You think some second hand exposure to all the Mary Jane is messing up your sleep?" Dave asked.

"I don't know. Maybe."

"Alright, listen, my man. I'll keep it in my bedroom after ten, how's that?"

"Would you mind?" I felt like a jerk for asking.

"It's all gravy, baby," Dave said.

"If they don't go away in a few nights, I'll know that wasn't the cause, and then you can resume your nightly weed-related activities."

"Sounds like a plan," Dave said, and he went back to playing his video game.

I took a quick shower, and by the time I was buttoning up my shirt and getting my notebooks together for the day, there was the familiar honk of a Mercedes in the driveway outside.

"Are you okay?" Vega asked. "You look like you've seen a ghost."

I shook my head. "I haven't been sleeping well the last few nights."

"It must be stressful," she said. "Away from home, the pressure of school, your car in the shop."

"Yeah," I said. "That's probably it."

"You're really pale, Nate," she said. "Do you want me to bring you back home?"

"Nah," I said. "It's a short day. I'd hate to miss it over some bizarre dreams."

"It's bad dreams keeping you up?" Vega asked. "Now I'm interested."

"They're nothing," I said, "they're just nonsensical, subconscious mish-mash. Like all dreams are."

"I don't think you're giving dreams enough credit," Vega said. "What were they about?"

I kept my eyes turned toward the passenger window and paused for a moment, trying to think of the best way to explain them. There was the impaled deer heads on the bank of the Mohawk River, a headless Joyce Nicholson haunting the halls of Marshall, and, most recently, Vega's murder of me. Where would I even start?

81

"Oh my *God*," Vega said. "One of them was about me, wasn't it?"

"Well—"

"Nathaniel Shaw, if you tell me you're having gross, boner-fueled wet dreams about me like some horny teenager, I'm pulling this car over and you're walking the rest of the way to Marshall."

My face flushed red. "In my dream last night," I said, "you chewed on my neck. You were drinking my blood like...like a vampire."

"Vampires, huh?" She giggled. "That's a little 2008, don't you think? I promise, Nate. I'm not a vampire."

"What a relief," I said.

"Seriously," Vega replied, "you've just got a lot going on right now. Between this stupid paper McManus is making us write, your car being in the shop with a gigantic repair bill, and not being able to see your family as much as you used to. You're a rubber band pulled tight." She smiled that radiant smile of hers. "It gets better, Nate. I promise."

ψ

That afternoon, after our day of classes had concluded, Vega drove me home. It was such a relief to have the next three days off. I could spend my Friday, Saturday, and Sunday working as much (or as little) as I wanted to. My first week of law school had been a whirlwind, not just because of the heavy load of coursework, but because of the bizarre dreams that had begun to haunt me. Vega made a good point that morning: I was getting overwhelmed. So, I did what all people do in times of stress.

I called my mom.

The phone rang six times before she picked up. When she did, she squeaked out a surprised little "hello?" In the background, I could hear a mechanical whirring.

"Hey," I said. "Did I catch you at a bad time?"

"No, honey, not at all. James is making frozen margaritas. But I can talk. How's kicks, kid?"

"Well," I said. "My first week is in the bag."

"Yeah?" my mom said, and in the background I could hear James laughing. My mom giggled, and whispered: "Knock it off."

"Sounds like a real party," I said, and I suddenly felt bad for calling. Who knew they'd be up to so much trouble on a Thursday afternoon? I'd always only seen them as parental figures, and maybe for the first time in my life, I was starting to see them as just…people.

"No, Nate, I'm sorry. Tell me, how was it?"

"A girl died."

"What? Nate?" On the other end of the line, the sound of my mom cupping her hand over the phone, then whispering to James: "One of his classmates died."

"Wait, no," I said. I didn't know why I blurted that a girl died. Looking back, I probably wanted to command some attention. And it worked. The sound of the blender in the background ceased. The line got quiet. "She died in 1988."

"Oh," my mom said. "Nate, I'm confused."

"She died in a car accident on the same stretch of road I take to campus each day. I don't know why, I've just been thinking about it a lot lately. There's a rumor that she was in love with one of my professors."

"That sounds very, ah, interesting. Nate—are you feeling okay?"

"I'm fine," I said. "It's also—just—well, remember when we talked last weekend? You said you had a dream. About you, dad, and me, on that day we had the picnic along the Mohawk River. You said that in the dream I was holding a black cat."

"Yeah, I remember."

"Doesn't that strike you as very strange?" I said. "What are the odds that you'd have such a peculiar and specific dream like that, two days after I take in a stray cat? I hadn't told you yet that my roommate and I had found a stray. So, how could you have known?"

"I don't know, Nate. Could be just a coincidence. You always said you wanted a cat. I didn't think anything of it."

"Mom," I said. "Have you had any more weird dreams since that night?"

"No," she said. "Nothing out of the ordinary."

"Okay. Good."

"Listen, hon. Why don't you drive down this weekend to visit? We'll all go out for dinner on Saturday. You can visit some old friends. You sound awfully stressed."

"I can't," I said. "The Beast broke down. It's in the shop. I don't know when it will be ready."

"What's wrong with it?"

"It's probably easier to list the things that aren't wrong with it."

"Well," my mom said, "it might be time to look into a new car. How are you getting back and forth to campus?"

I paused. "I met a girl. A friend with a similar schedule to mine. She's been picking me up and dropping me off."

"Oh," my mom said, and the cheer returned to her voice. In the background, I could hear the blender firing up again for another round of margaritas. "A girl, huh? Is she nice?"

"The nicest," I said. "Why don't I let you go? You two sound like you're in for a fun night."

"Sure, Nate. I'll talk to you soon."

"Talk to you soon."

"And if The Beast gets fixed, promise you'll reconsider visiting?"

"I promise," I said, and then I told her that I loved her and I hung up.

I spent the next few hours of the afternoon working on my research assignment concerning Dominic Bloom. I'd managed to stretch my paper from two and a half pages to five—not quite the thirty required for McManus the Anus, but it was a start. When I was just about ready to call it quits for the afternoon, my phone rang.

"Hey," I answered.

"Nate, kiddo," a raspy voice replied. "Good news, we finished the work on your Jeep. It's ready to be picked up at your earliest convenience."

"Great," I said. "How late are you open until?"

"Seven," Greg said.

I turned toward the digital alarm clock on my nightstand. It was already a quarter after six.

"I'll try to make it over tonight," I said. "What was the final total?"

"Don't worry about it. Just come pick it up."

"Well, no," I clarified. "I have to stop by an ATM before I get to your shop. I need to know the total."

"What total?" Greg said. "Don't worry about it. The work's done, free of charge."

"Uh—there must be some mistake," I said. "The other day you quoted me at least two grand worth of work."

85

"Nate, we gonna spend all night arguing over facts and figures? If I tell you the work is done, the work is done. If I tell you it's free of charge, then it's free of charge. A friend of Vega's is a friend of mine."

"I can't accept all of that work for free," I said. "You have to let me give you something."

"Nate, I gotta run. I've got a dozen cars to look at before I close up. You wanna do me a favor? Try to get here by close. Your Jeep is done, and it's taking up space in my lot."

Then, the click of his cell phone shutting.

I stood up from my desk. My head was swimming. Shadow stretched her front legs on the edge of my bed and gave me a curious, worried look.

"What the hell is going on?" I asked, half expecting the girl to answer.

Shadow simply blinked, then started to lick her paw.

I picked up my cell phone and dialed Vega. I was too excited by the fact that I'd just been gifted two thousand dollars of car repairs to realize it was the first time I'd ever called her. Up until that point, the two of us had only text messaged one another.

"Hey, Nate," Vega said.

"Who are you?" I asked.

"Okay," Vega said. "Kind of a weird way to start a phone call. What do you mean 'who am I?'"

"Are you some celebrity or something, living in Burlington under a fake name?"

"Nate," Vega said, sounding annoyed. "What is going *on?*"

"Greg—the car repair guy you got for me—just gave me a ring. He said the work he did on the Jeep is on the house. Said if I was your friend, then he was my friend too, or something…listen, I didn't really understand it."

"Wow," Vega said. "That was awfully generous of him."

"I hate to ask—you've done so much for me this week already, but can you— "

"Can I give you a ride over to Greg's so you can pick up your prehistoric Jeep?"

"Yes," I said.

"Sure," she said. "Hell if I've got anything interesting going on tonight. I'll be over in a few."

"Perfect," I said. "And one more thing. What's the nicest restaurant in Burlington?"

Vega laughed. "I don't know. Huh. The Rail Yard, I guess?"

"Great," I said. "We'll go there afterward. On me."

The line went quiet for a moment. Then, quite softly, Vega said: "Why, Nathaniel Shaw…did you just ask me out on a date?"

ψ

Vega got to my place in no time at all. With half an hour to spare, we made it to Greg's repair shop before he closed. When we walked in together, Greg was standing behind a counter, arguing with someone over the phone.

"I gotta let you—I gotta let you—listen! I gotta let you go!" Greg waved at Vega and I. "I have customers. We'll finish this some other time."

"Hey," I said. "I appreciate you fixing my car."

"No problem," Greg said. "Hey, maybe you'll leave me a good review on Facebook? All the kids love Facebook."

"Of course," I said.

"She's out back," Greg said, and he reached behind the counter and tossed me my keys. "Now you two get outta here."

"Thank you again," I said. "If there's anything else I can ever do—"

"Forget about it, pal. Hit the road."

I smiled and took the keys. Vega walked me back to The Beast. I unlocked the driver's side door, hopped in, and plugged the key into the ignition. One twist, and it started right up.

"I'll meet you at the restaurant," Vega said. "Deal?"

I gave The Beast's accelerator a little bit of pressure. The engine roared. It sounded brand new. "Deal," I said.

The Rail Yard sat on the shore of Lake Champlain, faced west and looked out over miles of endless water. The sun was setting fast, and I hoped that Vega and I might get a table before the night turned entirely dark. Tables in the back of the restaurant faced the water, and what a romantic sight that might be? Both of us, at a little table for two, a lit candle between our plates, sharing wine and enjoying the sunset.

My dreams were quickly dashed when I pulled into The Rail Yard's parking lot. Vega was waiting near the corner of the building, and ahead of her a line of thirty or so patrons stood, huddled together in clumps, waiting for their table.

"Well," Vega said, pulling her Wayfarers from her face. "You said you wanted to go to the nicest place in Burlington. It's not exactly a well kept secret."

I hurried toward her, my hands raised over my head. "It didn't cross my mind how busy they might be. I didn't think to ask for a reservation. I was so excited to pick up my car and—"

Vega reached a hand out, laced her fingers with mine. "Don't worry about it."

"Well, what will we do now? I'm starving. I saw a taco place a couple miles back—"

"Don't worry about it," Vega repeated, and she led me forward. We walked hand in hand toward the front doors of The Rail Yard. People glared and sneered at us as we strolled by.

"What are you doing?" I asked.

"You're adorable, Nate. You're like a little kid seeing Disney Land for the first time. But, you also worry too much. Just go with the flow."

I nodded, as if I understood what was going on or agreed with it. But I didn't understand it, and I couldn't agree with it. Were we simply going to cut all those people behind us in line? What was her plan?

The worry faded. Vega's hand was warm. Soft. Her fingers were so gently intertwined with mine that it suddenly became difficult to worry about anything else at all. Nuclear warheads could start dropping from the clouds above and I'd have walked on, grinning like a goof, swinging my hand with hers.

When we reached the entrance of The Rail Yard, I unhooked our hands and grabbed the door.

"Wow," Vega said. "A gentleman."

"I try my best sometimes."

I held the door open for her and we walked inside together. A young hostess in the front lobby greeted us right away.

"Good evening," the hostess said. "Do the two of you have a reservation?"

"No we do not," Vega said, plainly.

The hostess frowned. "Well, can I take your name? At the moment, there's a wait of an hour or so—"

"That won't be necessary," Vega said, and she peered over the shoulders of patrons and employees crowding the front lobby. She locked eyes with an older gentleman back by the kitchen. The gentleman handed the tray he was holding to another employee and hurried towards the front.

"Vega!" the waiter exclaimed. "We weren't expecting you tonight."

"Hey, Patrick," Vega said, and the two of them shared a quick hug. "Seeing as how it's not too busy, do you think you could grab us a table in the back? Overlooking the lake. I think my friend here would like that."

"For anyone else, the answer would be no. But for Vega—why, I'd lasso the moon if you asked me to."

"Thanks, Pat," Vega said.

Patrick led us toward the back of the restaurant. The three of us snaked between crowded tables and booths, and waiters and waitresses hurrying back and forth. After almost tripping over myself twice, we arrived at a neat little table with a plain white tablecloth that faced Lake Champlain. Patrick handed each of us a menu, told us to take our time to look it over, and left us.

"That's quite the trick," I said.

Vega was looking over her menu. "What was?"

"Wrangling us a seat on a night as busy as tonight."

"Oh," Vega said, and she laughed. "I've known Patrick for ages. Actually, the owner of this place and my father did some business together a few years back. We're family friends."

"You knew, didn't you?"

"Knew what?" Vega asked.

"That the place would be booked to capacity. That there'd be no way we could get in without a reservation. And yet, we came here anyway."

"Are you accusing me of trying to show off?" Vega asked.

"Maybe."

"And what if I was?"

I smiled. "You're full of surprises, aren't you?"

Vega smirked, looked up from her menu. "Oh, Nate. You don't know the half of it."

"How did you know that, if I had my choice of any table in the restaurant, it would be the one we're sitting at right now?"

Patrick returned to the table. He set a basket of warm, flakey dinner rolls between us and poured two glasses of ice water, then disappeared.

"You mentioned it to me," Vega said. "That night we met at the mall for coffee. You made a comment about the first time you'd visited the shopping mall—the morning you saw me—that you drove over to the shore and sipped on your smoothie and watched the sail boats come and go."

"Did I mention that?" I asked.

Vega picked up a dinner roll and took a bite. "No, Nate. I'm a psychic and I read your mind."

"At this point," I said, "that wouldn't come as a shock. I don't want to be nosy, but what is it your father *does*?"

"You know," Vega said, "that's very unbecoming. To say that you don't want to be nosy and then immediately be nosy."

"I'm sorry," I said. "It's just—free car repairs, easy dinner reservations…your dad seems to have a lot of pull in this town."

"I'm Emmitt Rowland's daughter, Nate."

"Emmitt Rowland? Should that name mean something?"

Vega sighed. "You're new here, so I suppose it wouldn't. He was one of those dot com geniuses in the 90's. He built his little empire in information systems. Ten years ago, Burlington awarded him a contract to engineer networking systems for the entire city. A few years after that, he dabbled in politics. He knows a lot of the locals. He's made a lot of connections."

"He must cast a very long shadow."

Vega rolled her eyes. "My father and I don't see eye to eye on everything. I wanted to get law degree. He had other plans in mind."

"Like what?"

"Have you been on many first dates?" Vega asked, and she took a sip of water. "Because, no offense, you're kind of terrible at first date conversation."

"Who said this was a date?"

"You did," Vega said. "Earlier, on the phone."

"No," I said, and I couldn't help but smirk. "I asked you out to dinner. *You* implied that made it a date."

"God," Vega said. "You're going to make a fantastic lawyer, aren't you?"

Patrick reappeared beside our table. "Can I interest the two of you in a bottle of wine?"

"Yes," Vega said. "Since my friend here is picking up the bill, how about a cabernet sauvignon?"

"Right away," Patrick said, and he vanished into the back of the restaurant.

Vega set her menu down on the table, an indication that her mind had been made up. "You always look so serious, Nate."

"What am I thinking about right now?"

Vega laughed. "The whole psychic thing was a joke."

"I'm not sure it was."

She flipped her hair over her shoulder. "Fine. Think of a question and I'll answer it."

If you can read my mind, I thought, and my thoughts raced forward, turned juvenile and crude, *you'll know I'm wondering what color your underwear is.*

Vega studied me for a moment, then leaned forward in her chair and whispered: "Black and lace."

I could feel my face turn red. I took a quick sip of water, then asked, "How did you do that?"

"I didn't read your mind, Nate! You're a man, and all men are pigs; it was just simple, deductive reasoning. A cold read. A parlor trick. For being so clever, you're so damn gullible!"

"Sorry to interrupt," Patrick said, and he reappeared beside the table. He poured two glasses of wine, then asked if we were ready to order.

"Who's in the back tonight?" Vega asked.

"Chef Garcia," Patrick offered.

"He's the best," Vega said. "Tell Garcia I'll have the flatiron, and please ask him to make it how I like. My friend here…" Vega winced her eyes, pretended to read my mind. "He'll take the ribeye."

"Maybe you're not a psychic after all," I said. "I'll have a New York Strip. Well done, please."

"Well?" Vega asked. "That's a crime."

"Well done," I insisted.

Patrick nodded and smiled, then took our menus and walked off.

Outside, the sun sank low over Lake Champlain. Half of it had dipped into the water. The sky rippled with streaks of purple, orange, and blue. Sailboats, kayaks, and the occasional jet ski dotted the horizon.

"You were kind to me," Vega said. "Before you knew who I was. If only you knew how rare that sort of thing is nowadays."

"I'm still not entirely sure I know who you are," I said.

"You probably don't," Vega said, and she shrugged. "But isn't that grand? Getting to learn about someone is one of life's little treasures."

"You never told me why you want to get into law," I said. "That night at the mall I told you my reasons for it. But I've never really heard yours."

"I want to practice contract law," Vega said. "I grew up watching my father make deals left and right. He had a very hard nose for business. When it came to negotiations and compromise, he'd always say, 'the sign of a good deal is when both sides feel like they've been screwed.' That always stuck with me. He was graceful at it. There was an art to it. It may not be as noble as your motivations—wanting to be a champion for the little guy—but it's kind of funny, now that I think about it, how each of our fathers helped shape the kind of law we want to practice."

I took my glass of wine and held it in the air. We'd both yet to take a sip.

"To justice," I said.

"Yeah," Vega said. "Whatever that is."

Vega raised her glass too and clanked it against mine. Together, we drank. When we sat our glasses back down, I puckered my lips.

"It's kind of sweet," I said. "Not bitter at all."

"It's good, right?" Vega said. "For one hundred dollars a bottle, it better be."

I dabbed my napkin against the corner of my lip.

"You don't seem awfully shocked by that figure."

"How can I be?" I said. "My car repair would have been over two grand. Dinner could be three hundred, five hundred, seven hundred dollars and I'd still have my head above water. Who cares what it costs? As long as we're having fun."

"So I can order anything I want? You truly don't mind?"

"Not at all," I said.

"Whatever is on the desert menu, if it fancies me, it's mine?"

"Only if you promise to order two."

"Are you trying to impress me Nathaniel Shaw?"

"I don't know," I said. "Am I?"

In no time at all, Patrick arrived with our meals. My steak was cooked to perfection, but it was hard to look at Vega's. Her flatiron looked like it was seared once on each side, then plated. When she slid a knife through the middle of the steak, it split open like a tab of butter. Dark red juices ran down the center of her plate, made a little river that trailed off beside her baked potato.

"It's an acquired taste," Vega said. "I can have Patrick bring a little divider for the table if it bothers you."

"It doesn't," I lied.

"Are you sure?" Vega asked. "You look a little pale."

"I'm fine," I said, and I focused on my plate.

As the sun vanished behind Lake Champlain, the bottle of cabernet emptied, as did our plates. We didn't leave a crumb behind for the dishwasher. I'd lost count of the drinks; I'd only had a glass or two of the wine. The rest had gone to Vega. By the time we were done, we were laughing and carrying on, perhaps a bit too loudly judging by the occasional dirty glances of our neighboring diners.

It was well into the night by the time Patrick arrived with our check. Lake Champlain was a dark pool underneath an equally dark sky. It was a challenge to tell where the horizon was, where the sky ended and the lake began.

"I hope the meals were to your liking," Patrick said.

"They were fantastic," I replied. "Send my compliments to the chef." I had always heard people in the movies say that.

"I'll be sure to," Patrick said. "Can I offer you anything else? A drink refill? Something from the desert menu?"

Vega patted her stomach. "I can't speak on behalf of my confidante across the table, but I couldn't eat another bite."

"Neither could I," I said, "but thanks anyways."

"Excellent," Patrick said, and he clapped his hands. "Then I wish the two of you a lovely night." He turned to walk to a neighboring table.

"Wait," I said, and I reached for the wallet in my back pocket. "Do I—do I, like, pay here or at the front?"

Patrick smiled. "Oh, your money is not welcome here. A friend of Vega's is a friend of ours."

Vega shrugged and gave me a goofy smile.

"Yeah," I said. "I've been hearing a lot of that today. Wait. Don't go yet." I pulled out my wallet. The wine and steaks should have easily added up to a couple hundred dollars. I plucked a crisp, fifty-dollar bill from my wallet, folded it in half, and placed it on the table.

"How very gracious of you, sir, but I couldn't accept," Patrick said.

"I insist that you do," I said, and I slid the bill towards him.

For some reason, he looked to Vega. She nodded, and he looked back to me and thanked me. "I appreciate your generosity," Patrick said, and he slid the bill into a pocket on the front of his apron and walked away.

"You knew the whole time," I said. "You knew they wouldn't charge us."

Vega's grin grew wider. "Nathaniel Shaw. A little boy at Disney Land."

"I better be a gentleman," I said, and I nodded toward the window beside us, "or that father of yours will have me at the bottom of Lake Champlain."

"You better be a gentleman," Vega clarified, "or *I'll* have you at the bottom of Lake Champlain."

I believed her.

Vega patted her stomach one more time. "I'm tired, Nate. And drunk. Now, give me a lift home. I'll come back to pick up my car tomorrow."

The directions were simple. Leave the restaurant, turn left onto North, drive for about ten minutes, then make a left at Anchorage.

Vega had curled up in the passenger seat of The Beast and started to nod off before we'd even made it out of the parking lot.

As I steered The Beast along the pine tree lined streets of Burlington, I took turns cautiously, always keeping an eye on the sides of the road. I thought of Joyce Nicholson and how she met her end in a collision with a moose that was roughly the same size as her little two-door. Could The Beast come out on top in the same type of crash? Maybe.

I didn't want to find out.

I'd successfully navigated us onto Anchorage by the time Vega woke up. Homes were few and far between. In fact, the word "home" was a somewhat disingenuous term to describe the buildings that cropped up every half-mile or so on Anchorage. Calling them estates or manors was probably more fitting.

"I'm just up there," Vega said, and she yawned. "Number six."

I cranked The Beast's headlight knob. The high beams blinked on, and the road illuminated brightly. Still, it was difficult to see. There were hardly any streetlights.

"It's easy to miss," Vega said. "Just go slow."

I eased off the accelerator. We were the only car for miles. On the right side of the street, a long brick wall appeared. In the center of it was a black, wrought iron gate.

"Drive up to it," Vega said, and she slid her cell phone from her pocket. She tapped at the screen and the gate slowly opened.

I drove The Beast up her long and winding driveway. House, estate, manor? None of the words seemed sufficient to describe the structure Vega lived in.

Calling it a castle seemed most appropriate.

The front of the brick home was covered in ropes of moss. On either side of it were two tall spires that pierced high into the starry sky. The rooms inside were gently lit; above the main doorway, I could see a hanging chandelier.

In front of the home, the driveway looped around an elegant slate fountain. I pulled The Beast alongside the fountain, shifted into park, and hopped outside to get the door for Vega.

"Thank you," she said, and she stepped out. Her foot landed on the pavement at an awkward angle. I caught her by the hand before she could trip.

"You live here," I said, "on your own?"

Vega nodded. "It's technically not mine. It's a part of my father's business. I don't know. It's all very complicated. But it's where I'm staying while I attend Marshall."

"Looks a bit cramped," I said.

Vega smiled. "Thanks for getting the door for me."

I walked her to the front door of her home. She pulled a key from her pocket and unlocked it. Before she stepped inside, she turned around.

"I bet I can still read your mind," Vega said.

"Oh yeah?" I asked.

"You're wondering if what I said earlier was true, or if I lied about the color of what I'm wearing, or if I'm just fucking with you altogether." She leaned against the door. "And now you're wondering if I'll let you find out for yourself."

I smiled. I did want to find out. I wanted to find out more than I wanted to breathe. But the night was late, and we'd both had a bit too much to drink—her more than me.

"There'll be plenty of other opportunities," I said, "for me to test your psychic prowess, Vega Rowland."

She smiled, draped her arms over my shoulders. "What a gentleman you are, Nathaniel Shaw."

I pressed my face forward and our mouths collided. The slightest trace of the cabernet was left on her lips, making the kiss sickly-sweet. We stayed like that, for a moment, suspended in time.

When I pulled away, I explained: "Not too much of a gentleman."

She had a dreamy smile about her, and she said, "That isn't necessarily a bad thing."

"I had a great night," I said, and I leaned back. Her arms left their place on my shoulders.

Vega nodded. "Get home safe, Nate." She turned around and let herself through the front door.

When I climbed back into The Beast, she was gone. The lights of the chandelier in the foyer had dimmed. I cranked the ignition and the Jeep started right up, first try. Up above me, in one of the spires, lights turned on. I figured that must be her bedroom, and before I wasted too much time imagining how she'd look slipping between cotton sheets, I shifted The Beast into drive. When I reached the gate at the end of her driveway, a sensor outside opened it automatically. I turned out onto Anchorage and started the quiet drive back home.

ψ

That Thursday night, I slept like a rock.

No nightmares. No dreams at all, for that matter. I piloted The Beast home, crawled into bed, and drifted off into a deep, dark slumber, the likes of which I hadn't had since moving to Vermont.

I woke up Friday morning to Shadow batting at my face. When my eyes squinted open, she started to meow. In the kitchen, Dave was cooking up his specialty, and it was clear that Shadow wanted to escape my bedroom and beg for scraps.

"I'll follow you," I told her, and I opened the bedroom door. She went dashing for the kitchen, and, true to my word, I followed close behind.

"Good morning," Dave said, cracking an egg onto a screaming hot pan.

"Hey," I said. "Stove's working."

"For now, at least," Dave said. He took a slice of cooked bacon, left drying on a paper towel, and tore off a square of it smaller than a postage stamp. He tossed it to the floor, and Shadow went sprinting toward it. In a flash, it was devoured.

"Got work today?" I asked.

Dave nodded. "Sure do. What about you, pal? What's on Nate Shaw's big to-do list?"

100

I shook my head. "I have a thirty page paper due in two weeks, so I should probably spend the day working on that. Or, at least pretending to."

"Thirty pages?" Dave said, and he let out a long whistle. He stirred the scrambled eggs in the pan before him. "What about?"

"A lawyer. I need to explain his significance to the legal profession. It's a bunch of busy work, honestly. Not at all the sort of thing you're supposed to deal with in law school. Some guy named Dominic Bloom."

Dave stopped stirring the eggs. "Dominic Bloom, huh?"

"Yeah," I said. "Have you heard of him?"

"How couldn't I have? You can't turn on a radio or a television in Burlington without hearing his name." He gave the eggs a flip then turned the burner off. "Well," he said. "Let's eat."

I grabbed a plate from the cupboard beside Dave and filled it with eggs, bacon, and toast. "You sound like you know him from more than just advertisements."

We took a seat at the tiny breakfast nook between the kitchen and the living room. Dave kept his eyes on his food, stuffed a slice of bacon into his mouth.

"Well," Dave said. "I don't know him personally. I hired his firm after my father passed away. There were some issues with the estate, with inheritance taxes, you know. All the red tape. Who wants to deal with that in a time of grief? His firm took care of it all for me. Sent me papers that needed to be signed, and a big fat invoice for their services when it was all said and done."

"Were you happy with them?" I asked.

Dave shrugged. "I had just become an orphan. Nobody tells you that, but even at age twenty-four, you can feel like an orphan. Like I said, I just didn't want to deal with any of it. They did a good job of easing my burden, sure."

I could tell it was a sore subject, and so I didn't press it any further. We sat together, quietly finishing our breakfast. By the time I was on my last slice of bacon, Dave was out the door.

With the house all to myself, I found it hard to concentrate. Dave's Nintendo called to me from the living room. I had laundry that needed to be folded. McManus's thirty-page paper hung high over my head. It's not that there wasn't anything to do; there was plenty. But picking the one specific thing to tackle? That was the rub.

I thought about Vega, wondered what she was up to. Had she woken for the day yet? Surely. I wanted to send her a text asking to hang out, but that seemed desperate. We'd seen each other plenty that week, between our time on campus together and the countless rides she'd given me while The Beast was in the shop. I reminded myself to take it slow and play it cool.

I was halfway through washing a plate when I'd decided on Nintendo—above the laundry or class work that needed to be done—to occupy my Friday morning. As I rinsed the plate, there was a sudden knock at the front door.

"I'll be right there," I called out.

When I answered the door a short, heavyset woman in her forties was standing outside. She wore a blue checked blouse, a white skirt, and a pair of black pumps. Short bobs of curly hair framed her face, a pair of wire-framed glasses rested on her nose.

"Oh, hi," I said, awkwardly. I assumed she was one of Dave's relatives. An aunt, perhaps? "If you're looking for Dave, you just missed him."

The woman at the doorstep paused. She folded her hands together, struggling to find the right words to say. "Dave?" she said. "No, I'm sorry. I'm not looking for Dave. I'm looking for Nathaniel. Nathaniel Shaw."

I froze. I'd never seen this woman before in my life. "How can I help you?"

"You're him, aren't you? You're Nathaniel. You look just like you did in my dreams."

I took a step back and started to close the door. It occurred to me that, in the even I needed to dial the police, I didn't know where my cell phone was. Had I left it in my bedroom? On the nightstand? I couldn't be sure.

"You know," I said, "I'm in the middle of cleaning. You caught me at a really bad time."

"Please," she said, and she looked ready to cry. "I know this is unusual, but if we could just talk for a moment, I can explain. I don't have to come inside. We can talk out here, or we can take a walk. We can meet up somewhere."

I kept the door open. Her eyes were full of sorrow and it was difficult not to feel bad for her. But, just because she didn't look like the machete wielding psychotic type, didn't mean she couldn't be. I thought of Dave, coming home, finding my body hacked to bits. A few days later, Vega would read my eulogy. "He was a sweet enough guy, but he held the door open for total strangers. What an idiot."

I was ready to close the door, to put on my shoes and tell her I'd meet her outside in a moment for that walk she wanted, when it occurred to me to ask her for her name.

"My name's Bethany Nicholson," the stout woman said, sadly. "But my friends all call me Betty."

I invited Betty to take a seat on Dave's couch, then strolled to the kitchen to reheat the morning's pot of coffee. She sat down, smoothed the creases of her skirt with her palms, and set her little white purse beside her. Shadow wandered up to her ankles.

"Sweet kitty," Betty said.

I raised my eyebrows. "She's a love."

"I don't know how to even begin," Betty said. "Or where to start. I know it will all sound so—so, well, crazy—but I couldn't live with myself if I didn't come to see you."

I had so many questions. How did she know my name, or where I lived? How did she find me? I hoped that, given the chance to explain herself, there might be some rational answers. But, I wasn't holding my breath.

I poured two mugs of coffee and brought them over. I handed one to Betty, then sat down across from her on the living room recliner.

"It will be twenty-four years next month," Betty began, "since my sister passed away. No matter how much time passes, I always get sentimental and melancholy this time of year. Like clockwork. But this year, Nathaniel, it was so much worse. So different."

I took a sip of my coffee, and Betty took a sip of hers.

"There's a lot of rumors that have gone around about Joyce over the years," Betty said. "For a big city, Burlington's awfully small, if that makes any sense. If you live here long enough, I suppose you'll find that out for yourself."

"I moved here a few weeks ago," I said. "How did you know I'm new?"

"It feels like I know a lot of things suddenly," Betty said. "I'll get to that, I promise. But first, I wanted to clear the air about Joyce."

"I'm sorry about your loss," I said.

"I appreciate that," she said. "It never hurts any less, it just feels a little further away. That pain goes away with time is one of the greatest lies ever told. It's never away."

I nodded and thought of my father. I could relate.

"Joyce was beautiful. Between the both of us, she was always the prettier of the two. She got—well, she got a lot of male attention, is what I'm trying to say. In the winter of 1987, she started dating one of the professors at Marshall. She was in her first year of law school."

"Ed McManus?"

"That's the one," Betty said. "Ed was a good guy to her, but…you know, they were skirting around some ethical grey areas. He wasn't her professor—he never was—but it was tricky, her being a student and him being a teacher at the same college. I think they tried their best to keep it secret."

"If you'll forgive me," I said. "There's some rumors that circle around McManus even to this day. A student in one of my classes said McManus taught her himself."

"Nope," Betty said. "I can tell you that's just one of the exaggerations that calcifies on a rumor after it goes around long enough."

"Huh," I said. I tried to picture a young Ed McManus and Joyce Nicholson falling hopelessly in love with one another. Then I tried to picture that love being so quickly and tragically taken away. It was easy, suddenly, to imagine how McManus the Anus could transform into the cranky old scrooge the student body at Marshall knew him as.

"There was a terrible snow storm that September," Betty said. "Sometimes, being this far north, it's not unusual to see a little early snow in the autumn. But that year was something else. The day before had a high of sixty-eight degrees, and the day after had a high of seventy. But the day of Joyce's accident, three inches of lake effect snow got dumped on Burlington. The temperature dipped to two below freezing. It just—well, it just didn't make any damn sense. The weathermen all called it an anomaly. Said it didn't have to make sense, that those things just happen sometimes."

Betty let out a long sigh, then raised her wire-frame glasses onto her forehead. She rubbed her eyes. I jumped up quick, grabbed a tissue from the counter behind me, and handed it to her. She thanked me, and I sat back down.

"She was on her way to class that September morning. They should have closed the campus, but they didn't. Not that it mattered anyway. A lot of kids stayed home. If it hadn't been for the snowstorm, if only the campus had closed, maybe she'd still be here. You gather a lot of ifs and buts in your life, but those are the two I think about the most. Had it not been for the ice-slicked roads, I think she could have braked in time to dodge the moose that leapt in front of her. That awful beast—it died, bled out on the broken glass from her windshield—but what it did to my sister....there was nothing left. We had to give her a closed-casket funeral, Nathaniel. We couldn't even say goodbye."

Betty paused, cleared her throat.

"She was pregnant. Eight months. She should have stayed home, but she was working so damn hard to keep her head above water at Marshall. She knew she'd miss a few weeks after the baby was born, but she truly believed she could stay ahead of it. She didn't want to fall behind a semester or let her grades slip. Now, what I have to tell you next is very hard to admit. It has gone unspoken in my family for years, but it's true, and I think that maybe, for some bizarre reason, it's relevant again."

"What's that, Betty?"

"We'll never be sure if Ed McManus was the father of Joyce's child. Earlier that year, around January, the two had a terrible break-up. They each saw other people for a few weeks. That's what Joyce told me. By February they were back together, and by February Joyce discovered she was pregnant."

I had no idea what to stay. I was so lost in her story that I'd almost forgotten what absolutely any of this had to do with me.

"Like I said," Betty continued. "I think about her dearly this time of year. But this time has been different. I haven't dreamt of my sister in ages. But, starting a few weeks back, I haven't gone a night without her visiting me in my sleep. How have you been sleeping, Nathaniel? Something tells me not very well."

I shook my head. "You're right. I've had my fair share of bizarre dreams the last couple weeks."

"When I see her, she's crying. She's holding a little bundle of blankets against her chest, and when I get close, I can see that they're empty. There's no baby there. Just the blankets, stained by her tears."

Betty set her mug of coffee down on the table between us.

"If it had stopped at that," Betty said, "I wouldn't have thought much about it. I obviously wouldn't be here. But it didn't stop at that. The dreams got progressively worse. More frequent. The last few times I dreamt of her, she didn't have eyes. Just dark black pits with tears streaming out of them."

I took a gulp of air. That's how McManus looked in the ghoulish dream I had of him.

"She kept repeating that she was blind, but 'he' could see just fine. I'd ask her who 'he' was, and before she could tell me, I'd wake up. Last week, she said 'Nathaniel.' I remember—in my dream, that is—saying to her 'there are an awful lot of people in Burlington with that name.' She wrapped a hand around my wrist—tightly—and screamed at me, in this awful, monstrous voice, '126 North.' When I woke up, there was a bruise the size of a dollar bill on my forearm. I turned on my computer, went to Google, and typed in the address. When your name came up, I almost fainted."

I crossed my legs. "Yeah, well. I changed my driver's license a few weeks ago, so an Internet search for this address could easily pull up my name."

"You think I'm crazy, don't you?"

"No—"

"I spent all week wondering if I'd come here, if I'd try to find you and talk to you. It took me days to work up the courage. I might have tried to forget the whole thing entirely, but last night she visited me one final time. She said she was tired, and that she needed to rest. Again, she told me she was blind—but Nathaniel could see just fine. We were standing on the side of the road where her accident was when she told me this, and above her a shooting star went streaking through the sky. And that bothered me."

"Why is that?" I asked.

"The morning of her accident," Betty said, "after the snow had fallen and the sky had cleared, a shooting star fell over Burlington just before dawn. It was still dark out. Hundreds of folks saw it. I didn't, I was inside at the time. It burned bright red, they said—a fireball—and reports of it went as far south as New York and as far north as Canada. I always wondered if my sister saw it, if Joyce was looking up at the early morning sky and it caught her attention just before the

108

crash. If not the snow storm, if not the campus being open, if not the shooting star—"

"Ifs and buts," I said.

Betty nodded. "Those goddamn ifs and buts."

I took a deep breath. What I wanted to tell Betty was that I had no idea why some strange series of dreams had led her to my front door, that I was sorry for the loss of her sister, and that I had absolutely no clue why I was suddenly involved in such a mess.

I *wanted* to tell her that, but it would have been disingenuous.

Perhaps I thought by not telling her—by not admitting what was going on in my own bizarre night terrors—that I could avoid having to admit I was having those bad dreams at all, that I could keep the whole thing swept beneath that proverbial rug and forget about it. But, I had a gnawing feeling deep inside of me that no amount of avoiding it could make it go away—whatever the hell "it" was—so I decided to tell Betty the truth.

"Betty," I said. "I don't understand what's happening here. I don't have the slightest clue. But, I've dreamt about your sister, too."

Betty gasped. "You have?"

"Yes," I said. "Just a few nights ago. I dreamt that I was sitting beside her in an auditorium at Marshall. Ed McManus was there, too. And I swear, I'm not making this up: he told me exactly what Joyce told you in your dreams. Just like her, he had no eyes. He told me that he was blind, but I could see just fine."

Betty's eyes widened, then glassed over. "What do you think it all means?" she asked.

I let out a long, exasperated sigh. "I don't have any earthly idea," I said. "But I want to get to the bottom of it."

ψ

When we were each done trading stories about our nightly terrors, Betty stood and we shared a long hug. From her little white purse she produced a business card with her name, phone number, and email address on it. As it turned out, she was a clerk at the Burlington Tax Collector's Office in the southern part of town. She'd taken an hour off of work that day to visit me, and thanked me for answering the door when I did. We were both glad our paths had crossed.

After Betty had left, it occurred to me how sorely I needed to speak with old McManus the Anus himself. But, I had no idea how to go about such a thing. I couldn't exactly visit him during office hours and ask if he'd had any strange dreams lately, or visits from ghosts. At least, I couldn't ask him that *outright*. I started to cook up a plan, and on my first Friday off from Marshall, I decided to do the unthinkable.

Visit campus.

ψ

On the drive over to Marshall, my phone rang. I was surprised to hear Vega's voice on the other side of the line when I answered.

"Hey," she said, and she yawned.

I looked at the digital clock on the dashboard of The Beast. 9:15 AM. "Did you just wake up?"

"Surely you wouldn't begrudge me for sleeping in a little, you know, one college student to another? It's a miracle I'm up before noon. What are you up to today?"

"Oh, Vega," I said. "I thought for sure you'd be smoother than this."

Vega laughed. "What do you mean?"

110

"Calling me twelve hours after a first kiss? It just reeks a little of desperation, don't you think?"

"Oh, shut up," Vega said. "No one follows that rule anymore."

"You're supposed to wait a day," I said. "At least."

"Sure," Vega said. "Whatever you say."

"I'm kidding. I'm glad you called."

"I bet you are," she said.

"You wouldn't believe me if I told you the morning I've had. And you wouldn't believe where I'm currently headed, either."

"Where's that?"

"Marshall."

Vega groaned. "Only Nathaniel, king of the nerds, would want to visit Marshall on his first day off from class."

"It's not where I'd prefer to spend my Friday," I said. "But I won't be there long. Afterward, I'll have the whole day to myself."

"What are you going to campus for, anyways?"

"I need to visit McManus. He has office hours on Friday."

Vega snickered. "What on earth could you have to bother McManus about today that can't wait until Monday?"

"It's about my paper," I lied. "I need to work on it over the weekend if I want any chance of finishing it on time."

"Whatever, nerd," Vega said. "Nerd, nerd, nerd."

"Is there anything else I can help you with?" I asked, sarcastically. "I don't like to talk and drive."

"Yeah. What are you doing tonight?"

"Nothing that I know about."

"Cool," Vega said. "There's an old theater downtown. The Capitol. They're running a series of Halloween movies and—"

"Wait," I said. "Halloween movies?"

"Yeah. Halloween movies."

111

"Vega, it's August."

"Who cares?" Vega said. "They play a different Halloween movie each weekend from the end of August until the end of October. Tonight's 'The Exorcist.'"

"Are *you* asking *me* on a date now?"

"God, Nate, it's no wonder you've been single. Do you want to see it or not?"

I hated horror films, but Vega could ask if I wanted to spend the night holding my head under water and I'd happily oblige. "Of course," I said. "Sounds good. But only under one condition."

"What's that?"

"We get free tickets. You've spoiled me. I'm not accustomed to paying for anything in the presence of the almighty Vega Rowland."

"Very funny," Vega said.

"What? You don't have any friends who work at The Capitol? There's no usher there who owes your dad a favor?"

"Spring the fifteen bucks for tickets, cheapo, or you can spend your Friday night alone."

"Fair enough."

"Shit," Vega said. "I just remembered—my car is still at the restaurant. After you visit The Anus, can you pick me up so we can go get it?"

"Absolutely," I said, and I told her I'd call her when I was finished visiting campus.

She thanked me for that, then finished the call by saying: "See you then, can't wait."

ψ

I arrived at McManus's office a little past 9:30 that morning. It was a shared office space, three smaller offices all surrounding the same secretary. A friendly enough woman at the central desk asked who I was there to see, and when I said McManus, she smiled and told me to take a seat.

About ten minutes passed before a girl my age stormed out of McManus's office, sobbing. Her eyeliner had smudged and smeared from her tears, and on the way out she screamed: "I hate this fucking school."

Not long after that, the phone at the secretary's desk rang twice. The secretary answered it, nodded, then hung it up right away. She smiled again and told me that McManus was ready to see me.

"I'm glad to see I caught him on a good day," I mumbled, as I stood and marched past her.

McManus was sitting behind an oak desk, his eyes focused on a laptop computer screen. Behind him were four tall bookshelves, each the same ugly shade of brown as his desk. They were crammed with law encyclopedias and legal texts. On some shelves were old photographs and framed diplomas.

I knocked on the outside of his door, left open by the previous student, and without bothering to look up from his screen McManus invited me in.

The room smelled bad, not in an overly disgusting way, but just in the sense that it hadn't been cleaned in ages. A whiff of something like sour milk hung in the air.

"What can I do for you this morning, Mr. Shaw?"

"Oh," I said, caught off guard. "I'm surprised you know my name."

"I memorize all of my class rosters during the first week of the semester. I'm old, not dim."

"That's a lot of students to memorize—"

113

"I'm terribly busy today, Mr. Shaw, so if you could cut to the chase I'd be greatly appreciative."

"Sure," I said. "It's about my research paper."

"Uh-huh," McManus said. "On Dominic Bloom."

"You memorized who my paper is on, too?"

"I could sit here all day and be charmed and flattered by your amazement at my rote memorization skills, but like I said, I am quite busy."

"Sure," I said. "I'm sorry. I'm just having some difficulty finishing the paper. Mr. Bloom wasn't involved in many landmark cases—"

"He wasn't?" McManus said. "How about Beckman v. Vidtronix Games Corporation? The Beckman family goes to pick their kid up from the local arcade, finds out a six hundred pound game machine tipped over on him. Boy needed sixteen surgeries just to walk a straight line again. That's a fairly landmark case, wouldn't you say? Better yet, it relates directly to the study of torts, which, if you've looked at your syllabus recently, you'd know is the class I teach."

"Yes, I know, it's just that—"

"Just what, Mr. Shaw? That you'd rather I sit here and write your paper for you, than for you to do the research yourself?"

I went on the defensive. "With all due respect, I've done the research. I'm familiar with Beckman v. Vidtronix. The problem is that the Beckman family filed suit against Vidtronix, when in actuality they should have filed suit against the arcade hosting Vidtronix's machine, since they were the ones who didn't have it installed properly. I didn't say Mr. Bloom wasn't involved in *any* landmark cases, I said he wasn't involved in *many*."

"Then focus your paper around the Beckman case," McManus said. "Mr. Bloom helped defend a company whose negligence injured many children. That should be enough to rant and rave about for thirty pages. Now, is that all?"

It occurred to me in that moment that Professor McManus wasn't simply familiar with Dominic Bloom, but had some deep-rooted resentment against the man as well. I didn't want our brief time together to be cut short, so I prodded at him a little.

"Bloom did a fantastic job representing Vidtronix," I said. "As he should have. Defending Vidtronix doesn't make him a bad man."

"Oh, you can be certain he is a bad man," McManus said. "Those stereotypes that lawyers are blood thirsty and vindictive? Bloom perpetuates those stereotypes everyday. A dozen times or more before he showers in the morning."

"All my research has painted Bloom in a very different shade," I said. "He's a top donor to the Burlington Children's Hospital, his firms offer legal aide to the needy, and he's worked pro-bono himself on local cases right here in our backyard. All of that makes your comments about him sound a bit…slanderous."

"You smug little bastard," McManus scoffed. "I can always smell the out of towners from a mile away. How long have you lived here? A week? And you dare question my judgment of a man I've known for decades? To sit there and try to tell me what slander is…the audacity of it."

I don't know what it was, but in that moment, the puzzle pieces in my head clicked together. McManus's voice faded away, the sickly sour-milk scent stopped bothering me, and it all made sense.

Dominic Bloom set up shop in Vermont in the late 1980's.

Dominic Bloom was the one Joyce Nicholson had an affair with during her breakup with Ed McManus.

All these many, many years later, and McManus the Anus still carried the grudge.

"Betty Nicholson visited me this morning," I blurted.

"What the *fuck* did you just say to me?"

I get it—McManus had tenure. He was untouchable. He could tell me to chain cinder blocks to my feet and hop in Lake Champlain, and there'd be nothing I could do about it. But still it felt weird, a person of his position and authority speaking to me the way he was.

"Betty Nicholson," I repeated. My voice waivered as the words left my lips. "She's hurting. Her whole family is. The anniversary of Joyce's death is approaching. You should reach out to her."

"Get out of my office," McManus shouted, and he slammed a meaty fist against the top of his desk. A stapler, a paper clip holder, and a coffee mug all jumped in unison. "I don't want to see you walk through my office doors for the rest of the semester."

The words gushed out of me; it was all happening so fast. "Do you have dreams about her?" I exclaimed. "About Joyce? Am I in them?"

He was seething, his front teeth grinding together, his nostrils flaring and his eyes widening. But I caught it there, in his expression. An affirmation hung on his face, if only for a moment. He wouldn't admit that he had, but he didn't have to. His eyes said it all.

McManus took a deep gulp of air. He'd made himself a master of beating down his students, but now it was a student that was riling him up. I think, honestly, he was surprised by it. He steadied himself, then stood from his desk and held the door open for me.

"Don't worry so much about your paper," McManus said. His tone was eerily calm considering the conversation that had preceded. "I'm entering a zero into my grade book as soon as I sit back down. Hand me a thirty page paper, a sixty page paper, or don't hand me one at all—in two weeks, you will have a zero for the assignment. That paper is worth fifteen percent of your overall grade, which

116

means—if you're not good at math, and I'm most certain you are not—the highest grade you can now achieve in my torts class is an eighty-five percent. A middle of the road B. That is the most you can aspire to. If you slip on other assignments, or do poorly on my exams, you will surely fail. I suggest you attend class regularly and try your damndest if you want any hope of passing my class."

I nodded and stepped out of his office. On the way out, the secretary at the central desk perked up her head, grinned, and in a cheerful voice told me to have a great rest of my day.

ψ

I pulled up to the front gate at 6 Anchorage Lane around 10:30 that morning. From the side of the road, I could just barely make out the silhouette of Vega's castle. She'd later tell me that she hated when I referred to her home as that, that it made her feel like some creepy monster housed away in a distant tower, where she couldn't harm the townsfolk.

The Beast idled and I waited there for a minute or two, and still the gate didn't open. I dialed Vega from my cell phone and she apologized, said that normally the camera's out front alert when someone pulls up to the gate but that they hadn't for some reason. She hung up with me, and right away pneumatic arms on either side of the gate pulled it open.

By the time I made it to the end of her driveway she was waiting outside, sitting on the slate colored fountain just beyond her front door. She had her Wayfarers on—a Vega trademark—a light blouse, a pair of cut up jeans, and black, high-heeled boots that went on forever.

Before I could park The Beast and get the passenger door for her, she had already climbed inside.

"You look like you're hiding from the paparazzi," I said.

Vega shook her head. "Nah, just creeps who drive old Jeeps."

We both laughed, then without warning she leaned over the center console between us and kissed me on the cheek.

"Thanks for the ride, Nate."

ψ

We made it to The Rail Yard soon after. There were only a couple of cars in the parking lot that morning and Vega's was one of them. I parked The Beast beside her Mercedes, then told her I'd pick her up later that night for the movie.

"What's the rush?" she asked. "In a hurry to get rid of me?"

I wasn't—if it was up to me, I could have spent the day with her. But I wanted to get home to my computer. There were hundreds of questions swimming through my mind, and perhaps a full pot of coffee and a few hours with Google could help answer at least a few of them. I needed to know more about Joyce, about her sister, Betty, and about the terrible accident that had shattered the Nicholson family twenty-four years prior.

Additionally, there was the matter of McManus's torts class. My morning meeting with him had all but made up my mind that I was going to withdraw from his course and retake it in the spring with that other professor—what was her name? —Harmon, that was it. It would set me back a little, but McManus was every bit the prick he was prophesized to be, and I had no intention of suffering through his class for the next four months.

"No rush to get rid of you," I said. "I just have a lot going on. There's some stuff I should take care of."

"Nate," Vega said. "You have all weekend to take care of stuff." She pointed out the windshield. "It's *beautiful* out, you're not stuck behind a desk, and you're in the company of a girl—a total babe, I might add—that actually wants to hang out with you."

"There's a lot on my mind," I said. "I don't know that I'd make very good company."

Vega nodded toward the shoreline. Near the edge of the lake, painted bright green, was a swinging bench.

"Come on," she said. "Spill your guts."

We strolled the shore of Lake Champlain for a bit, then took a seat on the bench swing. A cool, calm breeze was blowing across the lake, and even in late August, there was an underlying nip to it. Ahead of us, on the shore, children enjoying the final days of summer vacation flew kites, rode bicycles, chased each other playing tag.

"I'm jealous of the little bastards," Vega said. "Look at them. They don't know how good they've got it."

I grinned. "Remember how long summer break felt when you were ten? Felt like it would never end."

Vega kicked her feet at the ground and our bench swung gently back and forth. "I don't think you want to wax nostalgic about long past summer vacations," she said. "It looks like something's bothering you."

"I haven't really talked about it with anyone," I said. "You have to promise you won't think I'm crazy."

"I can't promise that."

"I'm being serious, Vega—"

"So am I!" she said. "I never make a promise that I'm not certain I can keep."

119

"Whatever," I said. "It'll feel good to get it out."

I sat there, and for ten minutes I told her everything. My dreams about Joyce Nicholson and Ed "The Anus" McManus. The visit from Betty Nicholson that morning. My theory that Joyce was having an affair with local businessman and attorney Dominic Bloom the year she passed away. I told her all of it.

When I was finished, Vega sighed. "I don't think you're crazy, Nate. Not one bit."

"That's a relief," I said.

"What do you think is going on? Why do you think you're in the middle of it all?"

I shrugged and gave our bench another swing. We swayed back and forth, and I said: "Do you believe in ghosts?"

"I don't know," she said. "I've never really thought about them. I think that most of what you see on TV is probably bullshit. Do you?"

"When I was ten," I told her, "I was playing in my garage one afternoon after school. Trying to fix the chain on my bike. I wasn't having very much luck with it, and I was thinking about how, had my dad still been alive, he'd have fixed it in a flash. I set my bike down, defeated, and got ready to go back inside, when something in the window facing my backyard caught my eye. I looked up and he was standing out there. Clear as day. He had his back turned to me—I couldn't see his face—but he was standing there. I screamed out for him and he didn't turn around, so I ran outside. I sprinted to the side of the garage. There was no one there."

"What did you do?"

"I ran inside, crying my eyes out, and told my mom."

"And did she believe you?"

120

"Yeah," I said. "So much so that she called the cops. She believed there was a man in the yard watching me as I worked on my bike. I pleaded with her, begged her to understand that it wasn't some pedophile or drifter. It was *him*. It was my dad."

"Who do you think it was?" Vega said, and she placed her hand on mine.

I shook my head. "I mean, who's to say—"

"No," Vega said. "Deep down in your heart, all these years later, you know one way or the other. You can't sit on the fence on this one."

When she put it that way, it didn't take any time at all to offer an answer. "It was my dad," I said, and my eyes started to burn. "No doubt about it. It was him."

"And what do you think your dad would have to say about all of this?"

"He was a romantic," I said. "He believed in fate. In things happening for a reason. He'd want me to get to the bottom of it."

"Sounds like an adventure, " she said. "Come on, then. Let's get to the bottom of it."

ψ

I walked Vega to her car, and that afternoon we drove back to my house. I parked The Beast in my driveway, then hopped into the passenger seat of Vega's Mercedes. Before we consolidated cars, I insisted that we should spend the afternoon in The Beast, but Vega refused. "My car is faster," she countered, and there was no arguing with that. Hers was the fastest, and Vega liked to drive fast.

Once I buckled my seat belt, we were off, although where we were off to, neither of us seemed to know.

"It's like there's a mystery to solve," Vega said, "but before we can solve it…we need to figure out what the mystery is."

"That's precisely the problem," I said. "There's obviously some unfinished business from the fall of 1988. But what is it? Joyce Nicholson wasn't murdered. She died in an accident."

"Are we certain that she did?" Vega asked.

"Uh, yeah," I said, and I couldn't help but laugh. "She drove into the broad side of a galloping moose. That doesn't exactly scream 'premeditation.'"

"You want to be a lawyer, Nate. Use your imagination."

I rubbed my forehead. "Vega, it's not like someone waited on the side of the road and pushed a moose out in front of her."

"Sure," she said. "That's unlikely. But what about her car? It could have been tampered with. A loose brake line would go an awfully long way on an ice-slicked road. Now, who do we know that could have *possibly* wanted to bring harm upon a pregnant woman on her way to class?"

"A scorned and bitter lover," I said. "Ed McManus. Maybe Joyce told him that their baby might not be his. Maybe that pushed him over the edge."

Vega tapped her nose. "God, I feel like Scooby-Doo and the gang."

I grinned at that. "Does that make me the Shaggy to your Scooby?"

"More like the Velma to my Daphne."

"Don't you mean the Fred to your Daphne?"

"Oh, please. Like Daphne would want anything to do with a square like Fred." Vega laughed, then let out a little purr. "You know Daphne and Velma were getting freaky in the back of the Mystery

Machine." She tapped my nose. "Like I said, Nate. Use your imagination."

Before we'd wasted too much time and gas, I suggested that we should visit a local police station. Maybe there were documents there, open to the public, that we could read over. We could see if there were any missing—or questionable—details about the morning of Joyce Nicholson's death.

A quick Internet search on my phone revealed that the accident would have been in the purview of the Vermont State Troopers. A second search revealed that the State Trooper office closest to Marshall was on the northern end of Burlington.

"What do you think?" I asked.

Vega nodded. "We'll drive over. More than likely, it was someone working in that office that responded to the scene of the crash. If there's anything worth finding there, we'll find it."

As luck would have it, there was plenty worth finding at the State Trooper's office that afternoon. Vega pulled into the station—a big, grey, square brick in northern Burlington—and parked her car in a civilian parking lot. To the left, behind a chain link fence lined with razor wire, was a gated parking lot with a dozen or so patrol cars. Ahead of us, on the front of the building, were two sliding glass doors.

"Ready?" I asked.

"Feels weird. Like when I walk in, I'll be arrested. Even though I didn't do anything wrong."

"Maybe you should wait here," I said.

"Why's that?"

"You're way above the legal limit of being cute—"

"Oh, shut up, you fucking cornball—"

"No, Vega, I'm serious." I held up my hand. "Here's a kitten chasing its tail." I held up my hand a little higher. "Now here's a little kid feeding an animal at a zoo." I held my hand up higher one more time, nearly touching the roof of her Mercedes. "And here's Vega Rowland."

"If you ever come at me with a cringe inducing line like that again, I might vomit. And I promise, I'll aim towards you when I do. Now, come on."

We strolled into the station together side by side. At a desk inside sat an elderly woman behind a computer. A nameplate on the desk read: Edna.

"Can I help you?" Edna asked, in a sweet, buttery voice. She looked a bit ridiculous, I thought, sitting there in her officer's uniform. It was easier to picture her at home, baking oatmeal raisin cookies for her grandchildren, than to ever have imagined her chasing criminals on a street or ticketing reckless drivers on the highway.

Then again, that was the year I finally learned all about appearances and how deceiving they could be.

"I'm wondering," I said, "if we could speak to someone about a crash from quite a few years back. September of 1988. A girl named Joyce Nicholson passed away out on Hampshire Road, by the—"

"Marshall College of Law," Edna said. "Oh, I remember. You kids look awfully young. That was before you were even born, wasn't it? Are you family members of the deceased?"

"Not exactly," I said. "I just wanted to see if I could learn a little bit more about the accident."

Edna nodded and leaned back in her seat. You could see in her eyes that she wasn't just at her desk, but that she had time traveled in that mysterious way that only memories can allow us to. For a

124

moment she was back in '88, reliving that September morning all over again.

"I worked that day," Edna said. "I was here in the station, but I remember it so clearly. Awful what happened to that girl. Just awful. Officer Dixon was the first responder to the scene."

"Does he still work here?" Vega asked.

"Oh, yeah," Edna said. "He spends most of his time at a desk now, just like me. I guess that's the way these things go. But he's here."

"Could we speak to him for a minute?" I asked. "If he's not busy, that is."

"You kids take a seat over there," Edna said, and she pointed to a row of chairs across from her desk. "I'll have him visit you in a moment."

Ten minutes passed before a square faced black man in his late fifties came out to the front lobby and greeted us. His hair was peppered grey and big, fat pillows of flesh had cropped up beneath his eyes.

"You the kids Edna paged me about?" His voice boomed, the words bounced off of the walls. Surely, I thought, he'd at one point had a career in the armed forces.

Vega and I nodded in unison. "We had some questions," I said. "About an accident."

"Edna told me. The Nicholson girl. '88."

Again, Vega and I nodded.

A sour look crept across Officer Dixon's face and he waved his hand. "Follow me back here," he said. "Let's hear all about it."

We followed a labyrinth of hallways before we arrived at a cramped cubicle in the rear of the station. Officer Dixon pulled out a pair of chairs for Vega and I to sit at, then took a seat opposite of us at his desk. Behind him, hanging from the cubicle wall, were newspaper clippings, awards, and a lifetime of photographs. Framed beside a certificate honoring him for his bravery was an American flag.

"What brings the two of you in today?" Dixon thundered. Any hopes of a private conversation seemed squashed. I jolted each time the man opened his mouth.

"We had a few questions about Joyce Nicholson," Vega said. "

"I know all about Joyce," Dixon said. "Not a day goes by that I don't think about her." He pulled a manila folder from beside his computer and set it on his desk, then opened it up. A quarter inch stack of papers had been stuffed inside. "I dug this out of records as soon as Edna paged me," he said. Miraculously, his voice had softened a bit.

"Thank you," I said.

"You family of the deceased?"

I shook my head. "No, but I've recently been in contact with Joyce's sister, Betty. I suppose I'd be considered a friend of the family's?"

"And you?" Dixon said, his eyes falling on Vega.

"Just a curious passenger, I guess," she said, nervously.

Dixon clicked his tongue. "I've been doing this for over thirty years now. Not a lot of things have stuck with me the way Joyce Nicholson's death stuck with me. It was my third year as a cop, but only my first year as a trooper. I'd been doing beat work for the city of Burlington beforehand, and at that point, hadn't seen much more than a bar fight."

Dixon fanned through the small stack of police reports. The papers were yellowed and tattered. The piles of pages, written in a

126

time before the Internet age, were crammed edge to edge with sloppy cursive writing and coffee stains.

The officer licked his thumb, then pulled a couple of pages from the stack. "The moose that ran out in front of her—big bastard—he crushed the front of her hood, then crashed through the windshield. The front of his antlers hit right about here," Dixon said, and he pointed at a dimple just beside the corner of his lips. "Tore her to pieces. Nothing left. One moment here, the next moment gone. Fucking tragedy."

"And the entire thing," I said, waving my hands at the mess of papers, "was summed up as an accident."

Again, Dixon clicked his tongue. "Now what would make you ask a curious thing like that?"

"It's an awfully long story," I said. "But I've just had this gnawing feeling that there's still something left of Joyce Nicholson's story. Something that has to be said."

Once more, Dixon dropped his gaze on Vega. "You some sort of psychic or something? We get plenty of you crazies dropping by here, wanting to help out with old cases, maybe get a two minute spot on the eleven o'clock news."

Vega opened her mouth, but before she could get a word out, I said: "We're college kids. That's all. Over at Marshall. To this day, lots of stories about Joyce swirl around. She was a student there. We've just—well, we've heard a lot of misinformation. And we want to learn as much about her and her accident as we can."

Dixon folded his hands together, rested them on the desk.

"Between the three of us, everything we talk about going forward is off the record, got it?"

We nodded. "Got it."

127

"Anything I say henceforth," Dixon said, "is my opinion and mine only. It's not reflective of the Vermont State Troopers. Do you understand?"

"Loud and clear," I said.

Dixon leaned back in his office chair, stared up at the tiled squares that lined the ceiling above him.

"The coroner came out not long after I showed up at the scene. Another student on their way to class had phoned the accident in as soon as they arrived on campus. Funny thing, the days before cellular phones. A short while after the coroner showed up, an ambulance and fire crew pulled up, too. Always bothered me that they showed up behind the coroner, even though there was no one left to save. So now there's eight or ten of us, standing on the side of Hampshire, freezing our jimmies off. Which means—of course—a news van shows up. And all I remember is, nobody could shut the hell up about that damn shooting star. Fireball, shot right across the morning sky. I missed it, because I was doing my job, but to all those rednecks standing around the crime scene, you'd think they'd seen the second coming of Christ. Beautiful girl, dashed to pieces behind her steering wheel, and these jackasses are standing around, bitching about the cold, sippin' their morning coffees, and carrying on and on about that shooting star."

Dixon scratched his chin, leaned forward again in his seat.

"The coroner had her out of there lickety-split. Had her declared dead on arrival and had her bagged. A fella named Rodney Curits. Real creep—then again, I've never met a coroner that didn't strike me as a creep. Gotta have a peculiar skill set to work a job like that. Curtis was gone in a flash, leaving me, the fire crew, and the paramedics to stand there with our dicks out."

The officer turned toward Vega and apologized for the vulgarity.

128

"Don't worry about it," Vega said.

"Anywho, it bothered me how quickly the whole thing was moving along. By the time I was starting a preliminary inspection of the vehicle, my sergeant was calling me on the radio, telling me to get back to the station. Said a wrecker would be on its way over to tow Joyce's car out of the ditch, and that forensics would sweep it later in the day. I didn't like that much, so while the lot of us waited on the side of the road for the wrecker, I started to dig around. I couldn't see much, you understand, because of the two-ton son of a bitch bleeding to death on her hood. But I know my way around a motor vehicle, and I wanted to learn as much as I could before the wrecker showed up. So I did a scan. I checked her power steering fluid: almost dry. I took a look at her brake cables: looked like a New York City rat ate 'em for lunch. Not a single airbag had deployed."

"You think someone tampered with Joyce's car?" I blurted.

"Oh, I know someone did," Dixon said. "Unofficially, of course. The real question is: how did she drive that far before there was a problem? She shouldn't have been able to back out of her driveway before realizing something was wrong, let alone almost make it to campus. I'm no dummy. Something about her accident smelled fishy from the moment I pulled up. Scratch that. It fucking reeked."

Dixon pushed the manila folder toward me.

"Am I allowed?" I asked.

"You tell me," he said. "You're the lawyer."

"Studying to be a lawyer," I clarified.

"I'm just fuckin' with you, son," Dixon said. "Anything in there is a matter of public record. You're free to poke around."

I opened the folder and squirmed in my seat. The very first photo at the top of the stack was in black and white, taken by Dixon himself. Strapped into the driver's seat of a little domestic two-door was a petite and pretty girl, save for the fact she was missing a head. A little bit of lower jaw hung like a flap from her neck, but that was it. The rest was gone. The interior was covered in dark stains, like someone jammed a firework into a watermelon and set it off. Her hands were still wrapped around the steering wheel.

The next photo was of the scene itself. Joyce's car, half in a ditch on the side of Hampshire, the other half jutting out into the driving lane, crushed beneath a monstrous creature. Just out of frame was an ambulance and a state trooper's patrol car.

I flipped through a few more photographs, then passed them to Vega. She didn't look at them with the same disgust and horror that I did—but then again, this was the same girl who *wanted* to see The Exorcist that night at the Capitol Theatre, so I placed my bets that she wasn't easily offended.

Beneath the stack of photos were piles of police reports, hastily written, many of them scribbled so full of sloppy handwriting and police jargon that they were barely readable.

"You kept quiet all this time," I said, glancing at a report that Dixon had filled out. The words on the page directly contradicted the story he'd just told me: "No foul play suspected."

"I was told to stay hushed," Dixon said, "by some very powerful people. People you don't say no to. Besides, I wasn't a forensic examiner anyway. Their testimony would be all that mattered, and their opinions were all the same: a simple case of being in the wrong place at the wrong time. And who knows, what if I was wrong?"

"You weren't wrong," I said. A sour puddle filled in the pit of my stomach. "You know you weren't."

I sorted a small pile of photographs and documents, everything I considered essential. "Can I make copies of these?"

"Up front, Edna can make a copy of your ass sitting on the Xerox machine if you wanted, kid. So long as you got the dough. Copies are a buck per page."

ψ

Vega and I sat in her car for a moment, the silence only punctuated by the humming of the Mercedes' air conditioner. Outside, patrol cars came and went.

"That was exciting," she said.

I opened the car's glove box and stuffed the folder full of copies I had made inside. "It was, wasn't it?"

"There's a thread here, Nate, and you've started to pull it. All of these strange dreams and weird crossed paths of yours are adding up to something. They haven't been for nothing."

"I don't think so either," I said. "For the past week, it's all felt so weird, like my tires were spinning in place. But now I've got some traction."

Vega shifted the car into drive.

"Listen," I said. "This is a big start to something. I can feel it. Thank you for believing in me, and for not thinking I was crazy."

She smiled and steered the Mercedes out of the parking lot. "It's nothing. Where to next, Velma?"

ψ

According to their website, The Capitol Theater would be screening the seminal 1973 horror classic "The Exorcist" at seven PM that night. And, even though it took good ole Edna a staggering amount of time to make the copies we asked for—twenty seven dollars worth in all—we had plenty of time to kill before the movie started.

Vega suggested that we drive on down to the Church Street Marketplace, and that was exactly what we did. It was just before four, so we had a few hours to spare, and nothing to fill the time. Walking the flea markets together and eating terrible food seemed like just as good of a suggestion as any other, so Vega parked her Mercedes in a cramped little lot on the eastern side of Pearl Street and we started the day's next adventure.

Along Main Street, crowds had started to form. Stages were set up and folk bands played live music. The smells of sausage and peppers, popcorn and cotton candy filled the air.

Townsfolk huddled beside each other, shoulder to shoulder, so when Vega grabbed my hand in the crowd it seemed less like a romantic gesture and more like a necessity, less we lose each other in the crowd.

"Come on," she said, "I see a little wine shop up ahead. After the day we've had, I could use a drink. Couldn't you?"

She made a good argument.

We wormed our way into a little bistro that sold wine, knickknacks, and tchotchkes, and took a seat at a cozy table for two that faced out onto the street. Outside, the denizens of Burlington walked, biked, and danced along Main Street.

A friendly enough waiter quickly greeted us. I was almost shocked, considering the events of the day before, when he didn't seem to recognize Vega or offer us a free drink. Truthfully, it was a bit refreshing. Even just walking around town with her felt like strolling with a celebrity; all eyes were always on Vega, and for once, it felt good to be treated like any other customer.

Vega ordered a red wine with some fancy name I had trouble pronouncing, and I ordered a beer. Something domestic and simple.

"I'm excited to go to the movie tonight," Vega said. "I can't believe you've never seen it before."

"Well that'll make it all the more fun, won't it? You'll know all the scares that are coming, and I won't know a thing."

She smiled. "You don't like scary movies, do you?"

"Am I that obvious?"

"Nate," she said. "I can read you like a book."

"They've never really been my cup of tea," I said. "Besides, look at today. My life has been a scary movie. I'm living it."

"A little dramatic, don't you think?"

"Strangers showing up at my door? Violent and bizarre dreams that seem to connect me to a car accident from over twenty years ago? Yeah. Mark it down as horror."

The waiter set our drinks down at the table. Vega picked up her glass, swished the wine around a bit, then sniffed it. "You've never watched a scary movie, therefore you're unable to classify your day as a scary movie. You're...hmm." She took a sip of the wine. "You're trapped inside more of a suspense thriller."

"I'd happily trade it for a romantic comedy."

"You'd happily trade it for a porno."

I laughed halfway through a sip of beer. I had to cover my face, or else risk shooting the lager out my nose and onto Vega.

"I'm not gonna lie, Nathaniel Shaw. You don't like scary movies. That irks me. Might be a deal breaker."

"Well maybe you can convert me," I said. "Make me a fan."

"If tonight doesn't convert you, I don't know what else will. The Exorcist is a masterpiece."

"Is it your favorite?"

133

Vega crossed her arms. "Hard to say. There's a spectrum to horror movies. It's hard to pick just one as a favorite."

"A spectrum?"

"Yeah," Vega said, her voice softening. "On one end, you have your typical slasher flick. Friday the Thirteenth. A Nightmare on Elm Street. Halloween. They're all great, sure. But it's hard to find a good slasher film with substance. Slasher films are a quick fuck in the backseat of an empty parking lot. Fast. Fun. But not a lot of romance to the whole thing, you know? No foreplay. Not very satisfying."

"You have my attention," I said.

"Horror films," Vega said, "*real* horror films, are a two year relationship. Sunday mornings spent eating breakfast then making long, lazy love in bed. No rush. Everyone takes their time. A real slow burn with a big bang at the end. True horror films leave you wanting more. They stick with you long after you've watched them. The Exorcist. The Shining. Alien."

"I've seen Alien. I liked it."

"Then you like horror movies after all," Vega said.

"Alien wasn't a horror movie."

"It absolutely was," she said, "and a masterful one at that. The art of the slow burn. For a film called 'Alien,' how many times do you actually see the Alien before the big climax?"

"Not many," I said.

"Exactly my point," Vega said, and she finished her wine. "Yet, it was there all along. And not being able to see it? Only made it scarier."

ψ

We finished our drinks and left, but before we walked out, I left a twenty-dollar bill on the table for our friendly waiter. The drinks were only eleven bucks, but I'd had so very few opportunities to pay for Vega, and I wanted to impress her.

The two of us had a nice, manageable buzz going as we stumbled through the Church Street Marketplace. Hand in hand, we passed by booth after booth of folks selling their wares. Vega found a hemp bracelet that she had to have, and I found an ashtray made out of old, melted down records.

"You don't smoke," Vega pointed out.

"No, but my roommate does," I said. "It reminds me of him."

When we were done strolling through the vendors and shops, we found a little corner café, the illusive source of the sausage and peppers smell that had tickled my nostrils since we first set foot out of the car. I offered to pick us up dinner and Vega accepted. We sat there, talking and laughing, swapping our favorite movies, and books, and songs. There was a spark between us, of that I was certain, but it was sometimes easy to forget how little we knew about each other. It was Friday, and we had only truly met the Monday before.

At a little after six thirty, we left the café and started our stroll to The Capitol Theatre. The Capitol was a grand building, as majestic as it was old. The marquee out front listed a community theater production of Fiddler on the Roof on one side, and the seven o'clock showing for that night's screening of The Exorcist on the other.

There was a long line of folks waiting to buy tickets out front, and only one usher, it appeared, to sell them. Vega and I took our place at the back of the line, and waited patiently for our turn.

When we finally reached the ticket window, a teenager with a rash of acne in the space between his eyebrows greeted us.

"Two tickets, please," I said, and I reached for my wallet.

"That'll be sixteen dollars, and I'll need to see your I.D."

"Are you serious?" I asked. We'd stopped for drinks twice that afternoon, once at the bistro and again with dinner at the café, and both times we weren't carded.

"The Exorcist is rated R," the teen squawked, "and as such, patrons under the age of seventeen cannot be admitted."

"This is a joke, right?" I pulled my credit card and freshly printed Vermont driver's license from my wallet. I slid both through a narrow slat at the bottom of the cashier's window.

The teenager looked over both assiduously, as if license forgery for underage movie patrons was suddenly a hot crime in Burlington, then slid my credit card into a device on the side of his cash register.

"Before I complete the payment," the teenager said, "I'll have to see hers, too."

"You just saw that I'm twenty-two," I said. "Isn't that enough?"

"Listen, guy. I don't make the rules. I was simply told that absolutely no children are allowed into tonight's screening. It's an adult only event."

"Adult only," I said. "Right. Tell me, does my companion here look like an adult? Does she look like a child?"

"I couldn't say—"

"It's no big deal," Vega said, and she reached for her purse. "Really, Nate. Don't worry about it."

Vega smacked her license face down onto the counter, then slid it through the narrow slat. The ticket attendant looked it over as carefully as he inspected mine, then slid all three cards—both of our driver's licenses, and my credit card—back through the slat.

Vega took her license in a flash and I slid my card and license back into my wallet. A twenty-year-old printer beside the cash register groaned and made a whirring noise as it printed out our tickets. The attendant slid them through the slat before apologizing for the misunderstanding.

"What a twerp," I said, and I put my arm around Vega and walked her into the theater.

ψ

Vega and I stepped into a long lobby that was somewhat lost to time, a relic of a bygone era. The staff of The Capitol wore red vests and bow ties, pleated slacks, and black tap toes that were shined so bright you could see your reflection in them. The carpet was a faded burgundy with a checkered pattern, worn from years of foot traffic.

Ahead of us was a concession stand, and on either side of that, doorways that led into the theater. I suggested we get some snacks, and Vega agreed. A clerk, much more agreeable than the one selling tickets, took our order, disappeared behind the counter, and returned with a large Coke and a bucket of popcorn big enough to carry newborn twins in.

"Too many more adventures," Vega said as we stepped into the theater, fumbling to carry our snacks, "and I'll have to double my time at Happy Body."

"I'll join too," I said, and I nearly spilled the cola all over myself as I smacked my belly.

We found a row of seats near the back of the theater that were entirely unoccupied. It's not that people didn't show up for that night's showing of The Exorcist—there were plenty of folks peppered through the rows of seats ahead of us—it's just that The Capitol was so damn *big,* and the house had no hope of reaching maximum capacity while showing a thirty-five year old film.

137

The two of us curled up together and the theater's old lights dimmed. Speakers on either side of us crackled and hummed to life, and the film began.

I'd never seen The Exorcist before that night, and I doubt I'll see it again anytime soon. I've never been much of a horror movie fan, but of the few I'd seen, The Exorcist stole the crown for scariest.

When Linda Blair came shuffling down the stairs of her family home, possessed by a demon, walking backwards on her palms and bare feet, I just about shot out of my seat. Vega let out a short snort, then laughed so hard the sip of coke between her lips spat forward. An older couple a few rows ahead turned around to glare at us, but we ignored them.

There was a flash of the devil's face midway through the film. It was only on screen for half of a second, but what a wonderful trick it was. The image was gone before the audience had a chance to process what they'd seen, and it was glorious.

And, of course, the infamous final act: a priest shouting at the demon to leave Linda Blair's body, and Linda Blair scoffing at the exorcism, her head spinning in place, spewing split-pea soup like a garden hose.

I heard more of those final scenes than I saw; my attention was focused elsewhere. In the last twenty minutes or so of the film, Vega and I had reclined together in our seats, pawing at each other like a couple of teenagers under the bleachers after junior prom, and—well, what more can I say?

You know how it goes.

It was like something out of a movie.

ψ

When The Exorcist's credits began to roll and The Capitol's theater lights brightened, the room started to empty. Dozens of moviegoers filed out of the exits behind where we sat, until it was only Vega and I left.

"That was nice," I said.

Vega bit her lip. "The movie?"

"Oh, sure," I said. "The movie."

We collided once more for one last kiss. It could have lasted an eternity, I thought, but it was quickly interrupted by a team of teenagers with brooms and dustpans that had flooded into the theater.

Vega leaned back. "I guess that's our cue to leave."

"Guess so."

We stood, Vega grabbed her bag, and we walked out of the theater arm-in-arm. The ticket taker from earlier in the evening, whose duties were now assigned to picking up empty boxes of candy and popcorn, sneered at us as we left.

We walked out the front of The Capitol and strolled down Main. The streets had emptied and hushed considerably; gone were the folk bands and the food vendors, and the flea market booths peddling their wares. The air had chilled, too, and when I felt Vega shiver, I pulled her even closer.

"Does it always get this cold this time of year, here?"

Vega shook her head. Her hand was warm. "Not usually," she said, and she yawned.

After a short walk we arrived at Vega's Mercedes. We sat together for a moment, in the mostly vacant parking lot behind The Capitol, laughing and catching our breath.

"You were a total whimp during the entire third act," Vega said.

"I don't care what I was. That was horrifying."

"That was glorious," Vega clarified. "Film making at its finest. Story telling at its most compelling. A sweet, beautiful girl, completely ravaged by some hell-sent beast. What more could you want?"

"I never knew you were such a cinema buff," I said.

"There's plenty you still don't know about me, Nathaniel Shaw."

Any time she said my name like that, start to end, it always *got* me. She enunciated it perfectly. She spoke it like it was hers, like it belonged to her.

"What's left to know?" I asked. "Is there some devil hiding underneath that girlish exterior?"

Vega smirked. Her chest was heaving. She unbuttoned the top of her blouse and quite dryly asked: "Wouldn't you like to find out?"

Time stood still for that moment. All I remember was the feel and the smell of the fine-grain leather of the passenger seat and the glossed wood trim of the Mercedes. The cabin of the car was dark, save for a narrow shaft of yellow light beaming in from a far off street light.

Vega tossed her car keys onto the dashboard and carefully climbed over to my side of the car. She straddled me there in the passenger seat, her face brushing against mine, her hands wrapped around my waist.

"I don't know if you're the devil," I said, and I took a deep gulp of air. "But I think you may be a witch."

"Why's that?" she whispered, and she nibbled at my ear.

"Because you've bewitched me," I said.

She leaned back and her jaw widened into a smile. She lifted her hands from me and crossed her arms.

"What is it?" I said. "What's wrong?"

"You just tried to use a stolen line on me."

"A what?"

"Oh, don't play stupid, Nate." She paused to snicker. "Johnny Depp says that to Christina Ricci in a movie. Sleepy Hollow. They're fighting the headless horseman, and he says to her, 'Are you a witch? Because you've bewitched me.'"

"You really are a film buff," I said. "Nothing gets past you."

Like I said—I haven't seen a lot of scary movies, but I've seen a few, and Sleepy Hollow was one of them. I felt like a kid caught with his hand in the cookie jar.

"I'll forgive it just this once," Vega said, and she pressed herself against me, initiating a kiss so long and otherworldly that I feared I might pass out.

Everything was moving fast, and my head was spinning—it really was. And just because it was moving fast didn't mean I minded the direction it was moving in. Through four years of college, I'd put so much pressure on *it,* and now I didn't care much about *it* at all. In a penthouse suite, or in the passenger seat behind The Capitol, I didn't care where I lost *it* once and for all. I was absolutely intoxicated by her, and wherever our strange and winding road would take us, I was ready to go there.

Vega leaned back and in one fast swoop pulled her blouse up and over her head. In the dim light, I could just barely make out the intricate patterns of her bra.

She leaned against me again and my hands, unsure of where to go, went to her back. Her skin was soft, smooth as silk.

I closed my eyes.

Then made the mistake of opening them.

Now at the time, I wasn't sure that what I saw standing outside of Vega's Mercedes was anything more than a trick of the eyes. How easy it could have been, between our heated exchanges in the

141

darkened parking lot, to mistake something as innocuous as a garbage canister or a theater attendant finishing their shift as something more sinister.

But I've seen enough now to know the difference between an overactive imagination and something that's there—something that's *real*—and whatever was standing at the edge of the parking lot that night was real. Of that, I'm certain.

I was halfway finished unhooking Vega's bra, barely able to control my finer motor movements, her lips tracing the path between my left ear and my shoulder, when I saw it standing on the opposite side of the parking lot.

Whatever it was looked like Joyce Nicholson, standing stoically beneath a street lamp. She was putting a hair clip into her shoulder length curls when her eyes caught mine. I had only seen her in photographs and dreams, but it was her, no denying it. She looked pretty, standing there, chewing at her bottom lip. It looked like she was waiting for someone.

Her eyes scanned the parking lot behind The Capitol, and when they locked onto mine, she grinned. Her face darkened, then caved inward, exploded into a burst of slush that rained down around her in the parking lot. She didn't seem bothered by that much, because instead of collapsing, she raised her right arm. It lifted with a janky, mechanical movement, and then it waved at me.

"Holy shit!" I yelled, and Vega leaned back quickly. "Turn around!"

Vega spun, but by the time she turned far enough to look out the windshield of the Mercedes, Joyce was gone.

"What is it?" Vega said. "What's wrong?" Her words were soft and breathy. "Was someone out there?"

"I thought I saw—I thought—I don't know what I saw," I said.

142

"Christ, Nate," Vega said. "The movie really spooked you, didn't it?"

"That must be it," I said, squirming in my seat.

"Maybe now isn't a good time," Vega said.

I nodded. "Yeah. Maybe it isn't."

Vega reached beside her, picked up her blouse from where it rested on the center console of the car. She pulled it over her head, adjusted it, and buttoned it back up. When she finished, she gently climbed back into the driver's seat.

"It was probably just some freak trying to get a free show," Vega said.

"I'm not sure it was," I replied. I didn't want to tell her who I'd seen. It was one thing to have dreams of the deceased, another to insist they were stalking you during waking hours.

"Probably some pervy teenager. Little boys are obsessed with tits from birth," Vega insisted. "Like I said—someone wanting a free show."

We sat in the car for a while, surrounded by an uncomfortable silence, each of us scanning the parking lot for movement.

There was nothing.

After what felt like an eternity, Vega broke the quiet, said: "I have to ask you something, and I want you to know, I don't care what the answer is—"

"I haven't," I said.

"You didn't know what I was about to ask."

I shook my head. "I haven't."

"Not once? Ever?"

"I've come pretty close," I said, and my eyes stayed fixed on the edge of the parking lot.

"What was her name?"

"Christine," I said. "It was earlier this year. It was a bad break up. We did everything but—"

"Everything but *it*," Vega said.

"That's about the long and the short of it," I said.

Vega huffed. "Is it like a…religious thing?"

I laughed. "No. Not at all. While everyone around me was out having sex, I just—I don't know. Decided to wait for the right one? It sounds lame, saying it out loud like this. It just became a thing of mine, something I wouldn't budge on. I started making a big deal out of it one day, then couldn't stop."

"And what about just now?" Vega asked. "We were going down a road that could have had a lot of different destinations—"

"It suddenly became not a big deal," I said, and we both laughed. "But the moment has kind of left, hasn't it?"

It had. And moments like that—well, once they're gone, they are gone for good.

Vega nodded. "I'll take a rain check on popping your cherry, Nate."

"When you put it like that," I said. "It sounds so romantic."

"Come on," she said, and she started the car. The Mercedes roared to life. "Let me take you home."

ψ

I hadn't spent much time wandering Burlington late at night, but the town had a charm to it, even after the sun had set. A few bars stayed open late to cater to the college crowds, and a McDonald's by the lake prided itself on being open seven days a week, twenty-four hours a day. Antique lampposts illuminated the narrow streets and dotted the shore along Lake Champlain. Alongside Vega, who at nearly every turn was treated like a celebrity, it felt less like driving through town and more like exploring a movie set.

We were rolling up to stop light on Hampshire, about to turn onto North, when we discovered the intersection ahead had been blocked. Sawhorses spray painted with the words BURLINGTON POLICE DEPARTMENT prevented oncoming traffic from getting onto the street. Ambulances, fire trucks, and patrol cars packed the narrow roadway, their emergency lights flickering.

Vega slowed the car to a stop and put her window down. An officer directing traffic approached her.

"Ma'am, you're gonna have to turn around, the road is blocked."

Vega scoffed. "I can see that. But my companion here lives on North and needs a lift home."

The officer leaned close into the window. "I have deputies setting up a detour now. You'll have to turn around."

"Can't we just get through?" Vega asked. "There's only, like, one street between here and his home."

"I'm at 126," I said.

"Ma'am," the officer said, sounding annoyed. "Turn back around on Hampshire, take a left at Niebolt, and follow that down a couple of blocks. Make a left onto Hersch and that'll bring you back to North. For now, you can't get through this way." He patted the car door and walked away.

"The fuck is going on?" Vega said, and she drummed her fingers on the steering wheel. "Things don't ever get this exciting around here."

"Things are getting more exciting by the day," I said. "Want to investigate?"

Vega smirked. "Nate," she said. "You read my mind."

145

Vega turned around, like the officer had instructed, and hooked onto Niebolt. She found a vacant lot behind Ned's Hardware and parked her Mercedes.

It didn't take long to hike back over to North. There were crowds standing around and a parked news van had raised its satellite antenna high into the sky.

"What do you think is going on?" I asked.

Vega stuffed her hands into her pockets. "The Frosty Boot is over there. Maybe a bar fight gone bad? A drunk driver?"

"I hope everyone's okay."

"I love that about you," Vega said.

"What?"

"Your naiveté." Vega shook her head. "You don't get a roadblock, a fire crew, and the six o'clock news if you're okay. No, someone's dead."

I felt a gust of wind pass right through me, and my face must have turned white, because Vega offered to walk us back to her car.

"I'm fine," I said. "Let's see what all the hubbub is about."

We got close to North and crossed the street. In front of The Frosty Boot stood a professionally dressed young woman holding a microphone. A guy in a backwards baseball cap trained a bright spotlight on her face, and another guy in a dirty t-shirt and jeans pointed a camera at her. It was hard to hear what she was saying over the murmurs of the crowd.

A ring of people had formed on either side of the street. A half dozen or so police officers kept them from getting close to the center of the road. They stood, slack jawed, cell phone cameras aimed at the center of the street.

"Oh my God," Vega said, as we got close enough to see what was going on.

I felt a queasy feeling creep deep into my stomach. On the double solid line of North was a white sheet draped over the outline of a person. The edges of the sheet were stained dark red. At the end of the sheet extended a pair of feet, one dressed in a pink sneaker, the other in only a sock. I scanned the road; ten feet away, the other sneaker rested on the edge of the street beneath a police barricade, still laced tight. A police officer was taking a photograph of it.

"It must have been a hit and run," Vega said, crossing her arms.

I studied the street for a moment. If a car had swerved out onto North, it was reasonable to think the driver would have braked before colliding with the unfortunate soul under the white sheet. If they braked, the tires of their car would have left long skid marks, burned onto the asphalt. I looked up the street, then down it, and up it again. There weren't any.

"Not a hit and run," I said. "This was intentional. Whoever was driving never even tried to stop."

"That's horrible," Vega said.

Behind us, the news reporter and her crew were loading film equipment into the back of their van. The satellite antenna atop the vehicle had retracted, and it was clear they were getting ready to leave.

"Come on," I said, and I grabbed Vega by the hand. We hurried over to the van, just as the guy in the backward baseball cap was hopping into the driver's seat. The reporter was helping the light operator carry a tripod through a sliding door on the side of the vehicle.

"What's going on here?" I blurted.

147

The news reporter smiled. "Doesn't take a rocket scientist to figure out. Hit and run."

"No," I said. "It looks like more than that."

The reporter shook her head. "Police are calling it a hit and run."

"Who's the victim?" I asked.

"Cops are telling us not to release a name until they can notify the family."

"Please," I said.

"My segment goes to air at midnight," the reporter said. "Tune into channel six and find out then. I really can't divulge that information until then."

Vega burst into tears. "My aunt works at The Frosty Boot," she said. The words were soaked in heavy sobs. "I've been calling her all night and she isn't answering." Vega pulled her cell phone out of her pocket and held it up in despair. "*I* could be her family," she said, "and the cops won't tell me anything. Please!"

The reporter grimaced, then flicked her wrist from her sleeve and glanced at her watch. "What the hell," she said, "it's less than an hour before the information goes to air. Swear on your life you're not one of those vultures working for channel four news?"

"I swear," Vega said, and she wiped a tear from her eye.

"Fine," the reporter said, and she sighed. "Victim was a female, late forties, leaving the bar for the night. Works at the county tax collection office right down the street. Name's Bethany Nicholson."

ψ

Vega had to hurry me back to her car. According to her, I started to breathe deep and heavy, and she was worried I might faint right there and then. The reporter, by virtue of her profession, caught on to all

148

of this, and immediately wanted to ask me some questions. She was expecting there might be a chance Vega was related to the deceased after Vega's fib, but she was shocked when I almost doubled over. Vega politely declined comment for me, then rushed me back to her Mercedes.

The fine-grain leather seat was cool against my skin—it really was getting unusually cold that week—and I really did feel like I might pass out.

Vega climbed into the driver's seat and started the car, set the interior thermostat to warm.

"Was this my fault?" I murmured.

"It's not your fault," Vega said. "It was an accident. A horrible coincidence."

"Except it *wasn't* an accident," I reminded her. "Someone intentionally ran her down."

"You're not a crime scene investigator," Vega said. "You don't know that for sure."

"She was at my house this morning," I said. "Sat right across from me in the living room. And now she's dead. She was Joyce Nicholson's sister, Vega, she said a series of dreams led her to my front door, and now she's dead!"

"Nate," Vega said. "Calm down. You're going to hyperventilate."

"There was no coincidence here," I said. "We started asking questions. We started to pull this thread. And now she's dead."

Vega put a hand on my shoulder and shook me. "Yes, Nate. She's dead. No matter how much you panic, that won't change."

"I need to get home."

Vega shifted the car into drive. "And I'm going to get you there."

149

The next five minutes were a blur. Vega followed the detour back to North and got me home safely. After we parked, she asked me—for probably the hundredth time—if I was all right.

"I'm not all right," I said, and I felt my front jean pocket buzz. I pulled out my cell phone, saw an unknown phone number appear on the screen.

"Who is it?" Vega asked.

"I don't know."

"You should answer it."

"Why?" I said. "They can leave a voice mail."

"There's too much going on tonight, Nate. Too much chaos. Just answer it."

I tapped the glass screen of the phone, then pressed it to my ear.

"Nathaniel?" a familiar voice boomed.

Officer Dixon.

"Y-yes," I said.

"Don't suppose you've seen the news tonight?"

"I know about what happened," I said.

"Good," Dixon said. "You home?"

I nodded, and the line went silent. After a short pause I realized how dumb that was—Officer Dixon couldn't hear a *nod*—so I said: "Yeah. I'm home."

"Terrific," Dixon said. "I'll be over in about ten minutes."

"What?" I asked. "How do you know where I live?"

"When you signed in at the station earlier," Dixon said, "you left your name, address, and phone number with Edna before she made copies for you. Remember?"

I did. Just barely.

"It's not a problem, is it?" Dixon asked.

"I'd prefer we did it tomorrow."

150

"I'd prefer we did it tonight."

I swallowed hard. "Okay. Okay then. See you soon."

I hung up the phone and slid it back into my pocket.

"What was that all about?" Vega asked.

"Officer Dixon. That guy from the station today?"

"What about him?"

"He's on his way over," I said. "I gotta get inside. My roommate is a total stoner, I need to give him a head's up—"

"I'll come in with you, Nate."

"You don't have to stay for this," I said.

"I should," she said. "I want to keep an eye on you. You're white as a ghost. You shouldn't be alone right now."

I said, "My roommate is probably home, I won't be alone," but Vega had already stopped listening and was opening the driver's side door.

The two of us burst into the front entrance of my house. Dave and Hannah were sitting together on the couch, each of them holding a Nintendo controller. A bong sat on the coffee table in front of them. A bowl of marijuana smoldered.

"Dave," I said, my voice exasperated. "You gotta get out of here."

Dave paused the game and looked over at us, smiling. His eyes were bloodshot and pink. "Is this...some kind of joke?" His glance fell to Vega. "Oh...is this the girl you've been talking about?"

I raced to the kitchen and grabbed a canister of air freshener. I held it tight and squeezed the button atop it. An endless cloud of flower scented mist emptied out into the house.

"Nate," Dave said. "If you ever want some privacy...or the house to smell good...you just gotta give me, like, a ten minute heads up, man. It's all gravy, baby."

151

"No," I said. "It's not all gravy. Nothing is gravy."

Hannah stood from the couch. "Okay, seriously, Nate. What is going on?"

"A state trooper is going to be here in less than ten minutes," I said.

Dave skyrocketed from the couch and stood beside Hannah.

"What did you just say?" Dave said.

"I hate to spring this on you," I said. "It's too much to explain right now. There was an accident downtown. They need to ask me some questions. I'm fine. Everyone's fine. This is Vega, by the way."

I pointed to Vega, and she sheepishly raised her right hand and gave a little wave.

It almost went by unnoticed, but I caught Vega and Hannah locking eyes for a little too long. One of them recognized the other; at least, that's how it felt to me, anyhow. Was it Vega that recognized Hannah, or the other way around? The moment lasted only a fraction of a second, and then they each looked the other way.

"Why don't we just hang out in your room?" Hannah said, and she gestured towards Dave bedroom. "Until whatever's going on here is...over."

"They can't, like, come in here, man. Not without like—a warrant. I saw that on Law and Order."

"I'll try to keep our conversation on the porch, Dave, I promise."

"You're like, the lawyer, man! Don't let him inside!"

"I'll really try not to," I said.

Hannah and Dave disappeared to the bedroom in the rear of the house.

"If you spray anymore of this," Vega said, "we'll suffocate." She took the air freshener from my hand. "Just be cool."

Outside the living room window, a pair of strobing red and blue lights slowed to a stop. For so many reasons, my heart was racing.

I was anything but cool.

ψ

Vega and I hurried out to the front doorstep. Officer Dixon was stepping out of his patrol car and putting a wide brimmed hat atop his head.

"That thing you did earlier, with the reporter, out in front of The Frosty Boot?" I whispered. "The spontaneous lying?"

"What about it?" Vega asked.

"That was a good trick. Anything else I should know?"

"There's plenty you *should* know," Vega said, and she smirked.

"Please don't lie to this cop like you lied to that reporter," I said.

"I'd never dare," Vega said. "Besides, what would I have to lie about?"

Officer Dixon approached the front steps of the house with a slow and steady gait. He nodded to us, then said, "Aren't you going to ask me in?"

"It's not a good time," I said. "If it's all the same to you, can we talk out here?"

"A little chilly out tonight," Dixon said

"We're babysitting his niece," Vega blurted, "and I *just* got her to sleep. She's three. If this one here," she said, poking me in the rib, "sneezes the wrong way, she wakes up."

So much for not lying.

"I know how that goes," Dixon said, and he laughed. "Got a two and a half year old granddaughter. Cutest thing."

Vega smiled and shrugged her shoulders.

153

The lines on Dixon's face creased, and his smile faded. "Listen, Nate. You strike me as a good kid. But there's some trouble going on."

"I know," I said.

"Betty Nicholson was killed. Run down while crossing the street. Now what are the odds of that? Almost twenty-four years to the day after her sister passed away." Officer Dixon scratched his chin. "She was standing right where I'm standing, just this morning, wasn't she?"

I nodded.

"I don't think you killed Betty Nicholson," Dixon said, bluntly. I would say that was a relief, but the thought never crossed my mind that he might suspect me to begin with. "But you're on to something. I don't know how or why, but you're on to something. You're piecing together what happened to Joyce back in '88. I know it wasn't an accident, you know it wasn't an accident, and Betty knew it wasn't an accident."

And now she's dead, I thought.

"And now she's dead," Dixon said. "You go to law school, Nathaniel. You're a smart kid. What does that say to you?"

"It says someone out there wasn't happy with what Betty knew, and they wanted to silence her. And, well. They succeeded."

"And until we figure out who that person is, neither of you are safe. Whoever knew Betty was on to something must know that the three of us standing here are on to it, too." Dixon groaned. "You own a gun?"

I couldn't help but laugh. "No, I don't—"

"I'm going to have one of my men drive by your house a couple times an hour for the next few days," Dixon said. "Until this gets straightened out. If you see anything weird—and I mean *anything*—

someone creeping around outside, weird phone calls, anything, I want you to call 911 right away. Got it?"

Vega and I nodded.

"Nathaniel," Dixon said. "You have any idea who could have done this?"

A name sprung to mind immediately, but it was impossible to say aloud. Could an old, balding torts professor at Marshall really be capable of running down Betty Nicholson as she crossed the street? He could if he killed her sister, Joyce, all those years earlier, and suspected Betty was getting wise to that notion. Would he go far enough to hurt me, next?

And if not me, then what if someone close to me?

I thought of my mom and James back at home in New York.

Then, I thought of Vega.

I licked my lips. "If I were you, Officer," I said. "I'd start by taking a peek at the hood of Ed McManus's car."

ψ

Officer Dixon pulled his patrol car out onto North. His siren made a quick, loud honk and the lights atop the vehicle flickered to life. In a blur, the car vanished out of view, the trees on either side of the road glowing a softer dim of red and blue until he disappeared.

Vega and I stepped back inside.

"It's safe to come out," I hollered.

At the end of the main hall, a bedroom door squeaked open. Hannah stepped out first, then Dave.

In the few weeks we lived together, I'd never seen Dave get pissed off about anything. He was as easy going as it came. But that night there was a madness to his eyes, and it wasn't just because of the copious amounts of marijuana smoke he had inhaled.

"What…the fuck…was that?" Dave said, the words spilling out between great, deep breaths of air. "What's going on?"

"It's okay, Dave. Everything is okay." I said the words, but didn't believe them.

Dave stepped close to me, until there was only a foot or so between our faces. He grabbed my hand and placed my palm on his chest.

"Do you feel that?" Dave asked.

Thumping behind Dave's ribcage was a heart beating so fast, I worried it might burst straight through his chest and race out the front door.

"I do, Dave," I said. "I'm sorry. I'm so sorry. Please, let me explain."

"Are you guys in trouble?" Hannah asked. She twirled a long length of curled hair nervously around her finger.

"No," Vega said, and she pointed to the couch. "Do you mind?"

"Be my guest," Dave said, and he let slip a sarcastic little laugh.

Vega plopped down on the couch. "No one's in trouble," she said. "There's just…a whole hell of a lot going on. Nate can explain it better than I can."

Hannah and Dave took a seat beside Vega on the couch. I sat down on the recliner opposite of them, and all eyes were on me. Bloodshot, tired, worried eyes—all waiting for an explanation.

"Keep an open mind," I said, and I cleared my throat and began the best I could.

Dave, Hannah, and Vega sat wide-eyed and slack-jawed as I did my best to explain what had been happening to me during the past few weeks.

I told them how it started, how each night I was visited by bizarre dreams. I explained how the dreams became increasingly unnerving and insidious, until they reached the point of being practically prophetic.

I spoke of how, just days earlier, I learned of Joyce Nicholson's tragic car accident back in 1988, and the twisted love triangle that had preceded it. I told them of Ed McManus "The Anus" and my theory that he was somehow responsible for her death.

I mentioned how Joyce's sister, Betty, had visited me that morning, convinced that I'd slipped into her dreams despite never having met her in my life. Dave let out an audible gasp when I informed him that Betty had passed away that night, runned down in the middle of the road in front of The Frosty Boot.

When I finished, a heavy quiet hung in the air. Without saying a word, Dave stood up, disappeared into his bedroom, and came back with his bong.

"I don't know about you guys," Dave said, "but after that...I need a smoke."

We all nodded in agreement. Dave lit the bowl of the bong and the glass chamber filled with smoke. He took a deep breath, exhaled, and passed the still lit device to Hannah. Hannah took her turn before passing it to Vega, and Vega indulged, too. As Vega exhaled a long cloud of grayish smoke, she passed the bong to me.

Dave tossed a lighter my way, which I caught from the air, then used to light what remaining bits of green plant matter were left in the bowl of the bong. I pressed my lips to the glass and took a slow, deep breath. I felt my lungs fill and burn, then exhaled, coughing the

157

entire time. In no time flat, my fingers and toes started to tingle, and a goofy wave of giddiness crept over my brain.

"Nate," Dave said. "I don't want you to take this the wrong way, but you should go home tomorrow."

I shook my head. "I can't run away from this."

"No one's telling you to run away from your wacky dreams or whatever bad juju you think is following you," Dave said. "But the reality is, a woman is dead. And from the sounds of it, dead because she was on to the same thing you're on to. It's not safe."

"I'm not going home," I said. "I'm staying right here. I'm seeing this thing through. The officer who was just here? He's out there, right now, probably interrogating McManus as we speak. And when he's done, McManus will be in jail, where he can't hurt anyone else. I'll need to be here to help. To corroborate my story."

"And what's that?" Hannah asked. "That a series of bad dreams led you to believe he might have murdered a woman almost twenty-five years ago? You're the lawyer, Nate. That'll never hold up in court. That'll never hold up on an arrest report. If anything, they'll be carting you off in a straight jacket."

I turned to Vega. "What do you think?"

"I think you should stay here—in Vermont—but my reasons are selfish, too. I don't want to be left alone in this."

I sighed. On the coffee table between the recliner and the couch was the manila folder that I'd brought in earlier. Stuffed inside were pages upon pages of old police reports, thoughtfully copied by Edna earlier that day at the State Trooper's station on the other side of town.

"Why you, Nate?" Hannah asked. "Let's assume the ghost of Joyce Nicholson has been inside your dreams this week. Why does she need *you* to piece all of this together, all this time later?"

"I've been asking myself that every day this week," I said. I flipped through the pages of black and white photographs. There was a blurry shot of the tow truck that arrived to pick up Joyce's car all those years ago. The photo was grainy and old, and details had been lost in the copy, but the decal on the side of the truck was clear as day: Greg's Auto & Towing.

I flipped through a few more pages. Near the back of the stack was Joyce Nicholson's official autopsy report.

The details inside were gruesome. According to the report, the coroner had brought the deceased to Burlington Regional Medical Center in a last ditch effort to save the child inside. An approximately eight-month-old male fetus was removed from Joyce's headless corpse, but the shock of the crash and the amount of time that'd passed was too much.

The child had died.

I felt my eyes start to burn from tears—maybe it was the weed—but the whole thing had made me uncomfortable and emotional. I wondered about who that child might have grown up to be if given the chance. What kind of cruel monster would rob the universe of that opportunity?

I glanced up from the autopsy report at Dave, sitting cross-legged on the couch. He never spoke of his mother, only of his father, who had passed away not long ago. He was just about as many years old as had passed since the accident.

"Dave," I said, quietly. "I need you to tell me your birthday."

Dave nodded. "What's that have to do with anything?"

"What is it?" I asked, plainly.

"It's a few weeks from now," Dave said. "September twenty-third."

"What *year*?" I asked.

159

"1988."

"That's crazy," Dave said. "You're wrong. It's impossible."

Vega and Hannah had sat together silently as I tried to explain the very real possibility that Joyce Nicholson was Dave's mom. At least, it felt like a real possibility to me. Vega and Hannah had looks of doubtfulness. Dave was downright flabbergasted.

"Joyce's car accident was the first week of September," Dave said. "My birthday is near the end of the month."

"If there was a cover-up," I said, "they wouldn't have used the date of your actual birth. They'd fudge the paperwork by a few weeks to avoid suspicion."

"You're crazy," Dave said. "Between your hands is a police report—an autopsy—that clearly states the baby Joyce Nicholson was carrying died the moment she did."

"Reports can be falsified. Facts can be altered. With enough money thrown at it, any story can be fabricated to fit a different narrative. Joyce Nicholson supposedly had an affair with Dominic Bloom. Bloom is a *huge* lawyer around here. If anyone had the means to pull off a job like this, it'd be him—"

"Stop," Dave said, interrupting me. "Dominic Bloom is not my father. My father was a good, honest, hardworking man, who raised me on his own. Right here in this house. Right until he drew his last breath."

"Bloom's law firm gave you the guidance you needed to settle estate debts after your father passed away," I said. "And this house being paid off, doesn't that strike you as odd?"

"Not one bit," Dave said. He was getting angry now, and why wouldn't he? I hadn't paused to think of how insensitive my accusations might sound. "My father paid for this house. Every penny. My *real* father. Dominic Bloom doesn't own this house."

"If all of this was true," Hannah said, "what on earth would the motive be? Why would Dominic Bloom want to cover up the birth of his child?"

I shrugged. "I have no idea. He has a kid, a daughter, about the same age as Dave."

"He does?" Vega asked.

"Yeah," I said. "There's not much about her or his family, but I've dug up all sorts of things on the guy while researching my paper. It's amazing what you'll find online. He already had one kid—why not two?"

Vega leaned forward on her couch cushion. "McManus assigned you Dominic Bloom as the subject of your research paper," she said. "There's a hundred students in that class that could have been assigned Bloom, but he gave it to you. He knew Dave was your roommate. Somehow, he knew. And he was counting on you putting all of this together." Vega clapped her hands. "The sick fuck."

"It's true," I said, looking over at Dave. "He seemed to be deliberate in assigning me Bloom as my research subject. Like he wanted me to find this all out."

Dave stood up suddenly, marched across the room to the Nintendo, and turned it on. "I don't want to think about this anymore tonight."

"You don't have to," I said.

"Let's come back to this in the morning," Dave said, and he handed Vega, Hannah, and I each a video game controller before taking one for himself. "After I've had some sleep."

161

The four of us quietly huddled in front of the television, and the screen flickered to life with cartoon characters. The silence between us was awkward at first, each of us contemplating the uncomfortable possibilities of the tangled web we'd been woven into.

But the silence slowly turned to laughter, and in the glow of Dave's old television, we carried on deep into the night.

It was the first—and last—night that the four of us would ever spend together.

ψ

The next morning I awoke in the living room recliner. A cramp crept down my leg from the odd angle I'd slept at all night.

Across the room, Dave was fast asleep on the floor. Hannah and Vega were each slumped over on opposite ends of the couch.

Shadow slinked out of my bedroom, squinted at me, and meowed. Surely, she needed to be fed.

I yawned and stood from the recliner, stretching. Beams of yellow sunlight flooded in from the front windows.

Shadow ran toward the living room, letting out little squeaks and meows as she ran. She brushed against my feet, then jumped onto the couch, where she curiously sniffed Vega as she slept.

Vega groaned and started to stir. As she raised her arms out ahead of her, the fur on Shadow's back stood on end, and the cat hissed loudly at her before jolting away at full gallop and disappearing into my bedroom.

"You have a cat?" Vega asked, sleepily.

"Yeah," I said. "She really seems to like you."

"I hate cats."

"What kind of monster hates cats?"

162

"The kind of monsters who are allergic to them."

Dave started to stir on the floor. He was face down on the carpet, using his left arm as a pillow, a Nintendo controller still clutched in his right hand.

Hannah woke up next, frowning and squinting at the rays of light that had landed on her face. "What time is it?"

I pulled my cell phone out of my pocket. The battery was nearly dead. It was a little after eight, and I had three missed calls from Officer Dixon.

"It's about eight-fifteen," I said, and I headed toward the front door.

"Where are you going?" Vega asked.

I said, "I need to make a call."

On the front steps of the house, I dialed Officer Dixon. As the phone rang, I tried to push away thoughts that just twenty-four hours earlier, Betty Nicholson had stood where I was standing.

And, now she was gone.

"Nathaniel?" Dixon said. "Been trying to reach you all night."

"It's morning, now—"

"I'm asking you to stay put. Wherever you are."

"What's going on?" I asked.

"It's Ed McManus," Dixon said. "We went to his house last night to ask him some questions. Maybe get a look at his car. He wasn't home. We've been looking for him around the clock, and he's gone. Poof. Into thin air."

"Well that's…worrisome," I said.

"Don't be too worried," Dixon said. "We're gonna find the son of a bitch. But until then, don't go far. Gotta go."

The line disconnected with a pop of static and I turned around, headed back inside the front door.

Inside, everyone was awake and moving around. Vega was readjusting her clothes, smoothing out wrinkles and combing her hair with her fingers. Dave was starting a pot of coffee in the kitchen.

"Someone turn on the news," I said. "I think this blew up over night."

Hannah bent over, found the television remote lost in a sea of empty potato chip bags and video game controllers. She thumbed at some buttons and the television clicked on, tuned to the local news.

Exactly as I suspected, a news segment began with McManus' face plastered to the right half of the screen.

A well-dressed woman in a blazer sat at her desk, speaking directly into the camera as the photograph of McManus floated beside her face.

"State authorities are asking for help this morning," the reporter said, "in finding the whereabouts of Edward Benjamin McManus, 62, of Burlington, Vermont. McManus is a local attorney and professor at the Marshall College of Law, where he was last seen yesterday afternoon. McManus is wanted for questioning in connection to the death of Bethany Nicholson. Nicholson passed away last night after having been struck by a car outside of The Frosty Boot bar in downtown Burlington. McManus drives a late model Cadillac Deville, cream colored, license plate number J76-HO4. Authorities suspect McManus' vehicle may have been used in the hit and run that killed Miss Nicholson. Viewers who have information concerning McManus' whereabouts should contact the Burlington office of the Vermont State Troopers at—"

"Turn it off," Vega said. "It's too sad. It's all too much. I can't listen to anymore of it."

Dave was shuffling around the kitchen. "What's everyone want for breakfast?"

Hannah groaned. "Thanks, babe. But I need to get home and shower before work."

Vega nodded. "I better get going, too. I still smell like The Capitol Theater. A hot shower and a fresh change of clothes could go a long way."

"We should all be staying together," I said. "Until the police find McManus."

"Whether the police find him or not," Hannah said, "won't stop me from getting a write up at my job if I miss work."

"Can't you call out?" I asked.

She was already halfway out the door. "That's sweet of you to worry, Nate. But I'll be fine." She blew Dave a kiss and left.

Vega stood in the hallway, fidgeting in her clothes.

"You too?" I said.

Vega nodded. "I'll come back in a couple hours to check on you guys."

"You can use our shower," I said.

"What, and have you creeping on me from the doorway the whole time?" She punched me lightly on the shoulder, then leaned forward and gave me a peck on the cheek. "I'll see you soon."

Vega was out the door in a blur, and the house felt big and empty again with just Dave and I inside.

"How'd you sleep?" Dave asked. He cracked an egg and spilled the insides into a waiting fry pan. "Any visions? Anything to help us out here?"

"I didn't have a single dream last night," I said, and that was the truth. I tossed and turned all night in the living room recliner. Standing there, it felt like I hadn't slept at all.

"That's too bad," Dave said, and another egg cracked and fell into the pan. "We could all stand to use some clarity."

165

"I'm sorry about last night, Dave—"

"You don't have to say sorry," he said. "I always wondered about who my mom was, who she might be. I didn't have so much as a picture of her growing up. My dad had girlfriends over the years, but it was never the same. I was only ever a novelty to them."

Dave stirred the eggs in the frying pan.

"Can I help with breakfast?"

"Sure," he said. "You can start making some toast."

I walked into the kitchen and did as Dave asked. I could tell by his tone that he wanted to talk more, but I didn't want to press the issue.

"Last night," Dave said, finally, "after everyone fell asleep…I opened up your folder from the police station. I flipped through the pages, looked at pictures of Joyce, wondered if she could really be my mom. I guess the two of us look alike, from certain angles. I was so reluctant at first, but now, I don't know. I almost want to believe it's her—that she's my mom. I don't know."

"Even if it means believing Dominic Bloom is your father?"

"My *father* was my father, regardless of who contributed to my existence. Biologically speaking."

"He already had a daughter and a wife. And he slipped up, had an affair with Joyce, and eight months later…the world got Dave."

"The world got Dave," Dave said.

"He wanted to care for Joyce and for the child," I said, "at least I think so. But McManus got in the way of that and frayed Joyce's brake lines, hoping that she'd run off the road on the way to class. When a moose ran out in front of her and she couldn't brake the car in time, that was even better, it made the whole thing look even more like an accident. It's how he managed to get away with it for all these years."

166

"And Dominic Bloom made sure I was delivered at the hospital," Dave said. "Even after Joyce had died."

"Yeah," I said. "Then had a mock birth certificate drawn up, and found someone to take care of you and raise you. The man you called your father."

"This is some heavy shit, man," Dave said.

"It is," I said. "But I think that's why our paths crossed, Dave. I don't know why it took me being here to piece this all together, but I'm glad we found each other. Of all the roommates I could have found in Burlington, I found you."

"If Joyce was my mom, then Betty was my aunt," Dave said, and a tear slid down his cheek.

"I guess so," I said, and I patted him on the back.

"And if Dominic Bloom is my biological father, then he owes me a couple decades of back child support. Cha-ching."

We both had a long, hearty laugh at that. Dave joked that he might buy a boat after confronting Bloom, and that one day soon the two of us could go sailing across Lake Champlain like a couple of aristocrats.

"Who cares about money," Dave said, after our laughter subsided. "This McManus asshole took a lot away from me." He swallowed hard. "I hope they catch the fucker."

ψ

Dave and I ate a mountain of scrambled eggs, then parted ways. He returned to his bedroom, and I returned to mine. He was scheduled for work that day, a shift from ten am until six that night, but—quite understandably—he called out. When the owner of the Quick Mart insisted he come in, that finding a replacement manager on such

167

short notice would be next to impossible, Dave just laughed. He said, "You'll figure something out," then hung up his phone, waved me a salute, and wandered off to his bedroom.

"If anyone knocks, calls, whatever," Dave said. "I'm not home. Only wake me up if the house is on fire."

"Understood," I said, and Dave shut his bedroom door with a *thud*.

I sat in my bedroom for a while that Saturday morning, my only companions Shadow and the poster of Kate Upton, thinking about all that had happened in the past week. My thoughts swirled like water in a drain, my head felt foggy and heavy. I tried listening to the radio, petting Shadow, and aimlessly clicking around the Internet, but nothing could distract me from the thoughts of my good friend two rooms over and the torment he must have been going through.

I tried to remember the last time I called home. What would I tell my mom? Should I tell her anything at all? I thought of what James might say to me at a time like this. Probably some well-meaning Army hoo-hah about staying strong and looking out for my friends and myself.

My desk chair squeaked as I leaned back in it. I pulled my cell phone from my pocket and tossed it onto my desk, then gave it a spin. After a short hesitation, I slid my thumb across the screen and dialed home.

There were three rings followed by a soft "Hello?"

Mom.

"Hey, mom," I said.

"Nate, what a surprise. Didn't expect to hear from you on a Saturday morning."

"Just wanted to hear your voice," I said. "It's been a hell of a week."

"What's wrong?" she asked. "You sound tired. Are you all right?"

I contemplated that question for a while. I wasn't all right, I hadn't been in days. I wanted to pop the cork from my mouth and spill, and spill, and spill; I wanted to tell her all about the past twenty-four hours, how I met Betty Nicholson on the day she died, how I helped solve a twenty-four year old murder, how I reconnected my roommate with his mother from beyond the grave.

Then, it dawned on me how pointless that would be. It would only worry her. I imagined what her reaction might be when I told her that ole McManus the Anus was still on the lam, leading the Vermont State Troopers on a wild goose chase. She would insist I drive down to New York for the weekend, or worse, that her and James drive up to visit me.

So, I lied. For the first time in my adult life, I lied to my mother.

"I'm all right," I said. "Just...got a pile of work, ten feet high." I thought of Vega and how easily lies rolled off the tip of her tongue when she wanted them to. It was a talent, honestly, and surely one that would come in handy in the legal field. But, it was a talent I had not yet mastered.

"Is that all?" she asked. "You sound upset."

"That's all," I said. "How are you and James? What have you two got planned for the weekend?"

"I picked up a shift at the hospital and James is going fly fishing with some old army buddies. Hey, you know, if you're bored, they're not heading out until later this afternoon. If you left now, you could join them. You're just a few hours away."

"I wouldn't want to intrude," I said.

"Nonsense," my mom replied. "He won't admit it, but he misses ya. Even if it's only been a few weeks."

169

"Like I said, I've got heaps of work."

"It's not too late in the day, so if you change your mind...just give him a ring and let him know."

"Sure," I said.

"I've got twenty errands before my shift, and you know how I feel about talking and driving. Can I take a rain check? Maybe give you a call back tomorrow?"

"That's fine."

"It's college, Nate. This is the best time of your life. Try to have some fun and enjoy it, yeah? It's Saturday. Go out, let loose. Don't lock yourself inside all day with that work. Promise?"

"I promise."

"Take care, Nate. I love you."

"I love you, too."

ψ

Is it still considered a nightmare if it visits you in the day?

I'd fallen asleep by mid-afternoon with Shadow curled up beside me on my bed, each of us under the watchful gaze of Kate Upton. With my desk lamp turned off and my blackout curtain panels pulled taught, it was hard to see my hand in front of my face. Sleep came easy after tossing and turning on the living room recliner the whole night before.

In the dream, I was standing outside of Vega's castle. I could see her in the second story window, where her bedroom was, looking down at me. She was standing still, twirling a ringlet of hair between her fingers.

Then, I blinked. And she was gone.

No puff of smoke, no dramatic exit; she was there one moment, then gone the next, and it terrified me.

I raced toward the front door of her home and pounded on it, but there was no answer. When I'd almost lost all hope, I felt a tap on my shoulder.

I spun in place, excited to see her, but when I turned she wasn't there. No, instead of Vega, two figures stood between me and the slate colored fountain in her driveway.

One of them was neatly dressed, but missing a head from the lips up. A flap of flesh dangled atop her neck, smacked back and forth as she approached me. Beside her was a woman who walked on broken legs and flailed broken arms. The left side of her head was crushed, the mark of a car tire imprinted on her face. A pulpy knot of flesh had swollen bright purple across her eyes.

It was Joyce and Betty Nicholson; sisters, united at last.

Betty brought her left hand to her face, traced crooked, broken fingers over the bruised skin that covered her eyes.

"Can you see for me?" Betty asked.

I swallowed hard. "I can, Betty. I did."

A jet of gleaming red blood squirted from the hole atop Joyce's neck, then landed on the pavement of Vega's driveway with a *splat*. I don't know why, but I interpreted it as a laugh. She was laughing at me.

"It's over," I said. "The truth is out. I'm sorry about what happened to you, Betty—I'm so sorry—but you have to leave me alone. The both of you."

Betty shambled toward me. Her twisted legs squeaked and cracked as she walked. "Not over, Nate. Not over until he answers for what he did. Not over until there's justice."

171

"They're looking for McManus now," I said. "As soon as they find him he'll be arrested. He'll answer for what he did to both of you."

Betty shook her head. "Now you're blind, too."

"What?" I asked, but it was no use. Betty jutted out her arms, grabbed the sides of my face with her jagged, shattered hands. Two broken, bony thumbs pierced my eyelids, dug deep into my skull. I let out a horrible yelp, could feel warm blood running from the corners of my eyes down to my cheeks, could feel it all—

I woke up in bed, screaming. Shadow leapt from the side of the bed and bolted to the other side of the room.

My pants pocket was vibrating. I yanked out my cell phone and answered it.

"Nate?" a sweet, lovely voice said.

"Vega," I murmured. "Speak of the devil."

"Were you sleeping?"

"If that's what you want to call it. What time is it?"

"It's quarter after five. I haven't heard from you all day, I've been worried."

"Vega," I said. "You just saw me this morning."

"No I didn't."

"I'm too tired for games, Vega—"

"Nate," Vega said. "I haven't seen you since yesterday morning."

"Wait...what's today?"

"It's Sunday."

"Holy shit," I said. I pulled the phone away from the side of my face, checked the time and date at the top of the screen. It wasn't a game, it wasn't some prank; Vega was right. I'd slept for nearly a day and a half without interruption.

"I want to come over and check on you," she said. "I'm worried about you."

I felt my stomach churn. I was worried about me, too.

"The last thing I remember," I said, "was having breakfast with Dave...then I came into the bedroom to lay down for a bit. I just wanted to take a nap. It's...it's getting bad, Vega. It's getting worse."

"I'm coming over now," she said. "Take a shower. Freshen up. We'll get something to eat, and you can tell me all about it."

I hung up my phone then clicked on my nightstand lamp. I'd been asleep for over twenty-four hours, so what happened next could have been my eyes playing tricks on me. But the days of ordinary excuses for extraordinary occurrences were long gone by then. That ship had sailed.

No, there was no doubt about it, no mistaking it. As my night stand lamp clicked on, I saw her there, Joyce Nicholson, her head missing from the lips up, neatly dressed and standing in the corner of my bedroom. Even with so much of her face missing, her bottom lip was upturned, and it seemed unmistakable that she was...that she was...

Smiling.

Before the scream forming at the base of my throat had a chance to escape, she was gone.

ψ

Dave had never before entered my bedroom, not once in the three weeks we shared his home together. There was a simple lock on the door, but nothing that couldn't be pried open with a butter knife. Still, he respected my privacy and I respected his. It was one of the dozens of reasons we got along so well.

173

When he heard my screaming, however, he came barging in without so much as a knock. The gold knob rattled and the door burst open so hard I worried it might have splintered.

"Are you okay?" he asked. His eyes were great wide moons.

I sat up in bed, staring at the corner of my room where only moments earlier Joyce Nicholson's corpse stood, watching over me.

"I'm not—I thought—I thought someone was in here with me," I panted.

"Christ, Nate," Dave said. "I didn't even know you were home."

"I've been home since yesterday morning," I said. "I haven't left bed since we had breakfast together." Suddenly, I felt like I might wet myself.

"You've been *home?*"

I stood up. "Hasn't my car been out front this whole time?"

Dave nodded. "I thought Vega picked you up."

I pushed my way past Dave and marched out to the bathroom. "I don't feel good," I said.

When I came back out of the bathroom, Dave was standing in the hallway, waiting for me.

"I didn't hear you, Nate. You didn't so much as snore. I mean—Shadow didn't even meow to get out. Were the two of you in a coma?"

"I don't know what's going on," I said. "I feel like...like I'm losing my mind."

Dave opened his arms wide then wrapped them around me. "Me too, buddy. The past twenty-four hours have been a whirlwind."

"Have they found him yet?" I asked. "McManus?"

Dave shook his head.

"I feel lightheaded," I said, and I turned toward the living room couch.

Dave said, "You should sit down."

I collapsed onto the couch. I was cold and shivering.

"You know, you should probably see a doctor, Nate."

"I can't," I said. "I can't miss a day of class tomorrow."

"McManus is your morning professor, right?" Dave said. "There's currently a state-wide manhunt for him. I'm not a betting man, but...I'd wager your morning class will be cancelled."

"They'll have an adjunct take his place," I said. "And besides, I have an afternoon class I can't miss, either."

Dave crossed his arms. "You've really been in there since *yesterday*?"

"I'm hungry," I said. Poor word choice. Really, I was starving. And, I was sick of being looked at like a science fair project.

There was a knock at the door. I stood up quick, and a field of blinking, black polka dots formed in front of my face.

"You look white," Dave said. "Don't stand up so fast. You're going to get sick."

"It's Vega," I said.

Dave walked to the door, opened it, and Vega stepped in. From where I sat on the couch I couldn't see them, but I could hear them whispering.

"Nate," Vega said, and she sat down beside me. She pressed a palm against my face; my cheeks were cool and clammy, but her touch was warm. Her touch was always warm. "What's wrong?"

"I'm hungry, that's what's wrong—"

"You've been passed out since yesterday morning," Vega said. "That's not healthy."

"I was tired," I said. "I slept like shit Friday night."

175

Dave was fiddling with his cell phone. "I was just about to order some takeout, anyways," he said. "I'll order extra. We'll all have dinner together. Sound good?"

Vega looked to me for an answer, and I nodded.

"Sounds good."

Forty-five minutes after Dave placed his order to Wok-n-Roll Chinese takeout, a delivery driver appeared at the front steps of our house. He was carrying two heavy paper bags of food and grinned happily after Vega paid and tipped him. There'd been a short argument between Dave and her about who would pay, but ultimately Vega won, and she insisted on picking up the bill.

The feeling was starting to come back to my extremities by the time the three of us sat down at the dining table to eat. I no longer felt dizzy and weak. After two egg rolls, I'd become downright talkative and jovial.

"You're looking better," Vega said. "You smell like crap, but you're looking better."

Dave swallowed a bite of fried noodles. "Why were you screaming earlier?"

I felt embarrassed by it. I pictured Dave sitting on the living room couch, watching television and rightfully assuming he had the house to himself, when suddenly my girlish screams pierced the silence.

"I had bad dreams," I said.

Vega scoffed. "What else is new?"

"There was more to it this time," I said. "When I woke up...I saw her. I saw Joyce. She was standing in the corner of my room, no different than how you're sitting across from me at this table."

Dave shivered. "I thought maybe the nightmares would stop," he said. "After you connected the dots with everything."

"Me too," I said. "But they're only getting worse. I think…there just has to be peace for Joyce. For her, for her family, and for her legacy. And as long as McManus is free, there won't be."

"Well," Vega said. "The entire state is looking for him."

"I know," I said, and I took a sip of wonton soup. "But it's hard not to feel like I should be doing more."

"You've done all you can," Dave said, and there was thankfulness to his words. It seemed he had started to accept the distinct probability that Joyce Nicholson was his mother. "You've done more than enough."

The three of us sat around the table, picking at white paper boxes full of stir-fry and noodles and rice, and after a short while I started to feel like my old self again. And when I felt like myself, we all were better for it. The conversation turned upbeat. In spite of everything we were able to sit there, the three of us, and laugh and joke around. We were a team, it felt like, a small circle allowed part in some elaborate secret that only we were privy to. There was camaraderie to it that I hadn't felt before, and have yet to feel again since.

When we finished our dinner Vega stood, said that she still had plenty of work to finish before class the next day, and I offered to walk her outside.

Dave was already washing dishes and packing up boxes of leftovers. When I asked if I could help him, he waved me away, not bothering to look up from the kitchen sink. "Walk your lady to her car," Dave said. "Be a gentleman. I can handle this. It's all gravy, baby."

177

I walked Vega outside. Her Mercedes was parked cockeyed in the driveway. When I pointed this out, she sighed.

"I came rushing over," she said. "No time to park perfectly. I'm worried sick about you."

She cupped a palm over my cheek and my mind flooded with memories of my most recent nightmare—Betty Nicholson's boney, shattered thumbs pushing their way into my eye sockets. I shuttered.

"Lately, Nate, it feels like you're somewhere else. Like you're on a far off planet."

"I'm beside myself," I said. "Until McManus is caught, I don't think I'll get a decent night's sleep."

"None of this was your fault. You have to stop acting like it was."

"It's never felt like my fault, but it's felt like my obligation to put it all back together. I know I'm not the reason Joyce Nicholson slid off the road in '88. I know I'm not the reason McManus went after Betty. But it's been up to me to put it all together."

"You're sweet," Vega said, and she kissed me on the cheek. "I'll be back first thing in the morning to pick you up for class."

"Are you sure?"

"You're on the way. We can get breakfast or something."

"Sounds good," I said.

Vega reached into her bag for her car keys. The sun was starting to set, the sky was turning fiery shades of red and orange. She clicked the remote to her car and the Mercedes chirped to life.

What happened next happened in a blur. There are moments in life where time literally slows down. Our mind stops working the way it normally does, stops tuning to the frequency it'd use to read a book or watch a movie. The moment before Vega was set to drive home was one of those moments.

It started with Shadow.

The cat had worked her way past the front door of the house, had somehow snuck out when I walked Vega to her car. Vega looked at the critter, said, "Isn't that Shadow?" and pointed.

I pivoted on one foot, turned back toward the house, and looked. Sure enough it was Shadow, her black fur shining beneath the recently lit streetlamps.

Shadow was found as a stray, after all, so the hedge bushes in front of 126 North probably smelled familiar to her, probably felt like home. The cat was brushing her face against a low hanging branch when she noticed Vega pointing at her. When the two locked eyes, Shadow lowered her ears, squinted, bared her teeth and hissed.

"She's really not a fan of yours," I said, and I took a few steps, bent over, and went to reach for her. Shadow hissed again, swiped a paw at my hand. Claws like razors, fully extended, grazed over the top of my wrist, leaving four white streaks. In seconds, the streaks turned swollen and filled with blood.

"Son of a bitch," I mumbled, and I shook my hand. Shadow's tail had fluffed to twice its size, was batting back and forth with anger.

I swung my hand back out to grab her, but she coiled her hind legs, and just before my hand caught her neck she sprung forward and dashed toward the road.

"Come back!" I screamed, like an idiot. Surely my yelling wouldn't help the situation, but I was too panicked then to realize that.

Shadow made four big leaps down the walkway in front of my house, then cut across the lawn, and sprinted past the mailbox.

"Get back here," I shouted again. I took off running, chasing after the damn cat. She was getting dangerously close to the road now.

Shadow made one last pounce toward the road and jumped into the center of it, came to a stop on the double yellow lines that divided North in half. I looked left, then right, then left again. The usually quiet street was—thankfully—devoid of traffic.

Shadow stayed perched in the center of the road, blissfully unaware of how dangerous her current surroundings were. Her ears raised, her tail flattened, and she meowed.

"Come here good kitty," I said, and I pressed my tongue against my teeth and made a clicking sound. Shadow meowed and spun in a circle, then sat down on her haunches.

"Nate," Vega said. "Be careful."

"I got this," I said, my eyes not leaving shadow. I approached the road and again checked for traffic.

Shadow let out a quiet chirp, then started to walk back toward me. I stepped out into the road, and she circled once around my feet. I waited for the perfect opportunity to drop down and snatch her, before she could become spooked and run away again.

She butted her head against my ankle, and I swooped. In a flash I knelt down, grabbed her by the folds of skin on the back of her neck, and yanked her upward.

Shadow growled from way down deep inside of her, but it didn't matter, I had her. I held her close against my chest and pivoted to walk out of the street and back toward the front lawn.

"Nate," Vega screamed, and in that instant time stopped moving entirely. An old pickup truck came barreling around the bend on North, its engine rumbling loud as it accelerated. The headlights of the truck shined bright on Shadow and me, and I froze.

180

I turned my head to see Vega running towards me from the front lawn. I picked up my left foot—it weighed a hundred pounds—and started what would have been the first step of a run, had it not been for the 1982 Ford pickup truck colliding into my side at fifty-six miles per hour.

I watched Shadow go tumbling through the air, released from my grasp. I felt the bones in my left leg crack and separate from one another. My left arm hit the hood of the pickup truck and I went rolling toward the windshield. There were the sounds of screaming and tires screeching, and glass shattering, and then—

"Walk your lady to her car," Dave said, "Be a gentleman. I got this. It's all gravy, baby." He was washing a dish in the kitchen sink.

I took a big gulp of air and twirled, found myself standing in the kitchen.

"Are you okay?" Dave said. "You went white again."

I pressed my hand against my leg, felt at all the bones and muscles exactly where they belonged, unbroken and untorn.

"Where's Shadow?" I said.

Dave shrugged. "I don't know. Probably sleeping in your room, like always."

I rushed to my bedroom. Shadow lay beside the door, licking her leg. I looked at her, then at my wrist. There were no lacerations where she swiped me with her paw, no cuts, no blood.

"Stay here," I said, and I slammed my bedroom door shut—trapping her inside—then went running toward the front door.

"Is everything okay?" Dave hollered.

"I don't know yet," I said.

I hurried outside and saw her there, lying on her back, convulsing on the front lawn. Her arms and legs were shaking violently, contorting into awful configurations.

"Vega!" I hollered, and I dropped beside her on the grass.

A small pool of white bubbles had foamed up around the corner of her lips. Her right arm stopped flailing just long enough to jut upwards and grab me by the collar of my shirt.

"Don't...call for help," she said, the words barely audible between short gaps of air. "Take...my keys...and drive...me home."

She was shaking wildly and the color had left her face. Her skin was pale, paper thin, almost translucent. The once unnoticeable tiny veins around her eyes and forehead were now bright blue and visible, a roadmap across her face.

"I have to call 911," I said.

Her eyes furrowed with anger and she yanked at my collar. "Do *not*...," she sputtered, "call...for help."

I looked forward, startled by the growl of an engine. On North, a pickup truck rumbled by, passed the front of my house and continued onward, until it turned the bend and was out of sight.

Vega's spasms had softened, but she was still writhing back and forth on the lawn. She jammed a hand into a front jean pocket and pulled out a key ring. She threw them in my face.

"Nate," she screeched. "Drive...me...*home*."

ψ

I unlocked Vega's Mercedes, then opened the passenger door wide and reclined the passenger seat.

Vega was shaking back and forth on the lawn. I returned to her, tucked one arm under her shoulders and the other under her knees, and lifted her.

Adrenaline coursing through my bloodstream, I carried her to the passenger seat and laid her down. I buckled a seat belt over her, then shut the passenger door, and hurried to the other side of the car.

I sat down behind the steering wheel of the Mercedes and panicked. There was no ignition on the steering column, nowhere to plug a key and start the car.

I slapped my hands against the steering column and felt around in the dark. Nothing. The instrument panel of the Mercedes was as luxurious as it was foreign, and I couldn't so much as find a switch for the headlights or the interior lights of the car.

"Goddammit," I whispered, and I slapped the steering column again. Vega was rolling back and forth in her seat, moaning softly.

I closed my eyes and took a deep breath. When I opened them, they focused on a small button in the center of the dashboard. It was silver, with only one word written on it, highlighted in green: "Start."

It's a pushbutton start, I thought. I pressed the silver button and the Mercedes roared to life. The headlights turned on automatically, sensing the darkness outside. Hell, for a second I thought the damn thing might drive itself.

"I'm getting you home," I said, and I buckled my seatbelt. "Just hold on."

Vega slumped to her left, facing me. Her eyes had rolled back in her head, leaving nothing but the whites showing.

I shifted the Mercedes into reverse and backed out onto North. As soon as the tires were in the road and straightened, I shifted into drive, then stomped on the accelerator.

What's that old saying—like a bat out of hell? I wasn't driving like a bat out of hell, I was driving faster. Bats, free of hell, only wished that they could have kept pace with me behind the steering wheel of Vega's Mercedes that night. I must have broken a dozen traffic laws or more as I raced out onto North and through town, barreling toward Anchorage.

I caught a yellow light at Niebolt—ran it—then a red light at Warsaw, and ran that too. Had a cop been near me, I could have been fined and ticketed ten times over.

In just a few minutes I was at Anchorage. I rocketed past quaintly lit mansions and driveways. There wasn't another car for miles.

The gate at the front of her driveway stood tall and still, a watchful guardian intent on not letting me pass through.

"Vega," I said. "How do I get in?"

Vega muttered and tossed in her seat. She pulled out her cell phone, tapped at the glass screen, and the gate in front of me swung backward. She didn't bother to return the phone to her pocket. Instead, it dropped from her hand and onto the floor of the car.

When the gate had completely opened, I carefully guided her Mercedes up the long and winding driveway that led to her front door. In the rearview mirror, I could see the wrought iron gate closing shut.

I pulled up alongside the slate fountain just outside her front door and parked the car. I exited the driver's seat, hurried to the passenger side of the vehicle, and opened the door. Vega was slouched, her shoulders and neck contorted in an awful and uncomfortable looking position. I grabbed her cell phone and pocketed it, then pulled her from the car and tossed her over my shoulder. Vega was a petit girl, but I wasn't very burly. We stood at almost the same height, and my lanky build—now exhausted of adrenaline—struggled to carry her.

I jammed a key into the deadbolt lock on her front door, and it slid halfway in before jamming. I yanked it out and tried the next key on the key ring. This one slid in fully and spun with a satisfying click when I turned it clockwise.

The front door of Vega's castle groaned open. Ahead of me was a wide atrium. The floor was checkered with black and white tile, and in the center of the room was a spiral staircase. Beside the staircase was a baby grand piano, and beside the piano was a potted aloe plant.

On either side of the atrium was an open doorway: to the left was a passage way to a formal living room, and to the right was a hallway that led to God knows where.

I grunted and stomped toward the formal living room. Pressed against a wall was a sofa upholstered in dark, smooth leather. In any other house it would have looked ostentatious and tacky, but in Vega's castle it looked right at home. As I set Vega down on it, I pondered at how many classes at Marshall could be paid for with just the cost of that couch alone.

Vega shivered as she stretched out on the couch. I stood, put my hands on my hips, and scanned the room. Draped over a wingback chair was a soft, plush throw blanket. I yanked it from the chair and pulled it carefully over Vega. She murmured something, then shut her eyes and turned away from me.

The color had returned to her face, and by and large the convulsions had stopped, but I still wondered if I should go against her wishes and call a paramedic.

What would I tell them?

"She stopped time," I would say. "No, I'm sorry—she *reversed* time, saving me from a likely fatal car accident, before collapsing on my front lawn."

Vega would get a ride to the hospital, and I'd get a one-way ticket to the nearest asylum.

I took a seat on the wingback across from Vega's sofa. Picture windows on either side of her offered a fantastic view of the valley below, painted by the sun's last rays.

In darkness and silence I sat, and watched, and wondered. An hour passed, and with nothing but my thoughts, I tried to piece together what exactly had happened that night. I relived the moment of the crash over and over and over again. Hitting the hood of the pickup truck, rolling into the windshield, my bones breaking like glass—it all felt so *real*. It was real, wasn't it? I could feel my broken body, tossed to the side of the road like a ragdoll, could hear Vega's screams and the screeching of car tires, and then—

Then I was inside my house, in precisely the same moment I had been just a couple minutes earlier.

What the hell had happened?

I'd set Vega down on the Sofa at a little after six. By ten o'clock she had started to stir. She rolled over, pulled the blanket off of her, and slowly opened her eyes.

"How long was I out?" she asked, calmly.

"Just shy of four hours."

"Not bad," she said. "Not the longest I've been down."

"You've been out for longer?"

"Oh, yeah," Vega said, and she chuckled. "After twelve hours it becomes a real bitch. But then again, you know how that goes, huh? Have you been sitting there the whole time?"

I nodded.

"That's sweet of you, Nate."

I can't imagine the look that must have crept across my face, but Vega's smile receded. She sat up and adjusted herself.

"If you promise not to think any differently of me," she said, coolly. "I can explain this. I can explain all of this."

186

ψ

Outside, a blanket of stars hung over the valley. Down below, the city of Burlington was falling fast asleep. Street lamps twinkled and buildings darkened. My gaze fell back and forth between Vega and the view of the valley below us as she told me her story.

"It started when I was five," she said. "At least, that's the first time I can remember it happening."

She paused, played with her sleeves. I could tell by her tone, by the way her eyes kept falling on the floor in front of her instead of on me, that this was a story she'd told very few times, to very few people.

"I had a video cassette tape—God, remember those? —of The Little Mermaid. I watched it every day after school. My dad was always so damn busy, my mom wasn't around. We had a housekeeper, Shania, and if she was half as interested in me as she was in stealing cutlery and jewelry from my father, maybe my afternoons wouldn't have been so dull. Every afternoon, at two-thirty on the dot, Shania stuck me in the sunroom on the back of our house. There was a purple beanbag chair planted right in front of an old television set. The kind that had the VCR built in.

"So, everyday, at the same time, I'd plug my copy of The Little Mermaid into the VCR slot on the television and press play. By the time the movie was over, my father still wouldn't be home. So I'd find the TV remote, press rewind, wait the two minutes or so for the tape to wind back, and watch it again. I had other movies—The Lion King, Aladdin, Dumbo—you name it, I had it, but I *loved* The Little Mermaid.

"One afternoon, while I sat in the sunroom and Shania pocketed some of our finer silverware, The Little Mermaid finished and I could not find the TV remote to save my life. It was gone. Without a remote, I couldn't rewind the tape. Without being able to rewind the tape, I couldn't watch the movie again.

"I panicked, and I started to cry, I'm sure, but Shania ignored me and I was left to suffer in my little bubble on the rear of the house.

"I sat out there, staring at the end credits of The Little Mermaid, tears stinging my eyes...I sat there and just *stared* at the TV. Like, *really* stared at it. The world around me hushed and it was like everything else on the planet—except for the television set— suddenly ceased to exist.

"In a blink, the movie was playing again from the beginning. I didn't need the remote, I didn't need anything. I wanted the movie to start again from the beginning, and it did. I didn't question it.

"The next day, after school, I came home to watch The Little Mermaid, and again the remote was still missing. The tape ended, I concentrated with all my might, and the tape started again from the beginning.

"I did this every day for a week, and each time I assumed I was rewinding the tape by my own force of will. Now, I was little, but I was still old enough to tell time. One day, I noticed the clock that hung from the wall on the other end of the sunroom. Just before The Little Mermaid finished, it read four-fifteen PM. After I rewound the tape, the clock read two forty-five. I was confused. Time doesn't necessarily make sense to kids in the first place, so I thought I was moving the hands of the clock back when I rewound the tape, not *actually* moving time itself.

"The next day, I set up an experiment—I pleaded with Shania for a glass of chocolate milk after the movie finished. Shania brought me one, and I drank it, and I returned to the sunroom to try my trick again. The VHS tape rewound, the hands on the clocks moved backwards, and I watched the movie again. When it was over, I walked outside of the sunroom, and again I begged for a glass of chocolate milk. With little convincing, Shania went to the kitchen and made me a glass."

I sat cross-legged on the wingback, my jaw agape. My face rested on an open palm, my elbow leaned against the arm of the chair. I didn't know what to say. The whole thing sounded so absurd, despite the fact that hours earlier Vega had somehow saved me from a car accident that could have ended my life, using the same technique she had just described. We sat there, in total silence, until Vega finally spoke.

"You're looking at me like I'm an alien," she said.

"Are you?" I asked.

"I'm not," she said, sounding offended.

"This is like…some kind of test? Or joke?"

"Jackass," Vega said. "I saved you from being hit by a truck, and you can't believe it?"

"I don't know what happened earlier," I said.

"I *saved* you," Vega repeated. "That's what happened."

"You got sick after."

Vega leaned back on the sofa. "Yeah. It started when I turned twelve."

"The convulsions?"

Vega nodded. "My father signed me up for a youth soccer league in middle school," she said. "He wanted me to socialize more, or some bullshit like that. We were playing a scrimmage during practice, and the coach put me in goal. I hated being goalie. Debbie Horner—fucking Debbie Horner—got put in midfield. Christ, she was such a

189

show off. Debbie scored a goal on me from fifteen yards down field. I was humiliated—"

"You used your ability to cheat at a game?"

"Don't act holier than thou," Vega said. "And let me finish. Yeah, I rewound. With surprisingly little effort, I turned back time, saw the shot coming right at me and blocked it. I remember holding the soccer ball, and looking down at it, and there were these little drip-drops of blood. I sniffled, tasted copper, and realized the droplets were coming from my nose, and then...then, I just went *out.*"

"Out?"

"Collapsed on the field. The next thing I remembered was waking up in the nurse's office. My dad was yelling at the nurse. It's kind of funny, all it took to get him to show up to my practice was a health scare. He was arguing with her, saying he'd sue the school, that he'd have all their jobs...it took him two minutes to realize my eyes were open, and when he did, he took me home."

"Does your dad—"

"Know about what I can do?" Vega asked.

"Does anyone?"

"My father knows. It's hard to keep that sort of thing hidden from a man like that. I told a boyfriend, once, during my freshman year of college. But he freaked out afterwards, didn't believe me, and so I rewound to the moment before I told him. I didn't get sick that time. Sometimes I do, sometimes I don't."

"You rewound before you told him your secret," I said, and that sensation of puzzle pieces clicking together in my brain returned once more, "and he *couldn't* remember that you told him?"

Vega nodded and grinned. She knew exactly where I was going with that question.

190

"You rewound me," I said, "and I remember *everything*—I can remember the truck hitting me on North, I can remember Shadow flying out of my hands."

"Aside from my dad," Vega said, "you're the first person I've ever met who can remember the time before the rewind. I always knew there was something special about you, Nate Shaw, from the first moment I set eyes on you."

I sat back in my chair, and I felt a lot of things right then—disbelief, wonder, anxiety. But what I remember feeling most was fear. A fear that wasn't alleviated by what Vega said next.

"Just imagine," she said, licking her bottom lip, "all of the things that we could accomplish together."

ψ

We sat in the formal living room together long into the night. The room was dimly lit, and there was just the two of us, sitting across from one another in the dark. I had one million questions to ask Vega and she had one million answers. I was surprised, given how few people truly knew her, by how open she was with me.

I asked if she really could read minds, and she insisted that she could not, but I didn't believe her. I asked how often she exploited her rewind for personal gain, and she offered a few scenarios that she was proud of. Once, during her sophomore year of undergrad, she rewound during a peer study group, just to answer all of the group leader's questions correctly and impress him. I felt a slight twang of jealousy at that, at the thought of her trying to impress somebody else, and the twang subsided when the reality of how dumb that was washed over me. Once she had rewound to play winning lottery numbers in the state lotto—"Just for the hell of it," she said—but that she immediately rewound *again* afterwards, to a point in time where she didn't buy the ticket, because she felt guilty about it. Her father had amassed such wealth, she pointed out, that the press would have been nothing but negative and harmful; but more importantly, she told me, it just didn't feel like the right thing to do. I was a bit impressed that, by and large, Vega carried some kind of ethical code alongside her unusual ability.

When I brought up that night at the mall from the week before, she blushed, admitted that some of the coffee I'd knocked over had hit her lap and it was scalding. After I stood up to find her napkins, she rewound right then and there in the mall, to a point before the cup had been spilled.

I asked her what the longest she'd ever rewound was, and she told me a number that I found surprisingly short—twenty-nine minutes—and that it drained her so badly she slept for a day.

Finally, I asked if she had any theories on why rewinding sometimes sickened her and sometimes didn't. She shrugged, said she had no clue, and there was something about the way her shoulders slumped back down that reminded me what a skillful and adept liar she was, how lies could just roll off the tip of her tongue without hesitation.

"You've been doing this almost all your life," I said. "Surely you must have some idea why sometimes you get sick after and other times you don't."

"I truly couldn't tell you," Vega said. "Honest."

An awkward silence again fell over the two of us, but this time it was I who broke it.

"I never said thank you," I said. "I ran out into the road for that cat like a fucking idiot. It all happened so fast."

"You love that cat," Vega said. "I'd have done the same thing for something I loved."

"I'd be dead if it weren't for you."

"I'm just happy I was there," she said.

"That night outside of The Frosty Boot," I said, "with Betty Nicholson—"

"We were too late," she said. "Trust me, I thought about it."

I crossed my arms.

Vega stretched and let out a long yawn. "Come on," she said. "Take me to bed. We'll ride to class together in the morning."

Class? I'd practically forgotten that I was a student enrolled at Marshall. So much had happened over the weekend. It was hard to think about class after all that had transpired. I wondered who would be waiting for us in McManus's auditorium to teach us about torts. Who would be his replacement? And how does one get chosen for such a thing? *One law professor needed—prior teacher was a murderous asshole and has been asked to resign.*

Vega stuck out her arms and I stood, walked over to her, grabbed her by the palms and helped her up.

"You can stay here," she said. "There's a guest room on the second floor. You can use the washer and dryer too, if you don't want to wear the same change of clothes for three days in a row."

"Are you sure?"

"It's not like I don't have the space," she said.

We walked arm-in-arm from the formal living room to the main atrium in the front of the house. Vega pressed a switch beside the doorway and the massive chandelier that hung above the staircase lit, casting one thousand little shadows across the foyer.

I walked her up the spiral staircase to a second floor landing that looked over the interior of the first floor of the home. There was a hallway with a railing that led to a series of rooms, and Vega pointed to the door farthest away.

"Aye aye, captain," I said, and I walked her to her door.

"Not going to tuck me in?" she asked.

"It's been a very long night," I said.

"Classic Nate," Vega said. "A gentleman to a fault."

"I might take you up on that offer to wash my clothes," I said. "I reek. I can't go to class like this."

"Washer and dryer are in the basement," Vega said, and she spun the doorknob to her bedroom and slipped inside. "There's a guest room you can crash in, down the hall and on the left. But, you know, if you get lonely…my door is always open."

"I'll keep that in mind," I said, and Vega sauntered off into the darkened room.

ψ

If Vega's home looked like a castle from the outside, it looked like a museum from the inside. The place was enormous, and it was hard to not get lost. Walls were decorated with oil paintings; statues like something out of a Greek theater lined the halls. There were plants everywhere you turned; hanging from hooks on ceilings, standing in room corners in their ornate planters.

With enough exploration, I found a door that led to a simple staircase and down into the basement. It took very little fumbling in the dark to find a light switch beside the stairs, and I walked down to the room below.

I can't be certain of it, but Vega's basement may have had more square footage than the gymnasium in my elementary school. Had it not been for the low ceilings and the occasional support beam, there would have been more than enough room for a game of basketball or field hockey.

There were boxes everywhere, and various items had been draped with white cloths to protect them from dust. Most notable was a pool table in the center of the room. A white sheet covered it, a pair of cue sticks leaned against it. Other items were more mysterious, left fewer clues as to what was hidden beneath.

I found the washer and dryer and stripped down to a pair of boxers. It occurred to me that I'd worn the same pair of underwear for as long as I'd worn all my other clothes—since the morning before—so why not wash them, too? It'd be uncomfortable, wandering nude through a stranger's basement, but the room was warmer than could be expected of a basement and it'd sure as hell beat wearing dirty underwear for three days in a row.

I pulled off my boxers, too, and filled the washer basin with soap and water. When the water had risen high, I tossed in my clothes, closed the lid, and set the dial on the machine to wash.

The washing machine hummed to life, leaving me with nothing but the body I was born with and a lingering stench of sweat and salt. I could use a wash just as badly as my clothes could, and so I decided my next adventure would be to find a shower in Vega's mansion.

I ascended the basement staircase and found myself back on the first floor. I tiptoed past the formal living room and to the rear of the house, where I found an oak door with a black doorknob. I opened it, and inside was a bathroom bigger than the bedroom I rented at Dave's house. There was a garden tub on the far end of the room, tucked beneath a frosted-glass window, an open shower in the corner, and a Victorian sink placed between the two.

"Holy shit," I said.

I walked to the shower, found a bar of soap and some shampoo, and turned the faucet handle to hot. A fine mist of water spouted from the showerhead and I stepped beneath it, savoring the warmth and softness of it. I scrubbed myself head to toe, and for the first time in forty-eight hours felt like I was back amongst the land of the living.

I closed my eyes, and couldn't help but laugh at the absurdity of it all. *I got hit by a car while chasing a cat.* And Vega, a girl I'd admired for weeks, saved me from it by turning back time? It was ridiculous. I recalled the terrible dreams I'd been having, and wondered if maybe this was one of them, too. Maybe I was still asleep in my bedroom on North, and this was all pretend.

I'd almost doubt the reality of it all, had it not been for the jets of hot water raining down on my skin. No, it was real, all right. Very real.

As the water hit my skin, sliding off in sheets, I thought about what I'd do if I could go back in time. I thought of the summer after my ninth birthday, just before my father's rapid sickness and subsequent death, and how I'd go back there. That July, there were no signs of the illness that would consume his life. They'd show up later that September, and by October, they would claim him. But that July was something special. My father, my mother, and I spent it together, camping along the Mohawk River. There was that picnic along the shore, when the deer visited us. There was swimming, and fishing, and the smells of campfire. But that had been fourteen years ago, hadn't it? And Vega could rewind reality like an old VHS tape to just shy of thirty minutes, and not a second longer. It didn't seem fair.

I had just shut the water off and grabbed a towel from the rack beside me when I heard a loud groan come from behind. The bathroom was thick with fog from my shower, yet even through the haze I could see that the bathroom door had opened just an inch.

"Hello?" I called out. I dried myself with the towel, then tied it around my waist.

There was no answer, only silence. I was certain I had shut the door tightly behind me when I first came in.

"Vega," I said. "Is that you?"

I walked to the end of the bathroom, opened the door, and peeked out. The formal living room was empty. The house was quiet and still.

I made my way back to the basement, where my small load of laundry was already finishing its cycle in the washing machine. I pulled dampened jeans, socks, boxers and a t-shirt from the washer and loaded them into the dryer. When I closed the lid of the dryer, I heard a choir of whispers, soft and indiscernible.

Beside the dryer was something tall and boxy. I couldn't tell exactly what it was, because like most of the furnishings and decorations in the home, it was draped in a single white sheet.

Whatever it was, it stood seven feet tall, and at least a couple feet wide. As the whispers continued their angelic chants, the sheet atop the monstrosity rippled. I reached out to touch it, overcome by a desire to yank the sheet right off and reveal what was underneath, but as I extended my hand the floor of the basement vibrated and the angelic chants turned to sinister screams.

I raced up the stairs of the basement as fast as my feet could carry me and, dressed in only my towel, ascended the spiral staircase like a blur, stumbling back to the guest room.

My clothes will still be there in the morning, I told myself, *and Vega can accompany me when I get them.*

I settled into bed and thought of what it might take to get me to venture down into that basement on my own ever again.

I couldn't come up with anything.

ψ

Sleep didn't come easy that night.

But, when had it?

I crawled between the blankets of the neatly made bed in the largest of four guest bedrooms in Vega's house. In an instant, I felt a sour homesickness for the little bungalow at 126 North. I thought of Shadow, curled up on my bed, wondering where I was. I thought of Dave, stretched out on the stained and tattered living room couch, a bong in one hand and a video game controller in the other. I hoped that they were well in my absence.

The guestroom was about as sterile and uninviting as any bedroom or hotel room I'd ever been in before or since. A full sized mattress rested atop a simple bed frame, dressed in plain colored blankets and sheets. There was a dresser pressed against the wall opposite of where I lay. To my right was a tall, narrow window with long mauve drapes hung in front of it. A slat between the drapes allowed only the slimmest sliver of moonlight to cast into the room.

I tossed and turned, pulled the blankets close to my face, struggled for peace. The frequent nightmares were one thing; I'd learned to handle them, after all. But the waking nightmare of the past eight hours? That was a new monster all in its own. No longer were the thoughts that tortured me subconscious, pressed between dreamscapes. They were real. They were tangible.

Vega's long soliloquy replayed on a loop in my head, over and over again. I'd known there was something special about her from

198

the first time I laid eyes on her, that afternoon at the gym in the mall. It went beyond her beauty, beyond her smile. There was a strange aura that hung over her like a grey cloud hangs low on a rainy day, and it seemed that, at last, that mysterious veil had been pulled back. She had trusted me with a side of her that the world hadn't seen. She had trusted me to accept her for who she was, nothing more, and nothing less.

The same that she had done for me.

And any time those worrisome thoughts wormed their way into my head—the ones telling me that I should be afraid of her, that whoever or whatever she was, or wherever she came from, was something I would never truly understand—I reminded myself of one simple fact: she saved my life.

"Are you out there, Joyce?" I said aloud. "Is Vega a part of this? Did I have to meet her to find whatever spiritual peace it is that you so desperately crave?"

I half expected a headless corpse to materialize in the darkened corner of the guestroom, laughing at me, mocking me, frustrated by my simple mortal mind and how long it took me to connect the puzzle pieces of the past week.

"They're searching for your killer, Joyce. Every minute of every day. McManus's life of freedom grows shorter with each passing second. Does that bring you satisfaction? When the bastard is brought to justice, will that bring you serenity?"

Again, there was no answer.

"Was that you outside my shower door, Joyce? Was that you in the basement? Are you following me? Because I never believed in ghosts much before this week. I thought I did, long ago, when I was a stupid kid grieving the loss of my father. I thought he'd visited me, but it was a short and fleeting moment, an awful waste of time for a

199

ghost, don't you think? If that was the ghost of my father so many summers ago, I wish he would have taken half as much time to pester me and annoy me as you fucking have."

I sat up in the bed, wrapped my arms tightly around a pillow. There were tears forming, burning in the corner of my eyes, slipping down my cheeks.

"I never cared much for ghosts—but from what I know, they haunt places, not people. And that's not true, is it, Joyce? Because that *was* you at the bathroom door, and that *was* you in the basement, so talk to me Joyce—just tell me whatever the *fuck* it is you still want me to do. Don't be shy now!"

The room went still, stiller than it had all night. But there was something new to it. Something unseen, but felt the same as the kiss of an early autumn chill.

It was as if all the air had been sucked out of the room all at once.

"You're so close," a soft voice whispered.

"Who is that?" I called out. "Who's there?"

The narrow shaft of moonlight entering the room darkened. I couldn't make out who or what, but something was blocking the space of bedroom between my bed and the window.

"I wish I'd known you in a different life, Nate. We would have been friends."

"Who are you? Where are you?"

I felt the mattress beside me dimple, watched the blankets crease the same way they would if someone had sat next to me.

"We could have carpooled to Marshall together, spent afternoons studying together in the library. Yeah. We'd have been fast friends, Nate. I'm sure of it. You're reliable. You have a good heart."

A silhouette appeared on the bed. She manifested from nothing, she glimmered with a pale glow. All at once, she was easy to see and difficult to focus on. She was a contradiction, but as surely as the moon hung outside the bedroom window, she was there.

She was young, beautiful. Long locks of red hair bobbed around her shoulders, and the freckles on her face were fair and plentiful, barely distinguishable in the soft light.

"You know who I am, Nate. Same as I know who you are."

"I've never seen you," I said. "Like this. Whole."

Joyce grinned. "Would you prefer the alternative? The way I looked in all of those police reports you've pored over?"

I choked. "I wouldn't. This is fine. If you've had the option, why would you choose the latter over the former?"

"Spirits at unrest have a flair for the theatrics," Joyce said.

"Just tell me," I said, "what's left to do. If I could drive out of here tonight and handcuff McManus myself, I would. I've done so much to piece things back together for you. I should be focusing on schoolwork and on my degree. But, my first week at Marshall...I gave it all to you, Joyce. I gave it all to you."

Joyce nodded. "I know, Nate. It's more than should ever be asked of one person. You've done so much. I'm thankful for it."

"So just tell me," I pleaded again. "Just tell me what's left to do."

"It's not that simple," Joyce said. "You wouldn't understand."

"Try me."

"I can't just outright tell you what to do," Joyce said. "I can leave you hints, I can leave you clues—but I can't tell you. My lips are sealed here, floating in this awful torment between worlds. Part of what will set me free—what will set Betty free, what will set you free—is you finding the right words for yourself, and putting them in the right order. There is a truth you need to pry out from the dirt all on your own, you must grab it with your hands and pull it from the sludge, Nathan, and you must scream that truth at the top of your lungs. Here, we're all blind, but you can see just fine."

"I'm sorry for what happened to you," I said, "and I'm sorry for what happened to Betty."

"There's no need for apologies here, Nate—"

"You should visit Dave," I said. "He wanted more than anything to know you."

Joyce shook her head. "Dave, huh?"

"He turned out to be a great person," I said. "A great friend. Caring. Strong. You'd be proud."

Joyce laughed. "I'm sure I would be." She clicked her tongue, shook her head again. "You're so close," she said. "Yet so very far away."

"What do you mean?" I begged, but she was already dissipating into the night. The dimples in the mattress evened, the moonlight once more filled the room, and she was gone.

I laid down flat on the bed, listened to the silence of Vega's enormous manor, listened to the sound of my own breathing. The only thought comforting enough to lull me to sleep that night was the prospect of how goddammned relieved I'd be when all of this— whatever *this* was—was finally over.

ψ

Maybe it was because Joyce visited me in person that night, face to face, that I didn't have my usual night terrors. I fell asleep around two in the morning, and a short four hours later, there was a light, whispy knock at the bedroom door. I had slept like a rock.

"Nate?" Vega called.

I opened my eyes. The faintest rays of sunlight were burning in the narrow gap between the mauve colored curtains.

"Hey," I hollered.

"Is it okay to come in?"

I pulled the blankets of the guest bed up over my chest, then leaned up against my pillows. "Yeah."

The door groaned open. She stood there, in the doorframe, wrapped only in a bathrobe, her face wiped clean of makeup. She absolutely glowed.

"How'd you sleep?" she asked.

"Wonderful," I said. "In some sick twist of irony, it was the hours leading up to sleep that were the true nightmare."

"Because of what we talked about?"

"No," I said. "Joyce...was here. In the house with me. She sat at the foot of the bed and talked to me. It felt as real as how you're standing there, talking to me now."

Vega shook her head. "Are you all right?"

"I'm fine," I said, and I laughed. "Any one else would accuse me of being crazy. You've kept such an open mind."

"With what I'm able to do, how couldn't I?"

She made a good point. Surely the girl who could shift time backwards wouldn't scoff at me for believing in ghosts and night visions, even if she hadn't experienced them herself.

"I better get ready," I said. "My clothes are downstairs in the dryer. Would you mind escorting me?"

Vega grinned. "After all you've been through, you're afraid of the basement?"

I couldn't help but smile. "You're fucking right I am," I said. "She was down there with me last night, Vega. I know that sounds ridiculous. There were sounds of chanting, the floor was shaking—"

"Say no more," she said, and she waved at me to get up. "Let's go. I'll be your tour guide."

I wrapped the top sheet of the bed around myself like a robe, and I must have blushed, because Vega used the opportunity to make a comment about my modesty as we walked together to the basement.

Early morning daylight spilled in through the narrow windows that lined the top of the basement walls. In the daylight, the room seemed smaller and less menacing.

Vega popped the lid of the dryer open and I pulled my clothes out.

"I'll give you some privacy," she said, "if you can handle being down here on your own for a minute."

"I think I can," I said, not amused by her sarcasm.

She turned back toward the staircase that led upstairs, but before she reached the first step, I called out to her.

"Hey," I said. "What is this?"

Vega spun around and I pointed at the seven-foot tall monolith, masked by the white sheet draped over it.

"A stack of boxes that my father keeps stored down here," she said. "Why do you ask?"

"Joyce, and whatever other spirits danced around me last night... they seemed awfully interested in it."

"I don't know why they would be," Vega said. "Now, don't be nosy. It's probably full of cockroaches and spiders. He hasn't been down here in years."

I nodded and Vega ascended the basement staircase. In the privacy of the giant room I dressed, and the entire time my eyes didn't leave that giant tower and the white sheet that masked it. I felt like a little kid told not to put their hand in the cookie jar. I wanted

204

more than anything to yank the sheet, to pull it off and see what was underneath, and understand why on earth the ghost of Joyce Nicholson would be so interested in it.

But I was a guest, after all, and I'd been asked nicely not to by a girl who claimed to have a time-shifting super power. So, I decided it was best to forget about the whole thing.

ψ

Vega's kitchen, like the rest of her house, was like something I'd only seen in a movie. Floor to ceiling windows made up the wall opposite of the kitchen table, peered over the valley and the city of Burlington below. Except for the stove and range, every appliance was disguised, covered in white paneling that masked it alongside the high cabinetry.

Vega had some cut up bits of melon, and I had made some toast. We sat at the kitchen table together, looking out over Burlington, and talked.

"If I knocked that over," I said, and I pointed at the carafe of orange juice on the side of the kitchen table, "would you clean it up? Or would you just rewind time by a few seconds?"

"Neither," Vega said. "I'd smack your hand and make you clean it up yourself. It's not something I like to do often, and even just rewinding for a few seconds can make me feel ill."

After breakfast, we hopped into her Mercedes together to start the trek to Marshall. The car pulled out of her long driveway, past the gate, and onto Anchorage. A short time after that, we were on Hampshire, the long stretch of road between our side of town and the university campus.

I kept my head pressed against the window, watched the rows of pine trees on the side of the road go blurring by. I thought about where I was a week ago that moment, behind the wheel of The Beast, driving myself to class, eager to learn, excited by the adventure that lie ahead. Law school had brought an adventure, hadn't it? Just not the kind I ever expected to find myself in.

It wasn't supposed to be like this, I thought.

A strange thought occurred to me in that moment, one that I'd never considered before. Maybe, just maybe, above all things—the truth of Ed McManus's insidious past, the truth about Joyce and Betty Nicholson's death—the universe was trying to tell me that law school just wasn't for me, that maybe it wasn't the path I was meant to follow. I thought about my mother and stepfather back home in New York. Would they be disappointed? How would they react if I phoned them, asking to take a semester off and crash at home?

My mother had so much trouble letting me go the day I climbed into The Beast and headed off to Vermont. But the last time I had spoken to her, she was happy—*really* happy—and enjoying the time she had with James. It was the natural order of things, I suppose. Parent raises child, child flies from the nest, parent relaxes with frozen margaritas.

I didn't want to ask to come home, I didn't want to upset that natural order. Not yet.

"You're awfully quiet," Vega said.

"There's a lot on my mind."

"What do you think will happen when we get to class?" she asked.

"I figure there'll be a replacement for McManus waiting for us," I said, "ready to teach us about the exciting world of torts—"

A siren rang out so loud, the interior of the Mercedes rattled. My eyes darted to the rearview mirror on the passenger door. Through it

I watched as a fire truck came rocketing up behind us at twice the posted speed limit.

"Pull over," I said.

"I know to pull over," Vega replied, and she steered the Mercedes off the road and onto the grass that ran alongside it.

The fire truck blew by, immediately followed by an ambulance, then a half dozen Vermont State Trooper police cruisers. The sheer force of each passing vehicle shook the frame of the Mercedes, rocking it back and forth.

We sat quietly as the convoy of emergency vehicles passed by, and a half moment passed before I realized where we were. The bend of the road, the contour of the tree line, the sign for Marshall just a bit up the road ...I'd seen each one of them before in photographs.

"We're parked where it happened," I whispered. "Where Joyce had her accident." I sat still in the passenger seat, scanned the tree line for moose. In the thick row of pines not far beyond our car, there was no movement.

"All those police cars," Vega said, "the fire truck, the ambulance...they're all headed toward Marshall."

In the tree line was the slightest sudden trace of movement; hard to see at first, but then undeniable. Someone stepped out from behind a pine, and though the morning sun was still low on the horizon, I could make out her features. Her bobbed red hair, her face full of freckles.

It was Joyce, and she stood there in the trees, watching us as we sat in the car. The flashing lights of the emergency vehicles passed through her, casted alternating shades of violet and red on the trees behind where she stood, and in that moment I could see that she was sobbing.

Before I could tell Vega to look, so that she might see her for herself, the Mercedes squealed back on to Hampshire and started its race toward campus.

We arrived soon after the fleet of ambulances and police cars. A barricade of police cruisers blocked the parking lot in front of the Bircham building. Just beyond the wall of cruisers and officers, a crowd of students and faculty had gathered. Each of them stared in the same direction—toward the roof of the building.

Vega hastily parked her car on a patch of grass near the front of campus, and together we stepped out.

"What's going on?" she asked. "Can you see anything?"

I cupped my hands around my eyes and squinted. It was hard to tell. We took a few steps forward toward the parking lot, and then it became clear: someone was standing on the roof of Bircham, arms wrapped around one of the high spires, the only thing separating them from a forty foot drop to the pavement below.

"Holy shit," I mumbled. "It's McManus."

ψ

Several students had their cell phones out and pointed at the roof of Bircham. They stood in awe and wonder as McManus held onto the high green spire, swinging back and forth like King Kong from the Empire State Building. He was yelling something, but it was hard to discern over the murmurs of the crowd.

I worked my way as close to the barricades as I could. When I was near, a young officer in his twenties crossed his arms, told me to take a step back.

"Is Officer Dixon here?" I asked. "I'm a friend of his."

"Officer Dixon is dealing with a house fire back in town. Some kind of explosion. Gas leak."

"Busy morning."

"Listen, kid, if you've got nothing to contribute here, I gotta ask you to move back."

"What are you going to do?"

The young officer sighed. "We're gonna call the circus and have them set up in the parking lot to cheer the guy up. Christ, are you a student here? We're gonna try to talk the bastard down."

I stepped back from the makeshift barricade, joined Vega in the crowd.

"He should do the world a favor and jump," I said.

Vega pursed her lips. "You don't mean that, Nate."

"He sabotaged a pregnant woman's car," I said. "He ran a woman down as she crossed the street."

"You're pursuing a law degree," Vega said. "Aren't you supposed to believe in justice, in fairness? In due process?"

"The only due process McManus deserves is the pavement when his body hits it."

Vega shook her head. "Let's hope it doesn't come to that."

An officer in the crowd grabbed a bullhorn from his cruiser, brought it to his mouth, and clicked the speaker on. It squealed to life with a high-pitched hum.

"Professor," the officer said. "We want to get you help—"

"You don't want to help me," McManus said. "You want to string me up by my thumbs, the lot of you. You want me to pay for what happened to Joyce, for what happened to Betty? I *loved* Joyce. Every day without her—my suffering—that is what I've paid for her."

209

"Please," the officer said. "No one here wants you to get hurt. All of us—your students, your peers—we all want a peaceful resolution."

"Peace?" McManus said. "You'll have no peace. This town has a curse upon it."

McManus released his grasp on the spire he clung to so dearly. He tumbled through the air in freefall, his body limp, spinning end over end. He didn't scream, he didn't yell, he didn't beg for help.

His head hit the pavement first, made the same sound a rotten pumpkin does when tossed into the street a week after Halloween. His body collapsed in on itself, folding like an accordion. A bucket of blood splattered outward from him, started to pool in a faculty parking spot in front of the building.

The crowd was silent for a split second, completely awestruck.

And then the screaming started.

"We shouldn't be watching this," Vega said, and she yanked me by the hand.

"Spirits have haunted my dreams," I said, "every day since I moved to this goddamn town. Restless. Unrelenting. All because of him, all because of what he did. You can go, if you want to. But I have to see this."

"If he's guilty of what he's accused of, he should have lived to stand trial," Vega said.

"You're the magic woman," I whispered. "A twitch of your nose and a clap of your hands, and you can rewind back to before he jumped. Give the police a second chance to get it right."

Vega bit her lip.

"You won't," I said, "even though you could. Because you know, deep down, that I'm right."

McManus's right arm twitched back and forth rapidly, as if some invisible puppeteer was pulling on it for one final performance.

"Let's get out of here," Vega said. "I just want to leave."

ψ

The two of us sat quietly in the car as it hummed back in the direction of town.

"Where are we going?" I said.

"I don't know," Vega said. "I'll drop you off at home, I guess."

"Should we talk about this?"

"I don't want to talk about this."

Vega's face had gone pale, and the thought crossed my mind that maybe she shouldn't be behind the wheel of a motor vehicle.

"I'd hope by now," I said, "you'd know you could talk to me about anything."

"It's the first time," Vega said, "that I could have prevented something truly awful from happening and chose not to."

"I'm sorry if I talked you out of it—"

"Don't flatter yourself," Vega said. "It was mostly my decision. I hesitated. I've had this ability all of my life, and it's the first time I've ever turned my back on someone."

"So do it now," I said. "You have a window of thirty minutes. Only four or five have passed."

"It's hard to describe," Vega said. "For it to work—for the rewind to work—I have to *want* it to work. I have to want it more than anything. When McManus hit the ground, it felt…good. All I could think of was you, and your nightmares, and the bizarre chain of events that led you to figuring out all the harm he's caused. I was

211

relieved that those would end for you. I was relieved that McManus couldn't hurt anyone else ever again."

"You can't hate yourself for this," I said.

"Oh, Nate. I can hate myself for plenty."

Vega hooked a left onto North, and way down the road, we could see a tall tower of smoke pluming from the street.

"One of the cops earlier mentioned a house fire," I said. "I wonder whose?"

Vega shook her head. We passed the convenient store where the bums hung out, then drove around the bend.

Parked in front of 126 North were two fire trucks, an ambulance, and a police cruiser. One of the fire trucks sprayed a wide fan of water onto the home, but I couldn't figure out why, because there was hardly anything left of it.

The home I shared with Dave—no, that Dave allowed me to stay in as a roommate and a friend—was gone. All that was left was a burnt frame, still smoldering, and the piles of ash and wreckage within. Most of the roof was missing. Debris had blown out onto the lawn and into the street. The Beast sat in the driveway where I parked it last, a charred husk of a machine.

A police officer standing in the road put his hand up, stopped Vega from driving any further, approached the car and told her to turn around.

"That's my house," I said, and I opened the passenger door, dashed out into the road. "That's my house."

"Sir," the officer hollered, and he started to chase after me. "Sir, stop! Sir, you can't go any further!"

I ignored him, pumped my legs as hard as I could. My lungs burned, my legs cramped, and still I ran harder.

In the shrubs outside of the house were the tangled remains of a black furred cat.

On the sidewalk, a team of paramedics pushed a gurney, atop which was a long black bag zipped tight.

I felt my knees turn to jelly, felt the horizon start to wobble to and fro. My vision blurred, then tunneled, and I collapsed into the street.

ψ

Officer Dixon's face was the first thing I saw when I came to. Vega was being held ten or fifteen feet away, they wouldn't let her near me. I was in the back of one of the ambulances. A paramedic was checking my blood pressure. He pumped his fist, and a black strap around my arm inflated and tightened, pinching at my bicep.

"He fainted," the paramedic said, and he nodded to Dixon. "He should start to stabilize soon."

"I fainted?" I said. "It's a wonder you weren't accepted to med school, being able to make such astute observations like that—"

"Nate," Dixon said, calmly.

"A wonder you're not a neurosurgeon, you fucking prick—"

"Nate," Dixon repeated. "Relax. Take a deep breath. You're in shock."

The paramedic hopped out the back of the ambulance, glared at me, and wandered off.

"What's happening?" I said. My eyes burned with grief. "Is he—was it—is he gone?"

Dixon's eyes fell toward the floor of the ambulance. "There was a gas leak. A bad one. There was nothing anyone could do."

I started to sob harder than I had in a very, very long time.

"And you're sure it was him? It was Dave?"

"His girlfriend was here a short while ago. She identified him."

"How long ago was the explosion?" I asked.

Dixon flicked his wrist, looked at the cheap silver Timex strapped to it. "An hour ago. Maybe a little longer. I've been trying to call you all morning."

I pulled my cell phone from my pocket. Dead.

"That's too bad," I said. "You see, I have a magic girl friend who can turn back time, but only by thirty minutes or so for some stupid fucking reason. So if I'd been here sooner, maybe I could have done more. Maybe I could have saved him."

"Okay," Dixon said, and a worried smile crept across his face. "You need to get hydrated, and you need some rest. I'm sorry about this, Nate. I'm sorry about all of this."

"Did McManus do this?" I asked.

"The fire marshal needs to sign off on some paperwork, but so far, the investigation shows no signs of foul play. It seems to have been accidental."

"The stove never worked right," I said. "And this weekend— God, this weekend—I slept an entire day away."

"For now, you should consider yourself lucky to be alive."

"We should have been able to smell it though, right? I mean, we should have been able to smell the gas. It never occurred to me that there could be a gas leak. See, I thought I'd slept for so long as a part of some curse put on me by the ghosts of Joyce and Betty Nicholson—"

Vega wormed her way toward the ambulance, pushing away the officers that tried to hold her back.

"He's babbling nonsense," Vega said. "He should be seen by a doctor."

"I'm fine," I muttered. "I don't need a doctor."

Dixon nodded, took a step back in the rear bay of the ambulance. "Why don't I give the two of you some privacy?"

"That'd be great," Vega said.

As soon as Dixon was out of earshot, Vega took a seat beside me in the back of the ambulance and clutched my arm.

"What are you doing?" she whispered. "I could hear everything you were saying."

"None of it matters," I said.

"I know this is a lot for you to process this morning, but you can't just go around telling people you know a time traveler, joking or not."

"You're not a real time traveler," I said. "You're no Doc Brown. This isn't *Back to the Future*. A real time traveler can move in distances greater than half an hour. You're just a hack."

"I can't imagine the grief, and the horror, and the sadness that you're experiencing right now," Vega said. "I truly can't. Which is why I'm giving you a free pass. Spit it out. Spit out all your venom. I can take it."

"It's not fair," I said, and the big, wheezy sobs returned. "He was my friend. It's gone, it's all gone."

Vega wrapped her arms around me, cradled me, held me tight. "I'm just so happy you're safe," she said. "And it's not all gone."

She stroked my hair, then patted my back as I wept. My face was pressed against the nape of her neck, my tears stained her shirt as they fell.

She kissed me on the cheek. "You still have me."

ψ

215

Vega drove me back to her house.

What else was there to do?

Where else was there to go?

I don't remember much about the car ride, except that the scenery of Burlington I'd once found so charming and quaint now repulsed me. The trees were once so green, their leaves so lush, ripened before autumn would have its wicked way with them. Now, they might as well have been made of cardboard. The town no longer felt like home, it felt like a movie set. We passed by Lake Champlain, and the children playing on the shore, careless, happy, laughing, no longer brought me joy. I envied them too much.

Vega's words were few and far between. I imagine she didn't know what to say. We'd only met each other a week before, and though it was clear we enjoyed one another's company, what was I to her now? A burden is what it felt like.

Her Mercedes rolled along North until it hooked left on to Anchorage. The street narrowed. The branches on either side of the street arched high above us, casting long shadows over the road ahead.

"We can spend the rest of the day doing whatever you want," Vega said. "Even if what you want to do is nothing. There's a pool in the back of the house, if you want to sit out there…or you can lock yourself away in the guest room, I don't know. But whatever you want, it's yours."

"I don't feel like swimming."

"You don't have to swim. We can sit out there together—"

"I don't feel like sitting outside."

"Then don't," Vega said. "I'm just letting you know that you can have whatever you want. I'm just trying to be nice."

I let out a long sigh. "I appreciate it."

I closed my eyes, thought of the last time I'd seen Dave. We were standing in the kitchen. He was doing dishes.

It's all gravy, baby.

"They're all gone, now," I said. "David. His mother. The man he thought was his father. I put the last puzzle piece together, and then it all exploded, right there in my hands. It's all my fault, Vega."

"It's not your fault."

"It is. I provoked McManus and he came after me. Came after me…and came after Dave. Dave, a living reminder of Joyce's affair from twenty-four years ago."

"There was a gas leak, Nate. How could McManus have planned for that? It was an accident. A tragedy."

"No," I said. "If I've learned one thing this week, it wasn't about torts, about family law, or about criminal procedure. It's that there's no such thing as a coincidence. Not in a million years does McManus throw himself from Marshall's rooftop and my house burns down on the same morning—within an hour of one another—and the two aren't related."

"You're trying to rationalize it," Vega said. "Which is understandable, because tragedies don't make sense, and our minds crave sense. They crave order. Sometimes, awful things happen and there's no one to blame."

We pulled on to the long drive way in front of Vega's home, passed through the wrought iron gate, parked beside the fancy slate fountain.

"I have to get a hold of Dominic Bloom," I blurted.

Vega shook her head. "Why?"

"He was Dave's father," I said. "I have to let him know what happened."

"Nate, everyone who watches the six o'clock news tonight will know what happened."

"I want to tell him how I got to know his son these past few weeks, and what a good person he was. They won't mention that on the six o'clock news."

"For now," Vega said, "you just need some rest. Let's head inside, and play it by ear afterward."

ψ

I spent the afternoon lazing about the guest room on the second floor. My cell phone battery had run dry, so I'd left it to charge while I paced the room, laid down, sat back up, knelt beside the window, and took turns crying loudly or thinking quietly. Vega had spent most of the afternoon downstairs. I think she sensed that I felt slightly embarrassed crying so much, especially in front of her, so she was doing one of the kindest things someone could do for someone in that moment.

She was giving me space.

When my phone battery had charged back to life, I scrolled through the logs of missed calls from the morning. There were seven from Officer Dixon, three from different local news networks, and one—most recently—from my mom.

I called her back, and before I finished saying hello, she could tell that something was wrong, in that way that only mothers can. She said she wanted to check up on me, had heard something on the news that weekend about a professor at Marshall getting into trouble, wanted to gossip with me and ask all about it.

"He's dead," I said, bluntly.

"Is that why you're upset?" she asked.

"No. I wouldn't piss on Ed McManus if he was on fire. The world is better without him."

"Then what is it?" she asked.

"The room I was renting…the house…my roommate…they're gone."

"What do you mean 'gone?'"

"There was a fire, mom. Something terrible. A gas leak. I was on the way to school when it ignited and—and nothing's left, mom. My roommate, my cat, even The Beast parked out front. It's all gone."

There was a long silence on the line. "Nathan, Nathan, Nathan. Thank God you weren't home. Nathan, no, I'm so sorry. James and I will be up right away to pick you up—"

"I can't come home right now," I said.

"Nathan, I want to see you, I want to know you're all right."

"I need a few days. I have to visit the admissions office and cancel this semester. I need to dot some I's and cross some T's, and I'll be on the next bus back to New York."

"Where will you stay?"

"I'm at a friend's house for now."

"As soon as we hang up, I'll call the hospital, I'll get someone to cover my shifts. I'll take vacation time if I have to—"

"Don't bother with all that, mom, please. Don't waste vacation time on this. I'll be home soon. Two days at the most. Maybe three."

"I love you so much, Nathaniel."

I could feel the lump in my throat working its way back up, another tidal wave of sadness curling from deep inside of me upward.

"I love you too, mom," and I hung up the phone.

ψ

219

The rest of the afternoon went by in a hazy blur. I took the time to call back the news outlets that I had missed calls from. I declined to meet with any reporters, or to allow any camera crews to show up at Vega's front door. Still, I gave a brief phone interview to WGAB, the local six o'clock news channel. I used the opportunity to tell them what a great friend and roommate Dave was, and that I'd miss him terribly, and that the world was worse off without him. I didn't mention the intricate family tree we'd pieced together that weekend, or my assumptions about Joyce Nicholson being his biological mother and Dominic Bloom being his biological father. Maybe, one day, there'd be a right time and place for that, but that day wasn't it.

When asked about Ed McManus, I declined to answer any questions.

Hours passed until five o'clock rolled around, and a gentle knock rapped at the bedroom door.

"Come in," I said.

Vega stepped inside, didn't look at the state of the room—or me—accusingly. The sheets were torn apart, the mattress hung off the bed frame cockeyed, my clothes were disheveled and hung loosely from me. I looked like how I felt, and how I felt was awful.

"Thought you might be getting hungry," Vega said.

"I can't think about eating."

"I thought you might say that," Vega said, "which is why I already took it upon myself to order a pizza."

I smiled, probably for the first time that day.

"Come downstairs," she said. "I wasn't sure what you'd like, so I got pepperoni and cheese. Can't go wrong with that."

She extended an arm and an open palm. I grabbed her hand and stood up from the bed, followed her out of the guestroom and downstairs to the kitchen.

On a granite bar top was a grease soaked pizza box, beside which were two barstools. We each took a seat.

The pizza was still warm, but not hot. Who knew how long it'd sat down there before Vega worked up the courage to ask me downstairs? I caught her looking at me the same way I must have looked at her, both when I discovered how adept she was at lying, and when she trusted me with the secret of her special skill.

"You're looking at me like I have three eyes," I said.

She set down her slice of pizza and rested her hand on mine. "I just can't fathom what you're feeling. And I'm just so thankful you weren't in your house this morning. I keep thinking…what if you hadn't stayed here last night?"

What if I hadn't stayed here last night? If I hadn't chased Shadow out into the road, and if Vega hadn't had to rewind for me, maybe there would have been hope for Dave. I pictured a world where I didn't have to drive Vega home, where I went back inside, helped Dave finish putting away clean dishes, stayed up late playing Nintendo with him. Maybe I'd have noticed it, then. The gas leak. The signs of trouble.

"Who knows," I said, and I took a bite of pizza. It took some convincing from my brain to force my throat to swallow it. It sat in my stomach like a rock. "If you start puling that thread, things can unravel quickly, right? But then again, I'm sure you know all about that."

"I wish I could undo what happened, Nate—"

"I'm not so unsure you can't."

221

Vega's eyes started to tear. "Trust me, Nathaniel. If I could, I would have by now."

"I don't want to stay here too long," I said. "I don't want to be in your way. I don't want you having to take care of me. Can I crash in the guest room for a day or two? Just until I get my affairs in order."

"Affairs?" Vega said. "What affairs?"

"I need to withdraw for the semester. The deadline is Wednesday. I need to withdraw and I need to go home. Maybe I'll take another crack at Marshall in the spring. But for now, the universe couldn't be more clear: I don't belong here, in Burlington, and I don't belong in Marshall College of Law."

"Don't say that, Nate. You can't withdraw. Classes have been postponed for the week, anyways. This McManus thing is a media nightmare."

"My mom heard about it, back in New York."

"It's national news," Vega said. "Take the week to reconsider. Promise me that much, at least. What happened to the Nate I knew, who wanted to get his law degree and be a champion for the little guy?"

"That Nate's gone," I said. "He needs to get away for a while."

"One week," Vega said, "and if you still want to head back to New York, then so be it."

I set down my slice of pizza, wiped the corners of my mouth with a napkin that sat beside the grease stained box. "One week," I said. "But only because you twisted my arm."

ψ

In an extremely short span of time, I had witnessed two major areas

222

of my life pull apart. McManus was gone. Home was gone. There was absolutely no preparing for something like that. I'd spent the day as a ghost, feeling absolutely outside of myself.

I wanted Vega to wave her proverbial magic wand and put it all back together again. But sometimes, that's just life. There were things even Vega couldn't fix, limits that even she had to abide by

By eleven o'clock that wretched Monday night, I had felt myself start to rematerialize. That is to say, I once again felt like a solid form, a collection of atoms constructed in the shape of a human. The ghost feeling had started to subside.

It's not to say that I felt any better, felt any warmth or happiness or levity that night. Physically I was whole, but deep down in my soul, pieces of me had been irreparably destroyed.

I thought of Dave.

I wished I'd had Shadow to hold on to.

Around eleven-thirty I crawled back into the bed in Vega's guestroom. I kept my eyes patiently focused on the mauve window panels draped in front of the bedroom window. I waited for some ethereal form to appear in the beams of moonlight, to guide itself towards the bed and offer some peace, some comfort, or some direction toward me.

No one came.

By midnight, my eyes—tired from hours of crying—had finally shut. I could have stayed awake forever, but my body was physically exhausted. There was no more fighting it. Sleep was coming for me, whether I wanted it to or not.

Such awful visions had visited me at the end of otherwise pleasant days over the past few weeks. I wondered, after all I had seen just that morning, what would come to visit me that night?

I hoped, whatever it might be, it might come peacefully and without ill will.

Those hopes would be answered.

That night, I dreamt that I was two floors down, deep in the bowels of Vega's castle, in the basement. It was so vivid, at first, so lifelike, that I wondered if maybe I had begun to sleepwalk.

I was standing in front of the washer and dryer, washing what was once again my only change of clothes. Funny how that worked out, wasn't it? Until that dream, it hadn't occurred to me that everything I had was truly lost. My clothes, my computer. Thousands of dollars worth of textbooks.

The spin cycle on the washing machine was endless. I stood there, watching clothes toss and turn in sudsy water, for what felt like an eternity.

"It's never going to stop," a familiar voice said.

I brought my gaze off of the front of the washer, turned it in the direction of the voice.

Someone leaned against the seven-foot tall stack of boxes hidden by a long white sheet. It was Dave. His arms were crossed, his hair was a mess.

"Dave," I said. "You're—you're—"

"Yeah," Dave said. "I know I am. Tell me all about it."

"I'm so sorry, Dave."

Dave shrugged. "It's lonely here, Nate. Joyce is here. Betty is here—"

"Then why is it lonely?"

"Because they're not my family," Dave said, coldly.

"I don't understand."

Dave just smiled. "I want to see my family. My real family. And there's something I want Hannah to have. Can you get it to her, Nate? Can you do that for me?"

"Whatever you want, Dave."

Dave traced his palm over the tall tower he leaned against. "In what's left of my nightstand drawer is a box. Its contents aren't much, but, it's what I could afford. Head over to the house and find it for me. And when you do, give it to Hannah. She's hurting something fierce, and this will help her with that."

I nodded. "Of course, Dave. Of course."

He tugged at the white sheet masking the tower, but it wouldn't give. "There's not much we can do here, Nate. We're all blind, but you can see just fine. You have to see, Nate. You have to see for us. One of these days, you're going to have to tear this goddamn sheet off once and for all."

"I'm afraid to," I said. "I don't want to know what's underneath."

"You gotta suck it up, man. But first, get that box to Hannah for me, won't you?"

"As soon as I wake up, I will."

Dave smiled. "You're gonna put this all back together, buddy. I know you will. In the end, it's all gonna be all right."

"It won't be, Dave. Nothing's ever going to be all right again."

"You felt that way once before, didn't you?"

My stomach pained. In a moment, I was once again a nine-year-old boy who'd just been delivered the single worst piece of news in his entire life.

"You want to fight for those who can't fight?" Dave said. "Now's your chance. It's not over yet, buddy boy."

He was vanishing right before my eyes. His body turned translucent, fading into the darkened basement.

"I'm so, so sorry, Dave."

He raised his left hand, spread his fingers in the shape of a peace sign, and before he entirely disappeared said:

"It's all gravy, baby."

ψ

I could still hear David's voice when my eyes opened up, but the guest bedroom was empty. Rays of morning light poured through the slat between the long, mauve curtains.

I groaned, checked the time on my cell phone. Nine o'clock.

When I stood and went to leave the room, I found a short pile of clothes left on the opposite side of the bedroom door, blocking my way. Atop them was a note, written in Vega's curly handwriting.

Nate –

I had my father's assistant pick these up early this morning. They're not much, but they're better than nothing. I hope the sizes are right.

♥ Vega

I scooped the pile of clothes up from the hallway and shut the bedroom door. I spread them across the bed and inspected them. There was a simple white t-shirt, a pair of jeans, a pair of boxers, and some socks. Tucked underneath it all was a brand new pair of sneakers. Every bit of it was designer and name brand. *They're not much?*

I dressed myself, and somehow everything fit just right. I made my way back out of the bedroom and surveyed the first floor from the second floor hallway. Vega was sitting cross legged at the kitchen table, a pair of reading glasses rested low on her nose, picking at a bowl of grapes and reading something on her phone.

Down the spiral staircase I went, wondering with each step how I'd ago about asking to use her car.

My dead roommate needs me to sort through the wreckage of our former home. He asked me to do so, last night in a dream.

And what if she asked to come with? Surely she would, she'd be too polite to flat out refuse my request, but regardless, she wouldn't want to leave her very expensive machine alone in the hands of a grieving person.

When I entered the kitchen, Vega set her phone down and pushed her reading glasses up into her hair.

"Hey," she said, softly. "The clothes fit pretty well."

"They do," I said. "Thank you. You didn't have to."

"It was nothing," Vega said. "Don't mention it."

"Listen," I said. "I need to ask a favor from you. You've already done so much for me, but I still have to ask. Feel free to say no."

"Shoot."

"Can I borrow your car for a bit? Just for an hour or two."

Vega smiled. "No."

I didn't know what to say. I just stood there, blank faced, like a dope.

"Come here," she said. She stood from the table, wearing nothing but a tight fitting tank top and a pair of pajama bottoms that

227

left woefully little to the imagination. "I have to show you something."

She walked past the table, took me by the hand, and led me to the front of the house. Together we pushed the tall, oak door open and stepped outside.

Parked to the left of the slate fountain out front was Vega's Mercedes. It gleamed in the early morning light; it must have been freshly washed and waxed that morning.

To the right of the fountain was a Dodge Challenger, painted hellfire red, its windows tinted a shade of black that surely wasn't legal in the state of Vermont.

"I don't understand," I said.

Vega stuffed her right hand into a pocket on the side of her pajamas, pulled out a single key, then tossed it to me.

"It's yours to use. For a little while, anyways."

"I can't—I can't accept this," I said. "I just needed to borrow your car for a short while. I don't need one of my own."

"I don't want to sway your decision too much," Vega said, "about whether or not you want to stay in Burlington. But whether you decide to, or decide not to, you'll need your own transportation while you're here. The nearest bus stop is two miles from where we're standing, and they never run on time."

I stood still, slack-jawed and flabbergasted. "How did you pull this off?"

"I didn't," she said. "My father heard the news about your house. He wanted to help out."

"A new Challenger, huh? Courtesy of Mr. Rowland. I'll have to meet him sometime. To say thanks."

"You've stayed two nights under my roof now, Mr. Shaw," Vega said. "There's only so much I can get past my dad, even as an adult. Trust me, the two of you will be meeting soon."

I clicked a button on the key fob, and the Challenger screamed to life. Its engine chugged and rumbled.

"And that's the sound it makes idling," Vega said. "Imagine what it does when you actually press the gas pedal. *This* is a car you can refer to as 'The Beast.'"

I winced, thought of the last time I saw my Jeep, smoldering in the driveway in front of my house. "Thank you," I said, and I hugged her. "I'll take good care of it, until I have to give it back."

"Don't worry about that just yet," she said. "Just drive careful. I'll be here the rest of the day, so I'll see you when you're done. We can get lunch."

"See you then," I said, and I climbed into the plush interior of the Challenger. The dashboard went on forever in either direction. The seats felt soft enough to sleep on. With the slightest tap of the gas, the mighty car lurched forward, and I was on my way. The gate at the end of the driveway creaked open, and I was gone.

ψ

A lump formed deep down in my throat the moment I pulled up to 126 North.

Gone were the emergency vehicles and camera crews. All that remained were the miles of yellow caution tape strung up around the property, draped over the tree branches and bushes outside. A sign that read DO NOT ENTER had been nailed to whatever was left of the front door.

Someone had the decency of picking up Shadow's remains. My Jeep had been towed away, leaving only a charred black stain on the pavement where it was last parked.

I parked the Challenger on the side of North and stepped out, then walked to the front door. My legs felt like rubber, my shoes felt like they'd been filled with wet cement. It was hard not to remember how the house looked the first time I had visited it. Now, all that was left was a hollowed husk, burnt beyond recognition.

I gave the front door one firm push and it fell backwards into the living room, falling clean off the hinges. A cloud of ash and dirt kicked up around it, and I carefully set foot inside.

The inside of the house looked like the testing site for an atomic bomb. The kitchen, where the brunt of the explosion occurred, was gone. Just...gone. The wall that faced east had blown outward and away. Most of the refrigerator still stood, but the cabinets, stove, and countertop were missing.

I couldn't help but peek into my own bedroom as I sneaked toward Dave's. I half expected to see Kate Upton smiling back at me as I passed by, but of course there was nothing. Some of my bed frame stood, still bolted intact. Everything else had turned to ash. The mattress and the pillows, my computer, my closet, my books. It was all gone.

The hallway past the kitchen was hard to navigate. Pieces of the ceiling and roof had collapsed inward, making the hall cramped and hard to squeeze through. I pushed myself through, scraping past fallen two-by-fours and burnt debris.

Dave's room was as much of a mess as the rest of the house. His window was gone; his furniture was blown to smithereens. In the corner of the room was what looked like the remains of a nightstand.

I crouched down to open the drawer, but the wood and rails of the drawer had fused shut.

"Just...open," I grunted, and I pulled on the little golden handle of the drawer. It squeaked and groaned, then finally gave.

When the drawer extended, I found burnt bits of paper cropped up around a little box. I pulled the box from the drawer and examined it; its velvet exterior had charred, but there was no mistaking what it was or what it held.

I pried the box open and the hinge gave a soft, satisfying little click. Inside, tucked between two small cushions, was a silver ring. Fastened to the top of it was a tiny diamond, not worth much.

I clicked the box shut and tucked it into my jeans pocket, then felt something brush against my foot.

I looked down and saw Shadow, purring happily at my feet. She rubbed her face against my ankle, then squinted her green, glowing eyes.

"Shadow," I said, and I crouched down to pet her; but, the further I lowered myself, the more she disappeared. By the time I was close enough to reach out and touch her she had vanished entirely.

I crouched there, for a moment, then rubbed my eyes. Surely the house was unsafe to stand around in; hell, it felt like the damn thing might fall around me at any moment. So I stood back up and left, carefully maneuvering myself through the collapsed hall and out the empty doorway at the front of the house.

When I sat down in the Challenger, I gave the house a brief wave goodbye. It would be the last time I ever saw it—at least, like how it looked in that moment, anyhow—and I think a part of me was acutely aware of that fact.

ψ

Dave had only ever once mentioned where Hannah lived.

"The Opera House," he said, quite nonchalantly, during one of our morning breakfasts together.

"The Opera House?" I asked. "As in, a theater?"

"No, no," Dave said, while whisking eggs and turning bacon over. "I'm not sure where the name came from, but it's a small row of second floor apartments in the old downtown district. Just across the street from The Capitol."

I could hear Dave's words echoing in my mind as I steered the Challenger toward downtown. I thought of the last time I visited Church Street; there was the fair outside, the food and drink, the screening of The Exorcist. That had been such a fun day, such a good day, and—it stung me quick, like a mosquito bite—that had been only a mere four days ago. It might as well have been four years.

The Challenger pulled onto Church Street and I parked in an empty spot in front of the neighborhood drug store. I stepped out of the massive vehicle and onto the sidewalk and began my stroll. Shop windows passed me at first, then the restaurant Vega and I had dined at before the movie, then the front steps of The Capitol itself.

It was beneath The Capitol's grand marquee (which was proudly advertising a showing of The Shining later that night) that I first noticed the apartment building across the street. It was three stories tall and sandwiched between a record store and an old five-and-dime. A white sign with black, painted lettering read: The Opera House. On either side of the sign were the faces of comedy and tragedy.

I looked up Church Street, then down it, then up again—Vega wasn't nearby to save me from disaster, here—and when it was safe, I walked across.

232

An unlocked glass door allowed me into the front of The Opera House, and it didn't take long at all to find a call panel next to a row of mailboxes in the main hall. I traced over them until I found a button with a wrinkled piece of paper taped beneath it that read "H. Reilly."

I took a deep breath, tried to gather the right words to say, then thumbed at the button. A short while later, a speaker beside the mailboxes crackled to life.

"H-hello?" a soft, broken voice called out.

"Hey," I said. "Hannah. It's me, Nate."

"Nate," she said, and I could hear her sniffle. "I'm on the third floor. Apartment B. I'll buzz you in."

"Thanks," I said, but the speaker had already silenced. There was a short moment of nothing, and then a second door inside of the building buzzed as the lock clicked open. I stepped forward, allowing myself inside, and started the long hike to the third floor.

The Opera House was old and weathered, a fixture of historic downtown Burlington. Each step groaned and creaked beneath my weight. The wallpaper that lined the halls was a putrid shade of green, and great lengths of it were peeling off here and there. There was a musty smell to the building that carried from floor to floor.

I thought about Hannah and how she hoped to move in with Dave the next summer—after her lease was up—in the bungalow at 126 North. I thought of how that was all gone, as were Dave's lofty dreams to move the two of them to Florida one day.

I tried to push those thoughts out of my mind as I knocked on a red painted door with a "B" affixed to the center of it. She'd been waiting for me on the other side and the door squeaked open right away. Hannah was standing there in a wrinkled set of pajamas, her

233

hair pulled back in a frizzy ponytail, her face caked with makeup stains and tears.

I didn't know what to say. Neither of us did.

"Hannah," I said, but before another word could leave my mouth or hers, the two of us connected into a long and awful hug; her sobbing was so hard her entire body shuddered. I started to cry too, and the two of us stood there in the third floor hallway weeping and holding each other for what felt like hours.

"Come in," Hannah finally said, breaking away from the hug.

I nodded and slid between her and the doorframe. Her apartment was small; a single bedroom, but nicely furnished and organized. I thought of how sloppy Dave and I sometimes left our house, and what a good influence she'd have been on him if given the chance. They'd have made a happy home together.

I asked if I could take a seat on the ottoman facing her living room couch, and Hannah nodded. She took a seat on the sofa, and the two of us sat there for a while, just looking at the floor.

"The funeral is Friday," Hannah said, the words cracking as they left her lips. "We should...we should get in touch with Dominic Bloom's office. If Bloom was really David's father, then he should know—"

"I think that theory was wrong," I said. "I don't think Bloom is David's father."

"But we sat there on the living room floor that night," Hannah said. "With all of those police reports and...and...it all felt so probable."

"I was wrong," I said, and I shrugged.

Hannah shook her head. "How can you be so sure?"

"Because," I said, and I took a deep breath. "Dave told me so."

"Oh, Jesus, Nate," Hannah said, and she stood up abruptly. "Not this again. What, did you see him in a dream?"

I nodded.

"Sure you did." The lines on her forehead creased. "You really need to get that looked at, Nate, I mean it. You need to talk to someone. I don't know what foolishness you've been going on about for the last week, or why Dave was so patient with you when he entertained it, but—"

"He told me, Hannah," I said, dryly. "Trust me."

"Why should I?" Hannah said. "Dave didn't visit *me* last night, in *my* dreams. We've been together for half a year. You've been his roommate for hardly a month. Why you and not me, huh? Why?"

"I don't know why it's me," I said. "I'm not sure if I'll ever know. But I saw Dave last night, and we spoke to each other. Of that much, I am certain—"

"Bullshit." She crossed her arms and rolled her eyes.

I cleared my throat. "He wanted you to have this," I said. "Before it was lost in the demolition of the house. Last night, he showed me exactly where to find it. When I went to the house to get it, it was right where he said it'd be." I reached my hand deep down into my pants pocket and pulled out the charred, velvet box. I stuck out my hand, offering it to her, but Hannah stood there, arms crossed.

"What is it?" Hannah said.

I nodded. "Just take it, Hannah. It was important to him that it got to you."

Slowly, she uncrossed her arms. She reached out toward me, her hands trembling, and took the little box. She knew what was inside; I could tell by the wave of sadness rolling across her eyes. She held

235

each side of the box for a moment, then clicked it open, and let out an awful cry.

I stood up quickly from the ottoman to catch her; I worried she might faint. I sat her back down on the couch, and she clutched the velvet box to her chest and wept.

"I met him at a bar downtown," she said, quietly. "It was a Friday. Some friends and I wanted to have a girl's night. There was an old jukebox in the back of the bar, and Barracuda—you know, that old song by Heart? —was playing at full blast." She stopped crying for a moment and smiled. Actually smiled. "Dave was dancing on a bar top, shoes off, slipping and sliding in his socks. He was singing into a beer bottle like it was a microphone and jamming on an air guitar. He was adorable up there—so full of life and energy. I don't want to say that I knew right then he was the *one*, Nate. I wasn't sure of that until later in the evening. But at the very least, I knew he was special. I knew before the night was over, I'd be getting to know him."

"He loved you so much," I said. "You were the apple of his eye."

Hannah bit her lip and nodded. "Who's going to sing me Barracuda now, Nate?"

I sat beside her and patted her back. She leaned her head against my shoulder and sniffled. "He loved you, you know. He was so worried about renting his old bedroom out to a weirdo or a narc. You guys were two peas in a pod. He told me more than once how happy he was to have found you."

"I was happy to have found him, too."

Hannah crossed her legs, leaned deep into the couch cushion. "I never even thought to ask…where are you staying, Nate?"

"With Vega," I said, bluntly. "She's letting me use a guest room in her house."

"Oh," Hannah said, and her eyes narrowed.

I thought back to the first time they had met each other, just a few nights prior. There was that odd moment—fleeting, yes, but undeniable—where they seemed to recognize one another.

"Hannah," I said, "do you *know* Vega?"

Hannah shook her head. "We've never met."

"Friday night...there was this moment between you two. Like you knew each other."

"I don't—it's silly. I don't really want to get into it."

"Nothing is silly anymore," I said. "Please, tell me. I won't judge."

"As a part of my nursing program," Hannah said, "I've had to do six-week internships at various hospitals, hospices, and health facilities around Burlington."

"Okay," I said. "Did the two of you meet during a job assignment or something?"

"No," Hannah said, and she looked down at the floor like it was very far away. "The only internship assignment I ever had that truly bothered me was my brief stay at The Weber Retreat. What people twenty years ago would call an insane asylum."

"Oh," I said.

"There was this one patient there, a younger guy, and he seemed like the most sane of all the orderlies. That is, his behavior wasn't bizarre, I never feared for my safety around him. He just seemed like a genuine, carefree kid. He kind of reminded me of Dave, a little."

Hannah leaned up on the couch and cleared her throat.

"I wanted to know what was wrong with him," she continued, " so one day I introduced myself to him and struck up a conversation.

237

When our talk turned toward his illness, he swore he had none. I told him that everyone between the walls of Weber had an illness, otherwise they wouldn't be there. He said—and get this—that he wasn't crazy, that people only *thought* he was crazy, because his girlfriend had super powers."

I swallowed hard. "What kind of super powers?"

Hannah laughed. "He wasn't sure. He said that anytime she showed them to him, she could make him forget that he'd ever been shown. Isn't that a riot? So, quite quickly, I was starting to realize what his issues were. That even people who appear normal on the outside can have very deep, troubling issues rooted within them. His theory was that she could travel through time, but that he 'couldn't prove that for certain.'"

"I'm sorry, Hannah," I said. "But what does any of this have to do with Vega?"

"This kid," Hannah said, "was an art student at U of V. And one day, as part of his therapy, he was given free reign to paint the afternoon away. When he was finished, he came up to me with two canvases."

"And?"

"And," Hannah said, "on the first canvas was something that I still see in nightmares from time to time. He painted a woman with long, sinewy hair, a skeletal face, fangs for teeth, her skin pulled taught against her cheek bones."

"What about the second canvas?" I said.

"A polar-opposite," Hannah said. "A woman with perfect hair, beautiful features, curves and lines in all the right places. I wondered how, in a place as devoid of beauty as The Weber Retreat, he could pull something as talented as that out of thin air. It was a face I'd never seen before. That is, until the night that I met Vega."

"So a guy in an asylum painted a picture of someone who looked like Vega?"

"Not looked like," Hannah said, and she shook her head. "I wish I had it here to show you. It could have been a portrait of her. When I asked him whom the paintings were of, he shrugged and said his girlfriend. 'Both of them?' I asked. He nodded. Both were of the same person, he insisted, just how she looked at different times of the day."

"Did this guy have a name?" I asked. "For his girlfriend?"

"Nope," Hannah said. "He wished he could remember it. So much so, I almost believed him. But, he said she made him forget her name, too."

I sat up from Hannah's couch and felt a shiver pass through me.

"Probably just a coincidence," Hannah said. "But it's crazy, isn't it?"

ψ

My drive back to Vega's castle on the hill was quiet. I left the radio turned off, and the only sounds to keep me company were the chug of the Challenger's eight-cylinder engine and the whispers of the pavement passing beneath its two-ton frame.

My conversation with Hannah weighed heavily on my mind, and for so many reasons. I felt terrible for her, alone in her apartment, grieving over Dave. We'd made plans to meet again sometime that week, before the funeral, but I think deep down we both knew we probably wouldn't keep them.

When I pulled into Vega's driveway, enormous thunderheads were cropping up in the sky behind her castle. They brewed dark and heavy with rain, dancing back and forth as the storms within them drew closer to Burlington.

I parked the Challenger beside the slate fountain in front of the estate and made my way toward the front door. Even from a dozen feet back, I could see her silhouette through door's oval shaped pane of glass; it was Vega, standing in the foyer, waiting for me beneath her gaudy chandelier.

She opened the door for me as I approached and stood there, studying my face, a look of worry etched across her own.

"I visited Hannah," I said, and I raised my hands high in despair. "She's a mess. I'm a mess. We're all a mess."

Vega glided toward me, put her palms on my shoulders. "Oh, Nate. I'm sorry. I'm so sorry."

"It's not fair," I said, and I felt my lower lip tremble. "They were—they were soul mates. They should have had their entire lives ahead of them, but they were ripped from one another."

Vega rubbed my shoulder. Her hair was down, and beyond the curls that fell in front of her face, it looked as if she was lost somewhere, deep in thought.

Outside, a crack of thunder unleashed with such ferocity that the windows of her home shook.

"It's not fair," Vega said, "but I'm sure she's thankful for every second she spent with him. That's what she has to hold on to now. What she has to cherish. I only met them for one night, but it was clear they made the most of their time together."

"Have we made the most of our time together?" I said. I was feeling a lot in that instant. Of what, I'll never be certain. Whatever it was, it was daring me to seize the moment, to never have the kinds of regrets Hannah was surely experiencing that afternoon.

240

"I think you and I have had a great time together," Vega said, and a flash of lighting illuminated the foyer. The rumble of the subsequent thunder vibrated the floor beneath us, sending shivers through our feet. Outside, a great and terrible rain started to downpour. It was as if someone twisted open an invisible faucet high above Burlington.

I pulled her close to me, and our noses brushed against one another. She wrapped her arms behind my neck, and we swayed there for a moment, quiet beneath the sound of the pounding rain.

"I care about you," I said; but I don't know why I did. By then, she must have certainly known that. Still, after all that had transpired in the past two days, it felt good to remind her. To say it out loud.

Vega nodded. "You're special to me too, Nate."

With each passing second, I was caring less and less about *it* and how long I had saved onto *it*; in a cruel world where love could be torn away so quickly and without warning, what good did it do to waste another second holding out for something that may never come? Whether Vega and I spent the rest of our lives together after that rainy afternoon, or if we never saw each other ever again, I suddenly cared very little about holding onto *it* any more.

There was a pressure building between the two of us since that first afternoon at the mall, and just like the lighting outside would surely strike at trees and buildings that afternoon, it seemed inevitable for that pressure to release.

She squeezed my shoulder and we pulled ourselves together very close. Her breath was warm and tasted sweet as our mouths collided, and after just a short few moments of eager hands exploring there were breathy gasps and short gulps for air.

We tumbled from the foyer to the formal living room, where just a few nights prior she revealed herself to me for who she was—who she really was—even though that was something I understood very little then, and even less now. Entwined, we plummeted onto the sofa, each of us exercising a charming amount of patience as we removed the others clothes.

For the next thirty minutes, we lived out every lustful fantasy we'd had of the other over the past week. Some moments were a blurred slow motion, others were a fast and rhythmic haze, but the entire experience—start to finish—was something otherworldly. At one point, Vega bit her lip and let out a short and stuttered moan that might as well have caused my soul to leave my body.

When we were done, we sprawled out on the living room floor, chests heaving, lungs begging for air. For four or five minutes we lay there, fingers tangled, catching our breath and staring at the ceiling.

When finally we regained our bearings, we both began to giggle and smile, and embrace one another on the short-pile carpet.

"First timer, huh?" Vega asked, and she kissed me on the cheek.

"Honest," I said.

She smirked. "Could have fooled me."

To the beat of drizzling rain we stood and, wrapped in nothing but blankets from the living room, marched into the kitchen. We ate cold pizza from the fridge, barefoot on the tile floor, sipping Cokes and smiling at each other. We made fast and fleeting eye contact and told lurid jokes, until finally Vega wiped her mouth with a paper towel and asked four simple words: "Ready for round two?"

Hand in hand we climbed the spiral staircase, and when we reached the second floor hallway, we glided past the guest bedroom that had become my surrogate home for the past two days.

Once in her room, we tumbled atop the canopy bed that—though king sized—only took up a small fraction of the floor space in her sprawling boudoir. Rain beat against the window and again we slipped into that primordial dance; but, when we finished the second time, each of us were pushed to the point of exhaustion. There was no giggling or kitchen exploration, just brief pillow talk and heavy eyelids.

There is an odd tradition in modern times to equate the loss of one's virginity as a passage into adulthood. But the truth is—and no one tells you this—the time in your life that you choose to cross that threshold has tragically little bearing on whether or not you are an adult. I became more of an adult the day my father passed away than I did that warm, rainy afternoon in Burlington, as magical as the moment may have been.

We sat together, curled beneath piles of heavy comforters and blankets, listening to the gentle tip-taps of the rain outside.

Before she fell asleep, she pulled my face close one last time and gave me one of those long, dreamy kisses of hers.

"You did great, champ," she said, and she yawned and rested her head on my chest.

I grinned. "You weren't so bad yourself."

Though the sky outside was clearing and narrow rays of sun were working their way through the window, there was little that the two of us could do to fend off sleep. Beneath the cool blankets and canopy above the bed we held each other, before we drifted off into a deep and wonderful nap.

ψ

Not long after my eyes shut and I drifted to sleep, lulled by the drum like, gentle rhythm of Vega's breathing, did the nightmares return.

Again, I was back in Vega's basement, and again, Dave was waiting for me. He was sitting atop the washing machine, legs crossed, waiting for me as I tiptoed down the basement staircase.

"The formal living room, huh?" Dave asked, and he smirked. "Nothing quite as exciting as leaving your DNA all over a twenty-five hundred dollar couch, is there? You know, Hannah and I were fond of the kitchen counter. Remember when I told you that? You didn't eat in the kitchen for a week."

I wiped my eyes, and Dave hopped off of the washing machine.

"I want to thank you for delivering that ring to Hannah," Dave said. "But, Nate, you really blew it this time."

"Dave," I said. "What are you talking about?"

"You gave her exactly what she wanted. Vega *always* gets what she wants."

"What do you know about Vega?" I asked.

"It's not important what I know about her," Dave said. "What do *you* know about her? I'm blind, but you can see just fine."

"Dave," I said. "I don't have it in me anymore. The riddles. The mystery. I just want my life to go back to normal."

"Oh," Dave said, and he laughed. "That's not happening any time soon, buddy-boy. The dead can't speak in truths, because it no longer means a thing to them. Lies, truths, they all stop mattering the second we're lowered beneath the ground. But for you? Nate, Nate, Nate. You've been sleepwalking since you set foot in Burlington. And—my guy—it is time to wake the fuck up."

I opened my mouth slowly. "What do you want from me?"

Dave grabbed the white sheet attached to the tall tower in the basement and yanked it hard. Before I could see what was underneath he threw it at me, shrouding me in darkness.

I stumbled backward through a sea of shadows. I tripped over myself, limbs flailing, before finding myself in a poorly lit room. In the center of the room was a long hospital gurney with stainless steel railings.

Crowded around the gurney were men wearing surgical scrubs and facemasks. They held scalpels and metal instruments with hands wrapped in latex gloves. A single lamp above the gurney creaked as it swung back and forth. The bulb cast long, sinister shadows across the room.

The men were murmuring to one another, and behind them machines hissed and beeped.

I slid between the doctors and nurses unnoticed, until I myself was standing before the gurney. Laid atop it was the body of a woman, disrobed.

Joyce Nicholson.

Her head, from the top lip up, was missing and dashed to pieces. Her body was bruised and still, and her stomach—swollen by the infant inside of it—protruded outwards.

"We're losing time," one of the doctors barked from behind a mint-green colored mask. He pressed a scalpel into Joyce's flesh, a few inches up from her belly button. Warily, he dragged the instrument slow and steady down her stomach. In an instant, he had carved a careful, perfectly straight trail. Doctors waiting on either side of her abdomen pulled and tugged. The narrow gash separated and the doctor yelling orders reached down deep, pushing his hands past flesh and organs.

"Have the nursery on standby," the masked surgeon hollered. "There are signs of life."

He twisted his arms further into Joyce's abdomen, wrapped his hands firmly around something, and pulled.

245

Covered in blood and placenta, a tiny infant emerged. The doctor held it up high beneath the single spinning light in the room. He gave the child a firm smack on the back, and immediately it started to scream and cry.

Before a nearby nurse whisked the newborn away, I had a clear view of it, squirming and fidgeting above its mother's lifeless body.

No, there was absolutely no mistaking it.

It was a baby girl.

I awoke with a gasp. Outside Vega's bedroom window, the sun was hanging low, painting the room with the colors of evening. Vega slept soundly, her head still on my chest, her right arm draped across my waist.

Carefully, I snuck out of bed. Vega mumbled something in her sleep. I feared she might wake up, but instead she grabbed at a blanket and tossed onto her side.

I tiptoed out of the bedroom and across the second floor hallway, down the spiral staircase, and through the formal living room. When I found the door to the basement, I opened it and carefully descended the stairs.

That damn tower stood in the rear of the basement, right where it always had. Vega had told me that hidden beneath the white sheet were moving boxes, and that they were nothing I should concern myself with.

But, Vega was great at being dishonest, wasn't she?

I walked towards it, and from somewhere far away I heard that angelic chanting once again. It whispered and cried as I reached for the sheet. I clenched both palms on either side of the tower and gave one, quick tug; all at once the chanting ceased, and the room went very still and quiet.

A cloud of dust stung at my nostrils and eyes as the sheet fell to the floor. Standing in Vega's basement was some tall, black monolith. It looked maybe like an old arcade machine; yet oddly enough, it was missing a screen. The buttons on it were worn and crooked, and there wasn't a single identifying mark on the thing, except for at the top. Spray painted in white lettering was one single word:

PHANTASOS

In an instant, my suspicions from my most recent nightmare were proven true. I pivoted on one foot to turn and head back upstairs. Standing at the basement landing, shrouded in darkness, was a figure blocking the way.

"You know, Nate," Vega said, and she tugged on the belt of her bathrobe. "You really shouldn't be playing with that. It's dangerous."

ψ

Vega inched closer toward me. "Most of them were destroyed back in the nineties. They kept tipping over on kids in arcades. Top heavy sons of bitches. Only a few survived."

"Why do you have it down here—"

"I can explain, Nate," she said. "If you want to listen."

"How will I know you're not lying?"

She frowned. "You'll just have to trust me."

I stood there, slack jawed, hands on hips. I no longer knew what to believe and what not to believe. My gut told me to leave—no, to run—and as fast I could. I could call a cab and be at the Burlington Greyhound terminal within the hour. I could ride a bus through the night, all the way back home to Albany. As for withdrawing from my first semester at Marshall, maybe I could handle those affairs from home. Maybe I could borrow my mom's car, or James' car, or, or—

Run? The thoughts of running subsided. She looked beautiful, there, painted by the light bulb in the basement stairway.

Who was she?

What was she?

Vega's intrigue was as alluring as the little grin she shot me from the bottom of the stairs.

"Go ahead," I said. "Explain. I'll listen."

"I've studied in Vermont, in California, in Washington…east coast, west coast…there's so many differences between those places, Nate. Topographical differences, political differences, social differences. The weather, the seasons. But do you know what stays the same, no matter where I go?"

"What?"

"My name, Nate. Vega Bloom. Vega Goddamn Bloom. My father casts a very large shadow everywhere I go. He's a negotiator, Nate. He gives people what they want, and he gets what he wants. People owe him favors, constantly."

I paused to consider Greg, the tow truck driver, and Patrick, our waiter at The Rail Yard. I remembered all the looks and stares thrown our way while strolling Church Street.

I sighed. "So, you use aliases?"

"All the time, Nate; more often than I'd like to. Vega Rowland…she's entirely made-up. Fiction, pure and simple. But Vega Bloom? You're looking at her, champ."

I held my hands up in frustration. The basement was dark and cold, but Vega blocked the way upstairs. I had the feeling neither of us were moving until this was settled, once and for all.

"I was new here, Vega," I said. "I didn't know who Dominic Bloom was. I wouldn't have had the slightest clue."

"I know," Vega said, and she smiled. "When we locked eyes through the window at the Happy Body, I could tell. You looked at me with pure adoration, and it had nothing to do with who my father was. That's rare for me. I figured you were worth a shot."

I rubbed my eyes. My forehead ached from the weight of thoughts pushing up against it.

"Do you know who your mother is?" I asked, bluntly.

Vega shook her head. "Her name is Melanie," she said, sheepishly. "She lives in California. I don't get to see her much. Why are you asking me that?"

"What happened between you two?" I asked. "And more importantly, what happened between her and your father?"

"She left when I was very little," she said. "I was too young to understand the logistics of it. My father had become quite successful in a short amount of time. There was something about a prenuptial agreement gone wrong, there was a very nasty divorce and—"

"She's not your mother," I blurted. "Whoever Dominic Bloom told you is your mom, it's been a lie."

Her eyebrows slanted and she looked angry. "*What* are you going on about *now?*"

My head was swimming. She had no idea, not the slightest. And how would I convince her of the truth? Because a dream told me so?

I let out a long, exasperated sigh, and it hit me all at once. Meeting Vega, the nightmares, the terror and the chaos. Every step of the way, I wondered why such awful things were happening to *me*, wondered what fate was trying to teach me with its all too typically cruel and horrid methods.

But it wasn't about me. No, it never was. Not even for a second.

249

It was about Vega. It was all about Vega.

And, it was about telling her the truth, no matter how difficult that might be.

"Joyce Nicholson was your mother," I said, and I could feel the corners of my eyes start to tingle. "She was your mom, Vega. Christ, the two of you even look alike."

"You're wrong, Nate. Dead wrong."

"It's true. The dreams, the nightmares, all of it has been pushing me toward this moment. So I could tell you. Because…you deserve to know."

She crossed her arms and glided across the basement toward me. "That's a horrible accusation to make, Nathaniel Shaw. No matter what your dreams told you. No matter what awful little prophecies you think you've had."

"It's true," I repeated. "Joyce couldn't rest until you knew. And now you do."

Vega stood there, silent and pensive. "My father," she said, patiently and carefully choosing her words, "is one of the best men I know. If what you're saying is true, then he was responsible for Joyce's death. Hell, that would make him the one behind Betty Nicholson's death and McManus's suicide, too. And while whether or not Joyce Nicholson is my mother might be entertaining for debate on its own, I cannot accept that my father would do such heinous things. It's an impossibility."

I took a moment to recall all of the articles I had read about Dominic Bloom while researching him. By and large he was a well-liked man, very much respected in Burlington and in the cities he set up shop in. But there was more to it, wasn't there? The message boards with the miles of text, the forum posts with their sinister

250

accusations; at the time, it was easy to dismiss such things as the cries of lonely conspiracy theorists.

Some went so far as to call him the Devil, ole Beelzebub himself. That was easy to laugh at, at the time. But I'd discovered so much more about Vega since then, hadn't I? Her strangeness. Her powers. Who better to have such otherworldly abilities, framed in the vessel of a beautiful young woman, than a person born to a mortal and…and…well, something *else*?

And who had assigned my research paper on Dominic Bloom in the first place? McManus the Anus. He knew. He *knew*. From far across the auditorium, behind his lectern, he knew Vega and I had become quite friendly with one another, the same way he knew the names of all his students, the same way he knew that Vega Bloom was merely using a tired alias to attend his class. He knew, and he assigned me a paper on Dominic Bloom because he trusted me to put those pieces together.

"I don't know anything about your father," I said. "I've never met him. I try not to judge people before I meet them. I try not to let rumors and gossip affect my opinion of them. It's a futile effort, I know. But I do try." I put my hands on her shoulders and rubbed gently. It wasn't much, but it was an olive branch; it was enough to get her to uncross her arms. "I do know *you,* Vega. I know that no matter who Dominic Bloom is or Joyce Nicholson was, you are a good person, and you are your own person, independent of them."

Vega started to cry. Her eyes welled and little tears slipped down her face. "You don't know me, Nate. You don't know that I'm a good person."

"What are you talking about?"

She removed my hands from her shoulders and took a step back. "I could tell two things about you that day at the mall. Just from how

251

you looked at me. The first was that you didn't recognize me, and the second was that...that you were a virgin."

I couldn't help but laugh at first. "Yeah, that was probably painfully obvious to a lot of people."

She shook her head. "You don't understand, Nate. I learned early in my teenage years that a virgin—a willing virgin—could, well....sustain me."

"Sustain you?"

She nodded. "That night on your front lawn, when you found me collapsed on the ground...it'd been months since I...well...you know?"

I felt my fingertips tingle and the pit of my stomach turn sour. "So what?" I said. "This has all been what? A trap to lure me in?"

"Not a trap, Nate. Not a trap. There was so much more to you than that. I knew you were special. From the beginning I knew. And that night in front of your house, when I saved you from the truck on North—"

When you *saved* me? I thought.

"—You remembered afterward, Nate. You remembered. No one has been able to do that. No one has been able to see me for who I really was and...remember. You were the first, Nate. The first."

"It's so easy for you to switch between lying and telling the truth, isn't it?"

She cried even harder.

I walked past her and up the basement stairs. When I was about halfway up them, I stopped and turned around. I looked at the Phantasos machine tucked away in the corner. I looked at Vega, her face buried in her palms, standing there in the dark.

"I'm driving myself to the bus station on the other side of town," I said, affirmatively. "I'll leave the car in the parking lot and I'll mail you the key when I get back to Albany."

"Please," Vega said. "Don't go."

I took one last look down the stairs, not realizing it would be the last time I'd ever lay eyes on that basement.

For whatever reason, destiny had chosen me to guide Joyce Nicholson's spirit toward peace. My short time in Burlington had a purpose—not to become some wonderful law school student, but to lay the dead to rest—and that purpose had been fulfilled. I didn't even bother to say goodbye. I headed up the stairs, then out the front of the house, and climbed into the Challenger parked out front.

I sat behind the steering wheel for a moment, watching the sun sink low across the valley. If Dominic Bloom was the man I thought he was, then I had tiptoed through a very dangerous game. A game wherein knowing the truth is a death sentence. And, despite how much it hurt and pained me to leave her there, crying by her lonesome in the basement, the time for games had ended.

It was time to go home.

ψ

I blew down Anchorage in the Challenger, past the posted speed limit sign for thirty miles per hour. I was doing forty, then fifty, then sixty. The steel body frame of the giant car didn't shudder or shake; no, it handled the acceleration like the marvel of engineering it was.

The sky was turning its nightly shade of cotton candy; hazy blues and purples clung above the tree line. Despite the early afternoon rains, there wasn't a single cloud in the sky.

I wondered if I might find the bus station on my own, or if I should slip my phone from my pocket and check for directions. I was reaching for it, patting the pocket on the front of my jeans to make sure it was there, when I felt the car suddenly decelerate.

My attention snapped upward and I focused on the dashboard of the car and the road ahead. The interior lights had dimmed, but returned with full brightness after a brief stutter.

It's a brand new car, I thought to myself, and I smacked the steering wheel with the palm of my hand.

Down Anchorage I glided, until the intersection with North appeared ahead of me. Just beyond North, running parallel to the road, was the shore of Lake Champlain. It looked beautiful, dusted with glitter, shimmering beneath the evening sun.

I thought of Vega. I thought of our dinner together at The Rail Yard.

Despite all the horror and tragedy that my time there had brought, a part of me, deep down, would miss Burlington. It always would. For one brief, shining moment, there had been an opportunity for a fresh start.

Now, all of that had been taken away.

I accelerated, and the Challenger lurched ahead. When I removed my foot from the accelerator, the motor of the car made a troubled sound. It was something like a rattling, and when the rattling ceased, the motor trembled.

"It's brand new!" I said out loud, to no one in particular.

As if responding to me, the Challenger hiccupped again.

"Just get me to the bus depot," I whispered, and the ride smoothed out once more. The engine galloped and the car sped onward.

Beside me, pine and elm trees passed by in a blur. The curving road straightened, and I could see that North was fast approaching. I figured I'd take one last drive by 126 before I left—who knew when, if ever, I'd return to Burlington, and I wanted to see the old house one last time. Or what was left of it, anyhow.

A stop sign up ahead warned me to slow before turning off of Anchorage, and so I slipped my foot from the accelerator to the brake. I pressed my toes against the brake pedal, and the car refused to slow. I applied more pressure and pressed harder, but the brake pedal sank to the floor, a hot knife through butter.

My pulse and breathing quickened and panic started to sink in. The Challenger was cruising downhill at close to sixty miles per hour, and I had no way of stopping it.

I felt something rattle beneath the hood of the car, and then emerge from the seam between the windshield and the hood. It was small and black, and at first I thought it might be the world's oddest colored squirrel. It climbed upward from the engine, then clutched onto the passenger side windshield wiper. It blinked its eyes at me—beady, black, endless eyes—and bared its teeth. They were long and crooked, and between them were bits of wire and metal, wedged deep down like a bit of spinach.

"What...the fuck?" I asked myself, and for a moment I forgot that the brakes on the car were failing, that I was coasting toward a busy intersection at fifteen miles beyond the posted speed limit.

The creature snarled before letting out a sinister little screech. A pair of wings, not unlike those of a bat, extended from its back. It beat them once, then twice, then took off into the night sky in a hurry.

I tried to follow it with my eyes, tried to watch it fly off into the tree line, but it had vanished too quickly.

As if awoken from a trance, I panicked once again, desperate to find a way to stop the car. I wrapped my right hand around the emergency brake, depressed the button at the end of it, and yanked upward. There was no resistance at all; the emergency brake pulled back with hardly any effort. The car didn't brake or slow. There was a sudden, awful stench of burning rubber, but it continued on its trajectory toward the intersection ahead.

My mind raced for a moment, but then it calmed. I thought of Dave, of Joyce, of Betty. Hell, even McManus the Anus. I'd be seeing them all shortly, I guessed, at whatever juncture waited beyond that mortal threshold.

I closed my eyes and took a deep breath, accepting that there was nothing I could do. When I opened them, the sun had almost entirely set, and the once shimmering Lake Champlain was now a widened, darkened pit. If another car didn't collide into me first, I'd drive straight over the shoreline and into the water.

Another deep breath, and I felt something heavy land on top of the Challenger. The frame of the car shook side to side. Four long claws pierced the roof of the vehicle, extending into the empty space above the passenger seat. They sawed through the metal, then peeled it back, a tin can. Something dropped into the seat, something sinewy, and winged, and fanged. It had glowing eyes, the color of crimson. It smelled rotten; like sulfur, like expired eggs.

I closed my eyes again, tried to ignore it. Whatever fate waited for me at the end of the road was far worse than whatever *it* was.

"Nate," a soft, peaceful voice said. "I'm sorry that you were ever dragged into this."

I opened my eyes. Sitting in the passenger seat was Vega. Her chest heaved fast, her eyes were wide and saddened.

"What *are* you?" I asked.

She shook her head. "If I could change everything, I would, Nate. If I could fix it. If I could put the pieces back together again."

My eyes moistened and the Challenger continued its careen toward the street below.

"I hate you," I said, and the words pained me as they left my mouth. I wasn't even sure that I meant them, but I *did* want to hurt her, and so I said them anyway. "I wish that I never met you."

Vega nodded. "I wish I could have shown you all the good we could have had," she said. "I'm sorry about Dave, I'm sorry about Betty. I'm sorry about your house."

The Challenger skipped across North. Miraculously, there was no oncoming traffic in either direction. I thought for sure I'd be t-boned as soon as I entered the intersection, but I was spared. The Challenger rocketed between a pair of elm trees on the shore of Lake Champlain.

"Nate," Vega said, and she placed her left palm on my right knee. "Remember me."

The two-ton car bottomed out as it hit a patch of sand, then fishtailed as it collided into the water.

Though the lake was only five or six feet deep there, it was high enough to submerge the car. We floated there for a moment, on the surface, and then a geyser of water burst through the air vents on the front of the car. Cold water flooded around my feet, and the car began to sink.

I unbuckled my seatbelt and looked at Vega. Gallons of water were pouring in over her, entering the vehicle from the torn apart hole in the roof above her head. She was calm and still, and her palm stayed attached to my knee with an iron grip.

"We have to get out of here, Vega," I said. "Wake up. Wake up!"

She couldn't hear me; or, if she could, she was ignoring me.

I jammed my hand into the door handle beside me and pulled it, but the door refused to budge. The water outside the car was pushing it shut.

"Vega," I said, and I shook her by the shoulders. "Vega we need to get moving."

The cabin of the car was filled up to our waists, now. The water was relentless as it gushed in.

I looked at the hole on the top of the roof. It was maybe wide enough for me to fit through. If I could pull myself out, I could pull Vega out behind me.

The water continued to find its way in, mercilessly. Before I had a moment to consider my plan, it had risen to my shoulders. Vega's lips bobbed across the surface. Her eyes stayed closed. She looked just like a porcelain doll.

I started to pound my hands against the window to my left, started to scream and shout and beg for help. Surely, someone must have seen the car run off the road and into the water. Someone would see us. Someone would call for help.

Vega's face was entirely submerged. I sat up in my seat, gulping for air. Cold freshwater lapped at my nostrils, and then rose even higher. I panicked, inhaled, and a pint of water rushed into my lungs.

I started to cough and wheeze, and it became more and more difficult to pound at the windows and cry out.

The water was dark. The sky outside was dark.

Everything was dark.

I thought: *this is it, this is the end.* I thought of the police finding my body, bloated with lake water and pecked at by trout. I thought of my mother, crying at a closed-casket funeral.

I closed my eyes and slipped beneath the surface, waiting for the inevitable, waiting for the worst.

I felt a sudden and unexpected warmness, could see something glowing in the darkened depths, and then there was nothing.

"Mister," a voice called out. "Mister...why are you wearing all your clothes?"

I could feel sunlight on my face, but I dared not open my eyes.

"Are you okay?" the voice asked again. It was coming from a boy. Young. Maybe eight or nine.

"Mommy," the boy cried out. "Mommy, come quick."

I was floating on my back. I kicked out my legs and tried to stand. The water was shallow, maybe three or four feet deep.

"How did you get here?" the boy asked.

I stood and opened my eyes. Judging by the sun's position over Lake Champlain, it was early morning, and a hot morning at that. The sun's rays burned as they landed on my face.

A stout woman in her forties waded through the water toward me. "Sir," she said, apprehensively. "Sir? Are you all right?"

I rubbed my eyes and spun in a circle. Not far from me, back on shore, a crowd of onlookers had started to gather.

"There's a car," I mumbled. "There's a car...out here...under the water."

"A...car?" the mother asked.

"Yes," I stuttered. "You have to help me find it. She's trapped inside."

A look of confusion crossed the mother's face. "*Who's* trapped inside?" she asked.

"Veronica," I yelled. "Veronica is in there!"

The woman took a step back and grabbed her child by the hand. Up on North, I could see approaching lights and sirens.

"Veronica," I mumbled, and I splashed at the water. A fish went darting by, then swam between my legs. No, her name wasn't Veronica. "Vanessa," I hollered. Va. Vuh. Veh. Vuh, veh, vuh—

"Vega," I screamed, and I dove beneath the surface. My eyes were opened wide, but there wasn't a trace of her or of the Challenger.

When I surfaced, a lifeguard was walking toward me. His hair was bleached blonde, his face was freckled, he had more muscles than I knew the male anatomy was capable of.

"Come on," the lifeguard said, and he placed a mighty palm on my shoulder. "Let's get you out of here."

"Not without *her*," I shouted, and I swatted his hand away. "Why aren't you listening?" I said. "There's someone else out here—there's someone *in the water*—and she needs help, too!"

The lifeguard nodded, then scanned the surface of the water. It was still, save for the few families who waded in the shallow depths together.

"We'll start a search as soon as possible," the lifeguard said. "But for now, you have to come with me. Are you feeling ill?"

"I'm not leaving this goddamn lake," I said, "without her. Do you understand?"

The crowd on the shore had doubled in size, and parked beside the police cruiser was an ambulance, its rear double-doors opened wide. A pair of paramedics marched over the sand and into the water.

"Please," I begged. "Please help me."

"We're going to help you," the lifeguard said, nodding. Humoring me. Placating me.

The paramedics approached me, stood on either side of me.

"Let's help you back to shore," one of them said, and I swatted at him too as he tried to guide me by the waist.

"Don't make this combative," the other paramedic said. "We just want to help. Don't make this worse."

"I'm not leaving here," I said. "You'll have to drag me out."

I closed my eyes and tried to picture her. She was short, and blonde, and just a bit overweight. She always wore that same ratty hooded sweater. She was funny, too, wasn't she? God, how she made me laugh.

No—no, that wasn't right. She was blonde, but she was a bit taller than I could remember. She could have worn contacts, but she always wore those Buddy Holly reading glasses, the kind with the boxy frames. She was thin—so thin. I used to ask her all the time if she was eating enough, and she'd get mad at that. Not *really* mad, playfully mad.

No! That was wrong, too. We never talked about her weight or my weight. No...what was it we talked about? Who knows, but the laughing, that was for certain. She could make me laugh—she could really get me going. Once in a while, I could make her laugh, too.

She had a beautiful laugh.

There were the Wayfarers, her favorite pair of sunglasses, always resting on the bridge of her nose. Her big floppy hat. Her red hair.

Yeah, that was her.

Remember me.

Vega.

Remember you?

How could I ever forget you?

Vega. Vega, Vega, Vega.

I felt the tip of a thin needle press into the side of my arm. Immediately, I felt woozy, and I started to collapse backward into the water. Before I could fall, the paramedics grabbed me.

My legs turned to rubber and I felt silly and goofy.

My last thoughts of that morning were being guided across the sand and toward the back of the ambulance; its doors opened wide, waiting for me.

They'd always been waiting for me.

ψ

The hospital bed I woke up in was quite comfortable. The sheets were starched and pulled tight over me. The mattress was firm, but not too firm.

My first instinct was to lean up and stand, but my head felt like it was stuffed with tissue paper. When I moved, I felt a slight sting from my inner elbow, where an IV had been inserted.

I groaned and patted at the bed. I found a buzzer and pressed the button, waited patiently for someone to respond.

In the silence, I sat and surveyed the room. The walls were painted mint-green and eggshell white. A window on the other side of the room faced an endless expanse of trees and wilderness.

A short while later a nurse entered the room. She wore teal scrubs and kept her grey hair pulled back in a tight bun.

"Mr. Shaw," the nurse said. "You've returned to the land of the living."

"How long was I out?" I asked. My throat was scratchy and my voice crackled.

"You've been dozing in and out for a couple of days now. Do you remember meeting me?"

"No."

"I suppose you wouldn't. My name is Liz Schroeder, and I've been taking care of you since you've joined us."

262

"Nurse Schroeder," I said. Had we met before? I wasn't sure. The past few days had been a blur. She looked familiar enough.

"Now," she said, and she clapped her hands. "What seems to be the problem?"

"There's no problem," I said, and I glanced at the tube sticking out of my arm. "I just...want to go home."

"Oh, Nathaniel," Nurse Schroeder said. "You can't leave. Not until we've cleared you. We've been over this."

"Where am I?"

She let out a short, impatient sigh. She must have told me a dozen times before. "The Weber Retreat, Mr. Shaw. On the southern end of Burlington, Vermont."

"The Weber Retreat. Sure."

"You've been showing signs of improvement, that's for certain. Your mother arrived in town yesterday morning. As soon as the doctor says you can have visitors, you two will be allowed to see each other."

"My mom is here?"

She nodded.

"I want to see her," I said. "Right away."

"Tomorrow morning at the earliest, Mr. Shaw," she said, and she tapped the tip of her nose. "Remember—let's be on our best behavior."

I kicked my feet out, but felt that they were strapped to the end of the bed. "I need to get up. I need to stretch." I'd never considered myself a claustrophobe, but my current arrangements were testing me.

"It's three forty-five in the afternoon," Nurse Schroeder said.

"So? What does that have to do with anything?"

She smiled. "You know the rules. We've been over them. Three PM 'til six PM is reflection time. At six, you'll have dinner. After dinner, maybe I can escort you to the rec room for a while. Burn off some steam."

I shook my head. "You can't leave me here all afternoon," I said, "strapped to this bed with nothing to do." I thought of Vega. It was getting harder and harder to remember her, to remember all that had happened. "Bring me a pen," I begged. "And some paper."

"A pen would be prohibited," she said.

"Then anything!" I caught myself yelling. "Then anything," I repeated, this time in a whisper. "Please. Before I forget. I need to write it all down."

"I'll see what I can do," she replied, and she stepped out of the room.

I sat there, eyes fixed on the mint-green walls, an impossible to reach itch gnawing at my left ankle. It was miserable being there. I found myself wishing for more sedatives, jealous of the person I was the day before, numbed and uncaring about my current predicament.

A short while later, Nurse Schroeder returned to the room. In her hands, she carried a small wicker basket. "I checked with the doctor and he said these were fine," she said.

I took the basket from her and inspected what was inside.

"Construction paper? Crayons?"

"Baby steps, Mr. Shaw. Baby steps."

"You have to be kidding me."

Nurse Schroeder rolled her eyes. "I could take them back, let you lie here all afternoon with just the view of the window to entertain you."

"They'll do," I said.

She patted the foot of my bed. "I'll see you again come supper time."

"Sure," I said, only half paying attention to her. I was already busy pressing the waxy tip of a black crayon into a piece of yellow construction paper.

I wanted to get my story down. Every single unbelievable moment of it. I didn't want to forget a thing.

I dragged the crayon across the paper and began:

"I had a normal life, once."

ψ

From my hospital bed, deep inside The Weber Retreat, I could see that evening was approaching. The elms and firs, with their long, gnarled branches, darkened as the afternoon hours passed.

My stomach grumbled. It'd been hours since I was allotted a dry bologna sandwich, a half pint of two-percent milk, and a cup of slimy green gelatin. I hungered for dinner, even though I wasn't sure it'd fare much better than my lunch. Earlier in the day, a couple of patients passing by the hall outside my door had quipped that it was meatloaf night, then made a gagging sound and laughed.

Scattered around my bed were piles of construction paper filled edge-to-edge with the thick lettering from my crayons. I talked about Dave, about my cat, Shadow, and about McManus the Anus. I spoke at length about Joyce Nicholson and her daughter, Vega, and about what really happened to the two of them twenty-four years prior.

When my hand had started to cramp, I examined the sheets of paper stacked around my bed in messy piles, and was visited by an awful thought: Had I gone insane?

265

I thought of my mother, worriedly waiting to visit me at some hotel in Burlington, and how the two of us would only get to see each other upon a doctor's permission. Then, I glanced around at all my work. There were rough sketches of Vega, of how I remember her looking, there were dozens of pages of scribbles detailing demons that eat the wiring out of engine blocks and girls who could time travel on a whim.

Carefully, I shuffled the papers into a single neat stack, then stuffed them into the drawer of the bedside table beside my gurney.

When the last paper had been tucked away, there was a knock at my half-opened door. Before I could answer, Nurse Schroeder let herself in.

"Dinner?" I asked.

She folded her hands in front of her apron. "You have a visitor."

I leaned up on my gurney—as far as I could, anyhow—in anticipation.

A tall gentleman stepped between the nurse and the open door, removing the beige, wide-brimmed hat that sat atop his head as he did so.

"I'll leave you two alone," the nurse said.

"Deputy Dixon," I said. "I was expecting someone else."

Dixon looked at me long and hard, then glanced down at his badge and flicked it with his finger. "Hell of an eye you got," he said, "if you can read my name from across the room."

I didn't know what that meant at the time, but it'd all become clear to me soon.

"What can I do for you?" I asked.

"Listen, son," Dixon said, in that booming, gravelly voice of his. "I just need help putting a few things together."

"Like what?"

"I've had a team of Vermont's best forensic divers, searchers, and rescuers, dragging Lake Champlain for nearly two days now. All because of what you told the men who dragged you out of the water."

"And?"

"No cars, no bodies, no nothing. If there were, we would have found them."

"Oh," I said, and I slumped down on the gurney.

"But, uh, well, I just wanted to let you know," he said with an uncharacteristic stutter, "that we won't be pressing charges."

I couldn't help but laugh. "I didn't realize that was a possibility to begin with."

"Lying to the police? Yeah, that's some serious business," Dixon said. "Wasted a lot of time, resources, and manpower dragging that lake because of what you were prattling on about. But, judging by your current living arrangement..." He placed a palm on the mint-green wall. "It wouldn't seem right to arrest you. I don't know what happened to you the other morning, but whatever it was, you seemed damn well sure that someone else was in that lake with you. Can't fault you for that."

I nodded. I didn't know what to say or how to respond. "You think I'm crazy, don't you?"

"I think you need help," Dixon said. "And you're in the right place to get some. Ain't nothing wrong with needing a little bit of help."

I rubbed my eyes and my stomach growled.

"The nurse who let me in will be back any minute with your supper, but before she gets back, help me to understand something, would you? Been bothering me for two days now."

"Sure," I said.

"Little boy that found you in the water—fully dressed—an eight year old named Alley Bauer. On vacation with his mom and dad. Says he never saw you wade into the lake. Hell, no one did. You just appeared there. Poof. Says he saw some bubbles floatin' up from under the surface, and when he looked down, there you were. How'd you walk into the lake, son? How'd you manage that without anyone seeing you?"

"I wish I knew," I said. "More than you'd believe, I wish I knew."

ψ

That night, I ate a lump of supposed meatloaf with a side of cold, instant potatoes. It was salty, tasted awful, but it felt nourishing after hours of not eating.

Not long after dinner, around the time Nurse Schroeder said that she'd take me down to the rec room, a doctor visited my room. Very matter of factly, he asked me a series of questions from a slip of paper attached to his clipboard. After I answered each question, he'd check a box, occasionally stopping to nod or offer an "mhm." Within two minutes, his questions had ceased. He smiled, nodded, and said that I'd be released on my own recognizance the next morning.

I'd later learn that patients who experienced whatever it was I experienced would be held for a week or two at least before being released, and that my early dismissal from The Weber Retreat would be more suspicious, had it not been for the fact that the doctor who released me was a good friend of Dominic Bloom.

I slept on my gurney that night unrestrained, and at approximately seven o'clock the next morning, after a long and dreamless rest, my mother darkened the door of my room at Weber.

I'm not ashamed to admit that I cried when we hugged—she did too—and after a brief and awkward conversation, she helped me up and out of the bed and escorted me through the labyrinth-like halls of the institution.

That morning, the two of us went out for breakfast at a Denny's in western Burlington. I ordered a stack of pancakes a mile high with an extra order of bacon. She had a coffee and two eggs, sunny side up. Nothing else. Her face was etched with worry. She looked at me like I was no longer her son, but some alien who had assumed his identity.

"I don't know what to say," she said. "You could have talked to me if you needed help."

"Help?" I said. "Everyone thinks I was trying to drown myself. I wasn't."

"People who don't need help," she said, "don't walk into a lake fully clothed."

"Mom," I replied. "If I explained what happened for the next six hours, it still wouldn't make sense."

"What were you doing in there?" she asked. "In the water?"

"Maybe I wanted to go for a swim," I said.

"Not funny."

"It's all just one big misunderstanding," I said. "It'll never happen again."

She raised her eyebrows. "I just—I don't know how this will affect your upcoming semester at Marshall."

I laughed. "There is no upcoming semester at Marshall." I started to panic. Had I missed the last day to withdraw from classes? I prayed I hadn't. If the withdrawal deadline passed while I was at Weber, I'd be on the hook for a semester's worth of tuition that I'd never use. "What's today?" I asked.

"Friday," my mom said.

"The date," I said. "What's today's date?"

"It's the first of August, hon."

I felt my hands turn icy. I felt sick; like I was about to lose all of the bacon and pancakes I'd so greedily scarfed down.

Noticing that I'd turned a paler shade of white, my mom put her hand on mine. "What is it, Nate? What's wrong?"

"It doesn't make sense," I said. "I moved to Burlington on a Saturday. Why was I up here in the middle of the week?"

"You said you wanted to drive through town and check out the house you found online. You know, before committing to it," my mom said. "You were going to come back yesterday, finish packing, and move here."

"No," I said. "That never happened. It's really the first?"

"It is."

"Of August?"

"It is."

My jaw must have hit the table just beside my stack of pancakes. The past four weeks were gone. But *where* had they gone?

The thought of that terrified me.

"We need to go," I said. "We need to get out of here"

"We haven't finished eating. Nate, will you relax? Will you explain to me what's going on?"

I was already standing up from the table. My mom fished a twenty-dollar bill and a ten-dollar bill from her wallet and left them folded neatly between her coffee mug and plate.

"I'm driving," she said. "I'm worried about you."

"That's fine," I said.

"Where are we going?"

"126 North," I said. "As fast as possible."

ψ

My mom pulled her little four-door sedan carefully to a stop in front of 126. The house looked as weathered as I remembered it. The windows on the front stared back at me like tired eyes. Layers of worn green paint on the clapboard siding were cracked and peeling.

I leapt from the passenger seat of the car and raced up the driveway. When I reached the front door I knocked excitedly.

The door opened, and standing behind it was a man in his mid twenties. In his arms he held a black kitten. It was small—impossibly small—and it purred as he pet it, its tiny eyes squinted shut.

"Hey, man," Dave said. "You here about the cat?"

I felt myself shiver. I wanted to reach out and hug him; but how crazy would that have been? After all, I was a stranger. The two of us had never met.

"The cat," I said, my lower lip trembling. "You found a cat."

Dave nodded. He looked confused, but he was being polite. "Yeah, did you see the missing posters we put up? Is she yours?"

"No," I said, and I couldn't fight it any longer. I started to cry.

"Are you all right?" Dave asked. "Do you need to sit down? Need some water?"

"It's not my cat," I said. "But you should take care of it. Have you thought of a name?"

"Ah, felt weird to name it," Dave said, and he nodded back into the living room at the girl sitting on the couch. Hannah. "My girlfriend has grown attached to it, but what if we find its owner and have to give it back?"

"It looks like a stray," I said. "You should keep her."

"She wants to name her Shadow because she's black and she follows our feet—"

"Like a shadow," I said.

"Yeah," Dave said. "Like a shadow."

"I actually came by," I said, "because I believe I spoke with you not too long ago. About renting out a room."

"Oh!" Dave exclaimed. "Nate, right? Why didn't you say so?"

"Listen," I said. "I'm so sorry. Plans changed. I'm not attending Marshall this fall, so I'll have no reason to rent the room."

"That's a bummer," Dave said.

I reached into my pocket and pulled out my wallet. Tucked inside was a blank check that I held onto in case of an emergency, or if I had no cash and my debit card was lost or decided not to work. It must have hid in there for a couple of years now, sandwiched between old receipts and loose change.

"Do you have a pen?" I said.

Dave leaned from the doorframe toward the little table he kept inside the living room, opened the drawer, pulled out a pen and handed it to me.

"Great," I said, and I scribbled onto the check and handed it to him. "We were going to be on a month-to-month agreement, right? Well, there's my first month. Should soften the blow until you find another roommate."

Dave took the check, looked it over and shrugged. "Hey, man. We're cool. You don't have to do this. This is for way more than what a month's rent would have been, anyway."

"Keep it," I said. "I insist. Put what's leftover toward Shadow's litter box and cat toy fund. Just keep it."

"You're really twisting my arm," Dave said, and he chuckled.

I started to walk away from the front door, but before I did, I turned around one last time.

"You'll want to get the gas line checked out right away," I said.

"What?" Dave asked.

"The natural gas line. These older houses, sometimes they have leaks. Get it looked at as soon as you can."

"Hey, if you say so, bud."

"And Dave," I said. "I'm sorry for bothering you. And, I'm sorry our roommate arrangement couldn't work out."

He tucked Shadow into his elbow, and with his free hand he threw me a peace sign. "It's all gravy, baby."

ψ

I sat in the passenger seat of my mom's sedan, sobbing as she drove out onto North. Looking back, it's hard not to cringe at just how worried—how terrified—she must have been for me.

"I don't know what's going on, but we're going to get you the help you need, Nate," she said, during a long and awkward silence at a stoplight.

"You think I'm crazy."

"I've worked around people with problems long enough to know that's just an awful little word uneducated folks like to toss around. Real problems," she said, and she tapped her forehead, "can form up here. Can cram themselves deep down in the mind like moss-covered roots. But we can address them, and we can work on them, and we can try each morning to wake up a better person than we were the day before."

"They found me floating in Lake Champlain," I said. "That's going to follow me. For a long time, that'll follow me. Doesn't matter how many mornings go by. Doesn't matter how much better I get."

"It's a footnote in your story, Nathan." She lifted her hand from the steering wheel and patted mine. "It doesn't define who you are."

"I lived here for nearly a month," I said, and I kept my head downturned. "And in that month, awful things happened to good people. I watched it all, right in front of me, as real as you are driving this car."

"I believe you," she said. The words caught me by surprise.

"Really?"

"If that's what you feel happened," she said, "then it's real to you, and that's all that matters."

"I thought I saw dad once. After he passed."

Again, the car quieted.

"That day in the garage?"

I nodded. "You thought he was a vagrant who'd wandered into our backyard."

"I remember," she said, and her eyes shifted up and over the steering wheel, not looking *at* the road ahead so much as looking *through* it.

"It wasn't a vagrant," I said, and I cleared my throat. The sniffles had settled, the tears had dried. "It was him. There's no explaining it, but it was him."

"Again, Nate…I believe you."

"I would have done anything to have him with me in the garage that day. To help me fix my bike. To talk. He was there and gone so fast, I wasn't sure that it was him, or my mind playing tricks on me, or what. There and gone…so fast, I wasn't sure at first that I'd even seen him at all. There and gone. Like a…like a shooting star."

The streetlight turned green and my mom's sedan bucked forward, its little motor humming as we crossed the intersection.

"Let's go home," she said.

My eyes connected to a billboard standing tall on the side of the road. On the left side of it was the picture of a man—older, handsome—grinning a big, wide grin. To the right of his smile were the words: INJURED? ACCIDENT? CALL THE BLOOM LAW FIRM!

"Not home," I said. "Not yet. I still have one more stop to make."

ψ

Some attorneys rent out an office space in a strip mall or in a business complex. It's a common enough practice for the most successful or frugal of them. But, as I'd quickly learn, modesty was not Dominic Bloom's style.

The Bloom Law Firm building sat on the northwest corner of Welks and Hammond in northern Burlington. It was four stories tall and quite modern. All four sides of it were plated in mirrored glass, a thinly veiled attempt at camouflage. The idea behind mirrored buildings is that they reflect back the sky and clouds, makes the typical passerby forget it's even there. Really, all they do is cause birds to fly headfirst into them. There was no missing the Bloom & Bloom building. It loomed over Burlington like a modern marvel, its gaudy exterior in stark contrast to a city filled with century old buildings. I suspected Bloom liked it that way.

When I walked into the first floor reception area of the goliath building, I hadn't the slightest clue of where to turn or who to ask for. The floor was busy. Men in suits with briefcases shuffled back and forth.

I worked my way through the crowd until I was face to face with a chipper enough young man at a secretary's desk. From the looks of him, he could have been an intern at Marshall.

"How can I help you, sir?" he asked, and he studied me with his eyes. I was wearing an old t-shirt, tattered jeans, and a pair of basketball sneakers. I stood out between the businessmen in their suits no differently than the Bloom building stood out amongst historic architecture.

"I'm here to see Mr. Bloom," I said, very matter of fact.

The secretary stifled a giggle. "Without an appointment?"

"I don't need one," I said.

He nodded. "Well, I regret to inform you that Mr. Bloom is away on business this morning. Could I take a message?"

I laced my hands behind my back and craned my neck, scanning the offices and the hustle and bustle of the building. "He's here," I said.

"I'm very sorry, sir. He isn't. If you're seeking legal representation, I can schedule an appointment for you with one of our paralegals. They can take your information and—"

"I don't need fucking legal representation," I said. "I need to speak to Dominic Bloom."

"I'm going to have to ask you to leave," the secretary said, and he reached for the phone at the end of his desk.

"Tell him it's about his daughter," I said. "I have to talk to him about his daughter."

His forehead wrinkled and he stopped dialing halfway through the number he had started to punch in. He hung the phone up, then picked it up again, spinning in his chair so that I couldn't see his face. I heard mumbling, and then he nodded.

I stood there waiting for guards to appear at any moment and remove me from the building—or worse. How would an arrest look on my record, not less than twenty-four hours after being discharged from The Weber Retreat?

"Take the elevator to the fourth floor," the secretary said, and he gestured across the room. "When it lets you off, just keep walking. You'll see his office. There's no missing it."

I nodded. "Thanks."

I made my way between smartly dressed women and men and pushed toward the elevator. I bumped into an older attorney in a navy blue suit who simply glared after I offered an apology.

The elevator car was crammed edge to edge with clients and lawyers alike, all either talking to one another or mumbling into cell phones. The cacophony of it all was giving me a headache, and those familiar pangs of claustrophobia were creeping back again, when finally the elevator reached the fourth floor.

The secretary was right. There was no missing Dominic Bloom's office. When the elevator doors opened, the passengers scattered, until I was the only one left in the car. I stepped out into the main hall of the fourth floor and walked forward, and I couldn't tell for certain, but it felt as if each office hushed as I passed by it.

At the end of the hall was a steel door, nine feet tall and four feet wide. Emblazoned into the center of it in big, looping cursive letters were the initials D.B.

When I was face to face with the hulking door, I went to knock. But, before my knuckles could kiss the steel, the door groaned open

Standing in the doorway was a man in his forties. His hair was short, but curled and slicked back. A thick shadow of stubble clung to his angled face. He wore a pink, pinstriped button down, creased beneath a pair of suspenders, the sleeves of which were rolled up to the elbow. On his wrist was a gold watch; heavy, expensive. His slacks were jet-black, tapered at the ankles just above a pair of shoes that had been polished to a mirror-shine.

"Nathaniel Shaw," Dominic said, and he rubbed his palms together. "Come in, come in. I've been expecting you."

I walked through the doorway and he closed the door behind me. He extended his arm and offered me a chair at his desk. After I had sat, he sat, too. We were quiet for a moment, watching each other. I was too afraid to speak first.

"What," Dominic said. "You were expecting little red horns? A cape? A pitchfork?"

"I just want to know that she's okay," I said.

"My daughter?" Dominic said, and he smiled. His teeth were perfect, the color of ivory, each of them planted evenly beside the next. "Vega's fine. Just fine. Like a cat, she always lands on her feet."

"Where is she?"

"She studies abroad, Nate. Young girl like that, you can never keep her in one place for too long. I believe she's in Toronto for the time being."

I slumped in the chair.

"Are we here to talk about Vega, though? Really? I think we're here to talk about Nate. The Great Nate. I've heard a lot about you, kid. You look good. They treated you well at Weber?"

"How did you know I was there?"

"I have friends everywhere. Especially in this town. I know one of the doctors over there—why do you think you were released so soon?"

"I didn't realize I had been."

"No need to thank me," Dominic said. "You shouldn't have been there in the first place, right? You're just an innocent bystander. A casualty of Vega's magic. Although, I imagine not an awful lot of people would believe that if you told them, would they?"

I thought of my mother, waiting downstairs in her car in the parking lot. "You might be surprised."

He folded his hands together at his desk. "It might be hard for you, Nate, to get started in this town. Word travels fast. Marshall might take another look at your admission application once they hear about your stay at Weber…once they connect the dots that you were the boy found floating in Lake Champlain."

I shrugged. "They might."

"I'm willing to make you an offer, though. And it's a damn fine one, too." He opened the drawer of his desk and pulled out a neat stack of eight or ten papers. They were fastened together in the upper left corner by a paper clip.

"What's that?" I asked.

"You know, Nate, Vega told me all about you after that night on your front lawn. You're the boy who can remember! She twisted time—the way she does—and you remembered it afterward. That's rare. Very rare. As far as I'm concerned, from that day forward you were family. So, what's this?" He fanned the pages. "It's an employment contract."

I couldn't help but laugh. "An employment contract?"

"You'd start on the first floor, as an intern. You'd be paid—quite handsomely—and all tuition, fees, and textbook costs at Marshall would be waived by the firm, so long as you're under our umbrella."

I leaned back in my seat. From the fourth floor office, you could see much of downtown Burlington. Church Street was in full view. I could see the marquee for The Capitol Theater. From high up here, he must feel like a puppeteer, the world beneath him dancing as he pulled the strings.

"You killed Joyce Nicholson," I said.

Dominic clicked his tongue. "Hell of an accusation to lob at a man who just offered you a job."

"Does Vega know?"

He frowned. "What happened between Joyce and I is more complicated than you can imagine. We had an agreement, and she...didn't hold up her end of the bargain."

"She wanted to leave you for Ed McManus. Doesn't sound complicated to me."

"Shut your mouth—"

"And so you rigged her car with whatever awful beast you put in the Challenger you left for me, and you let her drive off. But you couldn't stand not having the child she promised you, and so you had your newborn daughter snipped out of what was left of her body in the county morgue. Does Vega know *any* of this?" My words were firm. They didn't waiver.

"Well, Nate. You just have all the answers, don't you?"

"No," I said. "I don't understand why you'd go after Betty Nicholson, and Ed McManus, and Dave, and then...me."

"How are all those people doing right now?" Dominic asked. "Dave is fine. So are Betty and Ed, if you'd like to give them a call. The only time they *weren't* fine is when you showed up in this town, scratching at scabs that healed over two decades ago."

"Joyce wanted Vega to know she was her mother," I said. "I made that happen."

"You did, and look at all who suffered for it. The only reason they're alive is because of Vega's mercy."

280

"She wasn't supposed to be able to move that much time at once," I said.

Dominic chuckled. "Oh, she's capable of all sorts of things after feasting on a fresh virgin. Not exactly a lady killer are you, Nate?"

I squirmed in my seat.

"This is how I see it, Nathan. The past four weeks? Consider them a test. A test of…faith and loyalty. You passed with flying colors, for the most part. And look at how you landed! Vega knows the truth you were so eager to reveal to her, and all those who paid for it are living their happy little lives, blissfully unaware of what would happen to them had it not been for Vega. Today's a blank canvas." He pushed the stack of papers toward me. "This is your chance to do it all over again."

I glanced at the top page. The print was fine, very difficult to read. Just the way Dominic liked it.

"If you don't, you'll never see Vega again. Is that what you want? You'll never finish a degree at Marshall, either. I'll make sure of that. Think about it, Mr. Shaw. Do you want to ride back home to Albany—a nobody—or do you want to try again?"

I picked up the pen and thought about signing. He was a master manipulator, that was for certain. The past four weeks had been expertly crafted by him. Each time I got close to figuring out the truth about Joyce, he sidestepped me—punished me—and with every punishment, I inched closer to being in his servitude. I could have applauded him, if I didn't loathe him.

"No thank you," I said, and I scooted the chair back and stood. "But please, when you speak to Vega next, tell her I'm sorry about how things turned out."

"You wouldn't," he said, chuckling, "*dare* say no to me, would you?"

"I'd say it again," I replied. "No."

I turned and headed for the tall, steel door of the office.

"If it wasn't for how much she cared about you," he called, "I'd have you thrown off the roof of this building. I'd have you strung up from the lampposts out front by your insides. I could make you suffer, Nate. Suffer more than you could imagine."

"I've suffered quite enough, thanks," and I reached for the handle of the door.

"Wait," he said, and he smacked his hand on the top of his desk. "What if I could sweeten the deal?"

"There's nothing you could do to me," I said, "to make me spend one more second in this awful office with you."

He pushed the phone on his desk forward. "Wouldn't you want some guidance? Some advice? Before you answered yes or no to such a big decision. Before you dared to risk offending someone like me."

"Who would I call?" I said. "Vega?" I laughed. "I'm pretty sure I know what she'd tell me to do, and you wouldn't like it."

"*Anyone,*" he said, and he tapped on the phone. "Living or dead."

I stood, frozen.

"Don't you want to hear his voice one more time? Don't you want to speak with him?" He scoffed. "What would your father have to say at a time like this?"

Slowly, I walked back toward Dominic's desk. I looked at the contract, and then the phone, and then the contract again.

I picked up the contract—all eight pages—and Dominic smiled. I tore the pile in half once, and then twice, separating each page into quarters, and then dropped the torn pieces back onto his desk like confetti. His smile faded.

"I know exactly what my father would have to say at a time like this. Thank you for your time, Mr. Bloom."

ψ

We were quiet on the drive back to Albany. For the first twenty minutes or so of the drive, at least. Once Burlington was far behind us, trapped in the rearview mirror, I opened my mouth to speak.

"The Beast?" I asked.

My mom shifted in her seat, startled. "James drove up with me," she said, "when we heard you were at Weber. I had him drive it back to New York while I waited for your release. He wanted to be there to visit you, but I told him that it'd probably be for the best if he left. I know how you two...are."

"I'm sorry," I said, "for never calling him dad. Or, not even pop, or anything paternal—he was always just 'James.'"

"You don't have to apologize for that," she said. "He understood. We all understood. It's difficult; no one asked any differently from you."

In all their years of marriage, I hadn't once referred to them as parents. They were my mom and her husband, or, my mother and stepfather, or, mom and James. Always.

"Sometimes I feel bad about it," I said. "That I never treated him more like a father."

"He knows you love him," she said. "And I'm certain by now, you know he loves you too." She shrugged. "In this crazy world— what more could you ask for?"

ψ

The week after I returned to Albany, I found myself a job at a local used video game store. I had decided that Marshall—or, any law school for that matter—was off the table. Something deep down gnawed at me, even before my summer with Vega, that it might not be for me. That August had confirmed those gut instincts, and it was time to find something fresh. Something new. The video game shop was fresh, and it was new. It was fulfilling, it took my mind off things, and it kept gas in the tank of The Beast. Fine enough by me.

I stayed in my bedroom that summer until September rolled around. After a few weeks of careful surveillance by my mother and stepfather, I was given the okay to leave. They were satisfied that I was happy, that I was healthy, and that they wouldn't have to worry about me mysteriously turning up in any lakes any time soon.

I found a little one-bedroom apartment across town. Not huge, not tiny. But, a place to call my own nonetheless.

There were many nights spent in that apartment—during my first couple of weeks, anyhow—that I laid awake, thinking about Burlington. The town that never was. The life that never was.

I'd be lying if I said I didn't think about Vega from time to time. Some nights, I wondered if she ever thought about me, too. I had remembered her, no denying that, exactly as she asked.

But, had she remembered me?

The web page for the Burlington Bugle became my best friend that summer. I checked it daily to snoop on the comings and goings in town. The Capitol continued its Halloween movie marathon straight through the 31st of October. The Excorcist, The Shining, all the classics. One night, they even played Alien—though I'm still convinced that doesn't count as a horror film.

What I was really checking for on the Bugle's homepage each morning were any alarming articles about accidents or explosions. There were none. Betty Nicholson was never hit by a car. Ed McManus never leapt from the roof of Marshall. The little bungalow at 126 North never burned to the ground.

Life went on.

By October, I had stopped checking The Bugle's home page. I was no longer concerned for the safety of Dave, or Hannah, or anyone else I'd crossed paths with during my brief time in Vermont.

I did, however, try to look up Vega. While I couldn't find any social media account of hers so to speak, no digital link to keep in touch, I did stumble upon an interesting search result in my brief attempt to find her:

VEGA (name): Origin – Latin; Meaning – Star

ψ

In November of 2012, New York experienced one of the most dramatic and beautiful autumnal transitions in the history of the state. During the first week of the month, the colors peaked—a little later than most years—and all at once, the state was blanketed in a sea of golds and reds and yellows. It was something else; it was like something out of a children's storybook.

To celebrate the beautiful foliage, James and my mom invited me out for a picnic trip along the Mohawk River. It was my mom who had called on the second of the month and suggested the idea.

"I know we haven't been there since—"

Since your father passed, she wanted to say.

"—but I was hoping we could go again. I think it's good to continue traditions, even if not everyone is there to carry them on. In fact, *especially* if not everyone is there to carry them on. It would be a shame to miss out on the changing leaves over a sore memory."

I couldn't have agreed with her more, so the following Saturday James, her, and myself all took off work to meet at the Mohawk and spend the day fishing and relaxing.

When I pulled up in The Beast, the two of them were already setting up collapsible chairs down near the shore, each of them dressed warmly.

"There he is," James called out. "Look at this stranger."

"Nathan," my mom said. "We're so glad you made it."

"Me too," I said, "but I think I forgot my swimming gear."

James laughed. "Didn't stop you last time."

"Don't joke about that," my mom said, sharply.

James and I both shrugged. We both understood that sometimes, during the worst of it, all you can help but do is laugh.

The three of us carried picnic baskets, fishing poles, tackle boxes, and chairs from the trunk of my mom's car down to the shore. After a couple of trips, the two of them settled in together, sitting beside one another and facing the water. The river lapped peacefully at the muddy banks, the surface of it reflecting the endless miles of gold and red hues painted atop the trees.

"The cooler," James exclaimed, and he smacked the side of his chair. "We forgot it. And, what I wouldn't do for a cold beer right about now."

"I got it," I said, and I stood up.

"No, no," my mom said. "You two stay here. I can get it."

I was already marching back toward our cars. "I insist."

When I made it back to The Beast, I unlocked the car and lifted the rear gate of the trunk. Tucked beside the rear wheel well was a Styrofoam cooler I picked up on the drive over, filled to the brim with ice and drinks, and even a couple of tuna sandwiches from SubTub. For old time's sake.

When the gate lifted, I knew she was there—I could sense it— no differently than the smell before rain, or the way the atmosphere changes just before a lighting strike.

I turned quickly on one foot, my heel grinding into the gravel, and I faced her. She stood there in the grass, in a black coat and a plum colored skirt. She wore boots that were almost as long as her legs. And, resting on the bridge of her nose, were a darkly tinted pair of Wayfarers.

"Nate," she said, and she slid her glasses off of her face.

My keys dropped right out of my hand and I took a step forward. We hugged, and we held each other there for a moment, shivering in the cool November air.

"Vega," I said. "I didn't think I'd ever see you again."

She smiled. "You're not that lucky, Nate."

I smiled too, but I didn't mean it. There'd been a sliver of me missing since that day on the lake, a sliver that she held on to, whether she knew it or not. Despite all the good and all the bad, it was hers and hers alone. I suspected she'd hold onto it forever.

"How are you?"

"I think the more important question is, how are *you*?"

"I'm fine. I'm keeping it together."

"Good," she said. "I wanted to see you sooner. I wanted to visit you. But, well. It's complicated."

"You don't have to explain," I said.

287

"You said no to my father," she said, and she laughed. "I still haven't decided if that was very brave of you or very foolish. Whichever it was, it took guts. I don't think anyone has ever said no to him before. The look on his face when he told me about it...it was priceless."

"Does he hate me?" I asked. "I worry at night, sometimes...that he'll come after me."

"You know who he is," she said. "If he wanted to come after you, he would have. No...he actually wanted me to give you a message."

"What's that?"

"Don't bother him, he won't bother you."

Ah. Well, for the devil, a surprisingly easy to interpret message.

"I don't think I'll ever cross paths with him again," I said.

Vega sighed. "I never got the chance to thank you."

"For what?" I asked.

"For telling me about Joyce—I mean, about my mother. For putting the pieces together. For all you did, and for all you went through."

"You don't have to thank me. I can't imagine ole Dominic is thrilled that you know."

"He isn't," she said. "But, like I said. It's complicated. I'm still his daughter, too. I can't just shut that off like a light switch."

"Complicated," I repeated. "I couldn't begin to imagine."

She laced her hands with mine. "When I think about you, I miss you. But, I know that it's better this way. That...this is the way things should be."

"Well," I said. "You'd be the expert on that, wouldn't you?"

She smirked, then tilted her head toward the sky and squinted. "There's an infinite number of worlds, Nathan, with an infinite

288

number of possibilities. In some of those worlds, your father lives until a ripe-old age, he takes your children to the park on the weekends."

I caught my breath.

"In some of them," she continued, "you and I don't ever meet. And in others we marry, we have children and we grow old together, and we make lazy love on balmy summer afternoons. We nap together with the windows open. Our joints creak."

I smiled, and her grip on my hand loosened. She put her hand on my chest, then took mine and placed it on hers.

"But those infinite possibilities don't matter, Nate." She pressed firmer on my chest. "*This* is all that matters. Right here. Right now. No matter how much I try or try not to change that. No matter what I can or can't do."

We stood there for a moment, silently. I didn't understand what she meant at the time. I do now. At least, I'd like to think I do.

"We're with each other," she said. "No matter what."

I smiled. "No matter what."

I could tell that this was a goodbye—a sweet, sorrowful one at that—but goodbyes are rarely anything but sweet and sorrowful. Still, I wanted to ask her to stay for a bit, to watch the river pass lazily by and to stare at the changing leaves for a while.

She wiggled her nose. "Maybe," she said. "For a little bit."

I turned back toward the trunk of The Beast and grabbed the Styrofoam cooler. The woods around me hushed. Gone were the trills and tweets of the birds; silent was the sound of the passing river. I didn't have to turn around to know that she had gone, but I did anyways.

I stood there for a moment, alone, and the sounds of nature returned. The birds whistled happily, the Mohawk splashed lightly against its muddy shore.

I drew a deep breath of that old, November air. It was cool, crisp, refreshing—it tasted of change, the inevitable change that touches us all, no more unstoppable than the passing of the seasons.

Down by the shore, I could hear the laughter of my parents, the sound of a fishing line being cast into the river.

I lifted the cooler against my chest and started my walk back, comforted by the fact that sooner or later all nightmares—even those truly awful, horrid ones—come to an end.

About the Author

Robert Barnard lives in Orlando, Florida. In 2014 he graduated from the University of Central Florida with a Bachelor of Science in Legal Studies. Aside from writing, he works for an incredible law firm in the Orlando metropolitan area.

When he isn't writing, he enjoys playing guitar, collecting retro video games, attending pop-culture conventions, and at least several other hobbies that you'd expect the author of horror and paranormal fiction to enjoy.

His other novels include HOUR 23, HOUR 24: ALL THAT'S LEFT, and PHANTASOS: A PARANORMAL THRILLER.

Robert would love to hear back from his readers. If you're interested in reaching out, you can visit him online at:

Facebook: www.facebook.com/authorrobertbarnard